please take my baby

BOOKS BY EMMA ROBINSON

The Undercover Mother

Happily Never After

One Way Ticket to Paris

My Silent Daughter

The Forgotten Wife

My Husband's Daughter

His First Wife's Secret

To Save My Child

Only for My Daughter

To Be a Mother

My Stepmother's Secret

please
take my
baby

emma robinson

bookouture

Published by Bookouture in 2023

An imprint of Storyfire Ltd.
Carmelite House
50 Victoria Embankment
London EC4Y 0DZ

www.bookouture.com

ISBN: 978-1-83790-332-0
eBook ISBN: 978-1-83790-330-6

For 13c
For making my last year of teaching an absolute joy

PROLOGUE

Erin was about to give up and go home when the crunch of tyres on gravel caught her attention. A small red Fiesta pulled into the car park and a woman got out. Long dark hair. It must be her. Erin followed as quickly as she could, calling out to her, 'Imogen.'

The woman turned towards her with a smile. Beneath her heavy black leather jacket, she was slim and attractive, her lipstick dark red and eyes ringed in black kohl. It was difficult not to stare, searching for a family likeness.

Imogen tilted her head to one side. 'Sorry, do I know you?'

Erin waited until she was right in front of her, slightly breathless, before she replied. 'I'm Erin. We spoke on the phone.'

Imogen's face paled beneath her make-up. 'What are you doing here? This is where I work.'

'I know. I'm sorry, but I need to know what happened. Between you and Mum. Why you haven't been in touch.'

Her face wasn't revealing any secrets. 'What has she told you?'

Their falling out must have been pretty awful for her to be

this defensive. 'Nothing. I don't know anything at all. Mum has dementia. Her memory is really patchy. And before I found a photograph of you, I didn't even know you existed. Please, I know you have to get into work, but can you spare me ten minutes?'

Imogen chewed on her lip, then nodded. 'Okay. We can sit on the bench here. But ten minutes and I have to go.'

At last, she was going to talk. 'Great. Thank you.'

The wooden bench was damp and uncomfortable. Imogen sat very neatly, her hands in her lap, not making eye contact. 'What was it you wanted to know?'

There were so many questions that Erin had to pick one at random. 'When did you leave home? How old were you?'

Imogen squinted far into the distance as if picturing the day she left. 'The first time, I was sixteen.'

The *first* time? 'Why did you go?'

Imogen sighed, turned in her seat and, at last, looked Erin in the face. 'Has she really told you nothing? Do you not remember?'

Did *she* remember? 'Was I born by then?'

Imogen stared at her. 'Yes, you were born.'

This just got more confusing. Was she trying to suggest that it was Erin's fault that she left? 'I don't remember you at all. That's what I've been trying to tell you. Mum hasn't mentioned you once. No one told me anything. That's why I wanted to see you. I want to understand and...' she might as well get it all out, 'and I hoped that maybe we could get to know one another. I've always wanted a sister.'

Imogen's face twitched, as if she was about to burst into tears. 'I'm not your sister, Erin.'

This was getting tiresome. Why was she punishing her like this? Whatever had happened between their mother and Imogen was not Erin's fault. Imogen couldn't deny that they were family. 'Look, I know that—'

'I'm not your sister.'

The edge to her voice silenced Erin, but when she spoke again, the hardness in her eyes conflicted with the tears on her face. She lowered her voice to a sharp whisper. 'I'm not your sister. I'm your mother. And believe me when I tell you that you're far better off not knowing me at all.'

ONE

Half of this country's history is stored in an old biscuit tin at the back of a cupboard.

This particular biscuit tin – a McVitie's Christmas Assortment – belonged to Erin's mother, Ava, and had been excavated by her daughter, Harriet, who'd spent the last three hours loudly and angrily clearing a space for herself in the wardrobe in Ava's third bedroom.

Erin herself was in the lounge, getting ready for work. Ava – repositioning the pillow behind her on her favourite armchair – had long been dressed and ready to go, her hair styled by a mobile hairdresser who'd been there that morning. Maybe it was the fresh colour she'd run through it, but today she looked younger than her eighty years.

She was also smiling as she watched Erin walking back and forth between the table, where her make-up bag had spilled its contents, and the oval mirror on the sitting room wall. 'You look very smart, dear. Where are we off to?'

'I'm going to work, Mum. And you're going to The Oasis. Remember?' Though Erin felt guilty at the look of confusion on her mother's face, it was difficult to keep the frustration from her voice. According to the consultant, dementia progressed in different ways and at different rates, but Ava's short-term memory was likely to be the biggest issue. Erin had to remember to be more patient.

Upstairs, the thump of boxes being dragged across the floor was a reminder that she hadn't yet told Harriet that she was going. She called up the stairs. 'Harriet. Have you got a minute, love?'

A muffled shout came back down to her, which may or may not have been 'hold on'.

Though she could do with the extra hours, Erin was annoyed at being called into work at such late notice. The only sweetener was Jasmine also being on shift this afternoon; after only two months of working together, they made a pretty good double act.

Her mother was still fidgeting with the cushion. 'Is Simon coming home soon?'

'No, Mum. He's not.' She didn't have the energy to remind her, again, that they'd been divorced for two years and he was now living in an apartment in north London with his new wife: a very attractive, and annoyingly pleasant, dietitian called Carmel. Yesterday, she'd had none of these questions. The memory loss was erratic; it was difficult to predict when she would be okay and when she wouldn't. It was a relief she was going to The Oasis today; Erin had started to get nervous about leaving her alone too long.

Erin lifted her blazer from the back of one of the dining chairs and shrugged it on over the thick blue work shirt. Ugly as it was, at least a uniform meant that she didn't need to think about what to wear. The divorce haircut she'd unwisely agreed to after two glasses of Prosecco had finally grown out and her hair was back to a sensible shoulder-length which she'd pulled back into a ponytail.

Her mother was still watching her every move. 'That jacket looks nice on you.'

She still wasn't used to this new version of her mother who paid her compliments. 'Thanks.'

'I used to have a suit like that, I think. Those were the days when teachers had to be smart. Now it's all trainers and sweatshirts.'

That part of her mother hadn't changed. She was still as smartly dressed now as she'd been when Erin was growing up. Her exacting standards had extended to Erin too; she'd had it drummed into her that she should always look her best, carry a comb, be the tidiest person in the room. One of the many quirks she hadn't passed onto her own daughter, who preferred to spend most of her time in Primark leggings and a paint-spattered crop top.

A pair of those leggings now hammered down the stairs and joined her in the hallway. Harriet looked her up and down. 'Are you going into work?'

Ordinarily, she'd have made a quip about wearing the aubergine blazer for a slap-up lunch at the Dorchester, but she'd been tiptoeing around her daughter since the move. 'Yes. Tim called. They're short of someone on reception. I'll only be there 'til five because I'll need to collect your gran from her club.'

That's what they called The Oasis respite centre. Her mother's doctor had suggested that Ava might like to attend. Out of her earshot, he'd told Erin that it would be a good idea for her to familiarise herself with the place 'because it might become a necessity' as Ava lost the ability to look after herself. Her mother would be appalled if she thought she was being babysat while Erin was at work.

Harriet shrugged. 'You could've left her here with me. I'm not going anywhere.'

Was that a kindness or another complaint that Erin had moved her an hour away from her friends? Best not to dig too deeply. 'Thanks, love. I've already arranged it and she's looking forward to it. It's apple pie day.'

Erin pulled a face and was rewarded with a laugh. 'It's all go when you're eighty, isn't it?'

'Apparently so. What have you got there?'

'It's a tin of photographs. I found it upstairs. Gran might like to look through it and tell me who everyone is. You know, before...'

She didn't have to finish that sentence with *before she forgets who everyone is*. How strange it was that Harriet and Ava got on so well. Especially considering how unimpressed her mother had been when Erin had announced that she and Simon were expecting. Yet they'd always had a special relationship. As if the affection that should've been Erin's had skipped a generation.

Harriet held out a rectangular royal blue tin decorated with a painting of a Christmas fireplace. It took Erin a few attempts to open it, until she prised her fingernails under the lip and it flipped off with a metallic clatter.

Inside, yellowed papers and squares of card had been crammed in so tightly that a few jumped out to follow the lid and Harriet had to scoop them from the floor. Some looked like legal documents, others were handwritten notes. Most interestingly, there were photographs that wouldn't have been out of place in a history textbook. Erin glanced at her watch. 'We've only got a few minutes. You can show her one or two and then we need to go.'

The photograph Harriet chose was creased in one corner, the black and white image bordered in white. Erin almost didn't recognise her mother. Was it the apron or the broad smile that was most unfamiliar? The absence of what Simon had christened 'The Frown of Judgement'. The baby in her arms was a heavy looking toddler with a knitted bonnet whose tight fit might explain the child's pained expression.

Harriet stood to the side of Ava's chair. 'Who's that, Gran. Is it Mum?'

Ava smiled at the photograph and nodded. 'Yes. That's my little girl.'

Her mother had never called her that in her life. Plus, that child was definitely not her. 'Let me look at that, Mum.'

When Ava seemed reluctant to give it up, Erin moved closer and looked over her shoulder. She'd seen enough pictures of herself as a skinny little thing with wispy curls to know that this dark-haired chunk of a child was not her. 'It's not me, Mum. It must be someone else's baby. Is it one of Auntie Marcelle's twins? Lindsey, maybe?'

She'd always been jealous of her twin cousins, Lindsey and Angela. Not only because they had each other, but because Auntie Marcelle was a warm pillow of a mother who constantly told them – and anyone else – how beautiful and clever they were. While her own mother used to say she was 'making a show of herself' if she mentioned she'd done well in a maths test.

Her mother was shaking her head. 'No. It's not Lindsey, it's...' she trailed off, but her lips kept moving as if she was hoping they might form the name of their own accord.

She let the photograph drop into her lap and Erin picked it up, turned it over. On the back in faint pencil was a name: Imogen.

'It says Imogen, Mum. Do you know who that is?'

Her mother seemed to get agitated. 'No. I don't know. I don't know.'

This was happening more and more. As the dementia stole her mother's memories, she'd get upset and frightened at the things she couldn't recall. Harriet looked concerned, too. 'It's okay, Gran. It doesn't matter. Does it, Mum?'

Harriet looked to Erin for confirmation. Intrigued as she was, it wasn't worth upsetting her mother over. Especially as she was about to leave her at the respite centre for the afternoon. 'She's right. Don't worry, it's not important.'

Erin gave the photo another glance. She'd never heard the name Imogen mentioned before, but her mother had seemed quite taken with her. She could always give Auntie Marcelle a call in Australia later and ask her. It had been a while since she'd called her mother's sister with an update anyway. She grabbed her bag and car keys from the chair. 'Well, we'd better be off, Mum.'

As Ava pushed herself out of the chair, Harriet nodded towards the hall and Erin followed her out. 'I was wondering what time you're due back. I want to talk to you about something.'

Those words were a stone in her stomach. People only told you they wanted to talk to you if it was bad news. If it was good, they'd just come right out with it. 'What is it?'

Harriet was clearly trying to look innocent. 'Not now. I'll talk to you tonight.'

She was annoyed that she was going into work at all on her day off. The text from Tim – a wet drip of a hotel manager – said that the new girl he'd hired had handed in her notice after three days and he needed Erin to 'just cover a few hours'. She'd resisted the urge to tell him that he needed to hire someone who'd actually worked on a hotel reception before. 'I'm going to be gone a while, love. Why don't you tell me now?'

'No, it's okay. It can wait.'

Ava's appearance from the sitting room cut their conversation short. Harriet hugged her grandmother goodbye and blew Erin a kiss before disappearing back upstairs.

Erin watched her go with an anxious prickle in her stomach. For the last few weeks, she'd had the move back here plus her mother's dementia and appeasing Harriet to deal with. Now she had two more problems to chew on at work. What did Harriet want to talk about? And who was Imogen?

TWO

The Oasis adjoined the local church and was a drop-in centre for dementia sufferers and their carers. With its large glass windows, kind staff and volunteers, it more than lived up to its name. Macy's welcoming smile met them at the door as soon as they arrived. 'There you are, Ava. We've been wondering where you'd got to. Come in. Ginny has a cup of tea ready for you. No more than a splash of milk, exactly how you like it.'

Erin's mother allowed herself to be led away to a long rectangular catering table where a couple of the volunteers were helping along a card game between two benign old ladies and a rather cross looking old man. It still felt strange to drop her mother there, like a small child to a play group, but needs must. 'Do you mind if I shoot straight off? I need to get to work.'

Macy shooed her away with long glittery fingernails. 'Go, girl. Go. We've got her. She's fine.'

From there, the drive to work was only fifteen minutes; so much easier than trying to commute between her mother's, the last hotel she'd worked at and their old flat in Sutton. When Erin arrived at The Marlborough, Jasmine was on the reception telephone with what sounded like a difficult customer. She mouthed 'tea' at her and got an enthusiastic nod in response.

Directly behind the grand rosewood reception desk was a small office with a computer, a tired leather sofa and a tiny kitchen. None of the deep red carpet or embossed wallpaper from the hotel foyer reached into this room, which looked as if it hadn't seen even a lick of paint this side of the millennium. Erin was used to this. In every hotel she'd worked, the staff facilities were vastly inferior to those seen by guests. She'd often thought that this – and not any kind of security reasons – was why they were all marked with a 'Staff Only' sign.

Even the kettle was ancient and took a while to rumble to a boil, so she'd only just poured the tea when Jasmine poked her head into the office. 'How come they've dragged you in again today? Weren't you supposed to have the day off? Did the twelve-year-old not come back?'

Erin shook her head as she passed over the mug of tea, handle first. 'She lasted three days at least. Better than the last one.'

Jasmine groaned. 'Tim's lucky he found you. Otherwise I might've given in my notice, too. He's got no idea how difficult this job is.'

'To be honest, I could do with the extra hours. And it's nice to get out of the house.'

Jasmine screwed up her nose. 'Is your mother still doing your head in?'

If only she knew. Erin hadn't said too much about her mother's dementia aside from saying she was getting a bit forgetful. 'A bit. There's a reason you leave home when you become an adult, and we were never that close to start with.'

'And what about your daughter? Has she forgiven you yet?'

Harriet loved her grandmother, but when Erin had suggested they move into her house – an hour away from her old school friends – she'd understandably been pretty unhappy about it. But Erin couldn't see another solution. The two-bedroom flat she'd bought after the divorce was far too small to move her mother in with them and, to be honest, she was struggling to make ends meet. Moving them into her mother's house was killing two birds with one stone. She winced when she remembered the many material promises she'd made to Harriet to appease her and soothe the transition. A shiny new MacBook for sixth form was probably only the start of it. 'She's coming around.'

Jasmine sipped at her tea and let out a long sigh of pleasure, stretching her legs out in front of her. 'This is the first drink I've had in about four hours. There's got to be easier ways to make a living.'

It was an exhausting job, but Erin wouldn't have it any other way. 'I don't know. I like being here, making sure everyone is happy and enjoying their stay. Wouldn't it be great to own a place like this? Run it exactly as you wanted?'

That had always been the pipe dream; her own hotel. Nothing grand, a few bedrooms and a restaurant. Having watched so many inept managers make wrong decisions over her years in hospitality, she'd easily make a better job of it.

Jasmine raised an eyebrow. 'Really? You'd want to own a hotel? Then why haven't you?'

Erin shrugged. 'Never the right time. When I first started working in hotels, I was too young and inexperienced. Then I got pregnant with Harriet and, well, family life took over, really.'

Her mother had tried to control that too, as soon as she'd told her that she was moving in with Simon. *You need to get your career going before you settle down or you'll never have anything to show for it.* Well, she had Harriet to show for it and that was good enough for her.

Jasmine was nodding again. 'Well, if you ever do go for it, I'll work for you.'

A flashing light on the telephone signalled another call and Jasmine picked it up. There wasn't much chance of her running a hotel now. Not with her mother to look after too. Dementia was unpredictable. Some days she was pretty on-the-ball, but others she was so vague that Erin was scared to leave her on her own. Trawling dementia websites and forums, she'd discovered that this was common in the first phase. It was only going to get more difficult. Thank goodness for The Oasis.

As she picked up a pile of papers from the desk to file them away, Tim himself appeared through the door, looking relieved to find her there. 'Oh, Erin. You're here already. Thanks for coming in. Who'd have believed that girl wouldn't turn up today? She handed her notice in over a text message.'

Erin kept her mouth shut, but she could easily believe it. They came thinking it was merely a case of sitting behind the desk and answering the phone. The first disgruntled pensioner and they were off. 'Maybe I could help you with recruiting someone? I did it before in my old place.'

He looked surprised. 'That would be great. It's not my favourite thing to do and, let's face it, I haven't got a very good track record.' He paused then his face changed. 'Except you, of course. You've been a godsend.'

She smiled politely as if accepting that as a compliment, but he didn't need to tell her. Even the state of the filing system when she'd arrived was testament to how in need of an experienced pair of hands the place had been. 'Well, make sure to remember that when it comes to bonus time.'

Once her shift was over, she had to hurry back to The Oasis to collect her mother. Macy was sitting with her this time and she could hear her deep warm laugh in response to something her mother said. They both turned as she walked towards them across the sticky floor, but Macy spoke first. 'Ah. Here she is, your lovely daughter.'

Erin smiled. 'Hi, Macy. Hi, Mum.'

Macy pushed down on her thighs as she stood. 'I'm going to take Erin into the office for a minute, Ava. We'll be right back. I have some paperwork for her to sign.'

Erin had no idea what paperwork there was, but she followed Macy into the small office and took the chair she pointed to. 'What do you need me to do?'

'Nothing. I wanted to talk to you and see how things were going at home. Your mother has been telling me lots of stories today about you when you were growing up. Her eyes lit up when she was talking about you. You can see how much she loves you.'

Of course, Macy would think that: she'd only met *this* incarnation of her mother. Not the mother who'd forbidden and judged and lectured until Erin had been desperate to leave home. Since the divorce, she'd wondered if she and Simon would ever have married if she hadn't been as keen to live somewhere she could make the rules. Erin's throat tightened. If only that love had been more in evidence when she was growing up. 'Really?'

'Yes. And she was talking about someone else today. Imogen? Is that a relative of yours?'

The photograph must have jogged something in her mother's memory. 'I don't know. Maybe? We found a photograph of my mum holding a little baby. The name Imogen was on the back of it, but she doesn't seem to know who she was.'

Macy frowned. 'Well, she's been talking about her a lot today. Saying what a good baby she was.'

This was curious. It would suggest that her mother had known this child well. 'I'll have to dig around at home. See if I can find any more photos. Maybe they might jog her memory?'

'Good idea.' Macy paused and tilted her head. 'And how are you? It's quite a lot for you to take on, caring for your mother. Especially if you're working, too. You need to look after yourself. Have you got friends down here?'

This was above and beyond Macy's remit, but she was the kind of woman who could mother the whole world. Hanging from the gold chain around her neck, a large gold heart was etched with the names of her children. She'd told Erin before how much she missed her own mother who was back in Jamaica. Were some people born with bigger hearts than others? 'Thanks, I'm... fine. She's quite affable these days. As long as she's got her programmes on and the jam tarts don't run out.'

Macy must know that she was joking, but her expression stayed serious. 'You know that it's likely to get more difficult. You need to prepare yourself for that. There are other services that can help if you need it. I can give you all the numbers and make a referral when you're ready.'

Erin did appreciate the support, but they weren't there yet. Most days, her mother was no worse than a little forgetful. Until a year ago, she'd been independent and strong. The decline of the last few months had been a surprise. It wasn't only the memory lapses, it was the loss of confidence. Suddenly her mother was old. 'I know. Thank you. When we get to that stage, I'll speak to you about it.'

It would've been nice to sit for a while when she got home, but Erin needed to start dinner. She'd planned a lasagne, but she was too tired for that faff; it would have to be spaghetti bolognese instead. As she was browning the mince, Harriet appeared at the kitchen door. 'Hi, Mum. Is this a good time to talk?'

The last couple of weeks had been difficult; she understood Harriet's anger at moving away, but what could she do? Since they'd arrived, she'd tried her best to keep her happy. 'Of course. What was it you wanted?'

Harriet leaned against the kitchen counter, watched as Erin

emptied a tin of chopped tomatoes into the pan. She was working up to something: never a good sign.

But Erin had learned to let her take her time. Trying to second guess Harriet never ended well. In the last couple of years, she'd been more and more emotionally unpredictable. Eventually, she started. 'When I was at Dad's at the weekend, he had some news.'

Erin's heart plummeted. She'd been expecting this. Though they'd divorced two years ago – and separated a year before that – the jealousy of how quickly Simon had moved on still prickled. Carmel was nice enough and, despite her glowing complexion and fabulous figure, Erin had to begrudgingly admit she was kind. Most importantly, she was good to Harriet, making sure she got time alone with her dad but also including her in their lives together. All in all, she couldn't ask for a better stepmother.

But she was only thirty. It was understandable that she'd want a baby of her own. And Simon had clearly been happy to grant her wish. How much easier it was for men to start again and build a brand-new family. For Harriet's sake, she tried to keep her voice light. 'Well, what's his news?'

'He might be moving to America.'

She froze with the wooden spoon mid-stir. That, she hadn't been expecting. 'America? Why? Where?'

'California. For work. Well, and because of Carmel too, I guess.'

Carmel was American. Her Irish heritage afforded her a British passport and she'd been here for years, though her accent was still as strong as the teenage sitcoms Harriet had loved growing up. 'Oh, I'm so sorry, love. That must have been a shock. I know how much you'll miss him. Both of them.'

But Harriet didn't look shocked; she looked guilty. 'Well, the thing is. He said that, if he gets the job, he wants me to go with them.'

The sound of the grandmother clock in the corner of the room seemed to grow louder as Erin struggled with how to respond. Had he been serious? *Bloody Simon.* 'I see. And what did you say? I mean, what do you think about that?'

Harriet shrugged and pulled at a loose thread at the hem of her shirt. 'I don't know. I mean, I haven't had a chance to think about it. What do you think?'

Head still down, she looked at Erin through her eyelashes. She hadn't had a chance to think about it? Why wasn't she saying a resounding no? How could she contemplate leaving the country, leaving her mother? 'I... er... I'm a little surprised to be honest. You say it's because of his job. What does that mean? Why is he going?'

Harriet shrugged again. 'I don't really know. He said it was an opportunity and he had to grab it.'

Erin could just imagine. This was one of Simon's favourite mantras. He was all for *grabbing life* and *maximising your opportunities* these days. 'I see. Well, when would he be going?'

Harriet wrinkled her nose as if to ward off a negative reaction. 'In four weeks' time.'

This was crazy. 'He can't move that quickly, surely?'

'He said he has to. A project he needs to start. He was talking architecture again which was really boring. But Carmel showed me the house that they'd rent. It has a pool and this massive porch and,' she paused, 'a bedroom for me which has its own bathroom and a walk-in wardrobe and everything.'

She must've got the wrong end of the stick. They'd looked at a house already? 'Surely, they mean a room for you when you come to stay? In the holidays?'

But Harriet shook her head. 'No. Dad said that if I'm changing school anyway, why don't I look at the schools in California. Can you imagine that, Mum? Going to high school in America?'

Dread crept over Erin at Harriet's excitement. Was she

really considering doing this? *Leaving* her? Going to live on the other side of the world? 'Do you want to go?'

For the first time, Harriet looked unsure. 'I don't know. It's a big thing, isn't it?'

No, it wasn't a big thing. It was a huge thing. A massively terrifying life-changing horrific thing. She wanted to call Simon right now and ask him what the hell he was thinking.

'Erin?' Her mother's reedy voice called through from the sitting room. 'Erin? Where are you?'

Her throat was almost too tight for her voice. 'I'm coming, Mum. One minute.'

Harriet slid off the kitchen stool. 'I'll go and see what she wants. It's probably the TV remote again.'

The way she rolled her eyes and smiled pierced Erin's heart. Though she wanted to return the conspiratorial smile – share in the gentle mockery of her mother – fear coursed through her veins like iced water. Harriet was more than her daughter; she was her whole world. Without her laughter and conversation and companionship, life would be hollow and empty. How dare Simon parade this exciting life in front of her with no care whatsoever of the consequences? Where had this need to be with his daughter been when she was six or eight or twelve and he was too busy at work to attend a school play or drive her to a playdate or take her shopping for school clothes? He'd been more than happy to leave all of those things to Erin since the day that Harriet was born. And now he wanted to swoop in and steal her away? How could he be that cruel?

THREE

Her childhood home had barely changed since Erin had last lived there. Her mother had never been one for interior design. Where other mothers had china ornaments or vases, their house was clear surfaces and functional furniture. The only thing her mother would allow on their shelves was books. Millions of them. Novels from every decade, from *Robinson Crusoe* onwards. As an English teacher, her mother had believed in literature like a religion. *Everything you want to know, you can learn from the pages of a novel.* It was one of her many disappointments that Erin didn't love reading the way she did, despite her having read to her every night since she was very small. To this day, Erin didn't know if her disinterest was genuine or borne from a desire to frustrate her mother in the easiest way possible.

Harriet, on the other hand, was voracious. Even before she could make sense of it, she would clutch a sticky board book in her hand and turn the pages with intent across her beautiful face. When she learned to read before she'd even started school, Erin was so proud of her that it was worth the look of smug pleasure on her own mother's face.

In the last few months, however, her mother had spent less time with a book and more time staring at the television. After dinner, when Harriet disappeared upstairs to FaceTime her friends, Erin poured herself a glass of wine and tried to find something to watch that would satisfy both her mother and herself. 'What do you fancy, Mum?'

'I don't mind, dear. You choose.'

She knew already how this nightly pantomime was going to go. '*Eastenders*?'

'No. Not that. Too much shouting.'

She flicked again. '*Columbo*?'

'I've seen them all a million times.'

'*CSI*?'

'Too violent.'

As luck would have it, there was an old episode of *To the Manor Born*. She'd always thought that Penelope Keith would play her mother in the film of her life. 'How about this, Mum?'

He mother smiled. 'Perfect.'

It didn't really matter what was on the TV, she couldn't think about anything other than Harriet's bombshell about living with Simon in America.

Was it possible that Harriet had misunderstood? Surely Simon wouldn't have made that offer without speaking to Erin about it first? What was she thinking, it was more than possible that he'd got overexcited and blurted it out. But did he really mean that she should go there to live? Permanently?

It'd been too much of a shock to discuss it in any depth with Harriet. Far better to call Simon tomorrow and see what he had to say. There was a world of a difference between visiting for the holidays and relocating to the other side of the Atlantic.

Whatever the truth of the situation, she'd be lying if she didn't admit to being hurt by Harriet's reaction. Though there'd been a few arguments over the last couple of weeks – when she'd had to explain why they were moving an hour away from all of Harriet's friends – they'd always had a good relationship. Could Harriet really leave her for the promise of a walk-in wardrobe and a pool?

And then there was this strange business with the photograph. Maybe, while her mother was transfixed by the war of words between Peter Bowles and Penelope Keith, she'd catch her off guard. 'Who is Imogen, Mum?'

She didn't take her eyes from the screen. 'Hmmm?'

'The girl in the photo that Harriet found. The baby that you were holding.'

'I don't know, dear. Listen to this bit. It's funny.'

How could her mother not remember a child she'd clearly been fond of, but she could remember a scene from a sitcom made over forty years ago? The brain was an enigma. Where were these memories stored? And which ones stuck like glue and which were discarded?

Erin glanced at her watch. It was about 8 a.m. in Sydney and Auntie Marcelle was an early riser. Her daughter Lindsey had got her onto Instagram and she was always posting pictures of her morning dog walks. It was worth trying to call her now while her mum was occupied. 'I'm going to load the dishwasher.'

Marcelle answered on the third ring. It still amazed Erin how clear the line was on the other side of the world. 'Erin! How lovely to hear from you. I'm out with the dog. How's your mum?'

The sound of her voice always tweaked something in Erin. Growing up, it was Auntie Marcelle who would reassure her that her mother loved her when they'd had an argument. 'It's just her way. She doesn't mean to sound so hard.' She could almost smell her favourite Charlie perfume.

'She's fine. Well, the dementia is progressing, but she has lots of good days. To be honest, she's nicer now than she was before.' That had been the strangest thing. As if the dementia was softening her mother's edges. It wasn't that she hadn't been kind before, but she had been... firm. There were clear rules and boundaries and a way that things should be done. The way she'd been these last few weeks – gentle, almost affectionate – made it feel as if a closer relationship might be possible. Or was it too late for that?

Marcelle sighed on the other end of the phone. 'I'd love to see her. Do you think we could try another FaceTime?'

'Of course. I'll take you into her in a minute, but I wanted to ask you something first. We've been sorting out some of Mum's things and we found some photos with people we don't recognise.'

Her aunt's familiar chuckle made her smile. 'I can imagine. I dread to think what ones you're looking at. Do we all look like extras from a period drama? Could you not recognise me when I was five stone lighter?'

'I'd always recognise you, Auntie Marcelle. No, it's a baby. And Mum is holding her. Well, a toddler I suppose. Mum seemed very fond of her. She called her Imogen. Do you know who that is?'

For a few moments, the silence at the other end was so profound that Erin wondered if the line had gone dead. 'Your mum said that?'

'Yes. First of all she said it was me. Then said it was her baby. And then we read the name on the back of the photograph. Imogen.'

There was a sigh at the other end. 'Was that all? Did she say anything else?'

This was getting more curious by the minute. 'No. When I tried to ask her, she got confused. She seemed upset so I didn't want to push it.'

Actually, it had been Harriet who didn't want to push it, but that was irrelevant.

'Okay. Look, I don't know if I should be telling you this, but I promised myself that if you ever asked... Bertie!'

The last was shouted so loudly that Erin had to take the phone away from her ear. Bertie was Aunt Marcelle's Highland Terrier and he was clearly doing something he shouldn't. 'Marcelle? Are you still there?'

'Sorry. Bertie was about to roll in something nefarious. Look, maybe we should have this conversation later. When I can concentrate.'

For the second time that evening, Erin's stomach tightened with a sense of impending doom. 'Can you just tell me now, Marcelle? You're making me nervous; I don't want to wait.'

Again, that sigh. 'Okay. But there's a lot of story and I don't want you to judge your mother harshly. You've got to understand, we're talking about half a century ago. Things were very different.'

This delay was not helping Erin's anxiety. 'Please, Marcelle. Who is Imogen?'

'Imogen is, well, she's your mother's daughter.'

Though the line was a clear as a bell, Erin must have misheard. 'Her daughter?'

'I knew I shouldn't have told you like this. Look, I have a friend who is having an eightieth birthday celebration in a couple of weeks and I've been debating about whether to come. This has decided me. I want to see your mum, too. Let's talk about it then. We can speak to your mum about it together and I can help her to explain. It's complicated, Erin.'

Complicated? That was the word you applied to a knitting pattern or a set of instructions for a DVD player. She had a sister? All these years and her mother hadn't told her? 'Was she born before my mum was married to my dad? Did he know about her?'

'Erin, it's not my place to—'

'Please, Marcelle. I can't ask Mum. Even if she remembers, she gets upset. You have to tell me.'

'Imogen is your father's daughter, too. She wasn't given away as a baby or anything like that. She left home. As a teenager. She... she ran away.'

Erin felt sick. Her whole life, she'd been desperate for a sister. That's why she'd been adamant that Harriet wouldn't be an only child and why she'd been so upset when it hadn't happened; she'd not been able to fall pregnant a second time. She'd been told – or had she just assumed? – that it'd been similar for her own parents. And now Marcelle was saying that she'd had a sister out there all this time and no one had considered telling her?

'Erin? Are you still there?' Her aunt sounded concerned.

'Yes, I'm here. Sorry, it's a lot to take in.'

'Of course it is, sweetheart. That's why I wanted to wait until I was with you. I've made it worse, haven't I? Your Uncle Ted always tells me off for crashing in like a bull in a china shop. I'm so sorry.'

'No. Not at all. I asked and you told me. I only wish that someone had told me, that my parents had told me, a long time ago.'

'I think it was difficult for your mum. It was a very painful time. Look, I'll book my flight this week and let you know when I'm coming. Please, hold on until I'm there and we'll all sit down. Get this straightened out.'

Erin needed to let all of this settle, work out what she felt and what she wanted to do. 'Okay. That's fine. Do you want me to put Mum on?'

'Actually, no. I need to get this dog home. How about I call tomorrow at about the same time? When I can concentrate properly?'

Erin was relieved that she wouldn't have to sit through a painful conversation between the two of them with these thoughts crashing around her mind. 'Good idea. I'd better go. Mum is calling me.'

Marcelle probably realised that she was lying, but it was an escape for her, too. 'Okay, love. I'm sorry if I upset you.'

'You didn't upset me, Auntie Marcelle. You're the only one who's told me the truth.'

She didn't sound reassured. 'Well then, we can talk it through when I come. And remember, it was a long time ago. Things were different.'

After she'd gone, Erin stared at the phone. Of all the things she'd imagined about that photograph, a secret sister had not been one of them. And her mum had looked so happy in the picture, too. What had changed?

It was all very well, Marcelle asking her to wait before she asked any more questions, but how could she? This blew apart everything she knew about her upbringing, about her mother, her father, her whole life. Why had her sister run away? And why had her mother not gone after her? She couldn't imagine ever letting Harriet walk out of her life and not come back; she would hunt for her for the rest of her days. Her gut twisted at even the idea of Harriet going to live in America with Simon, at not being able to see her every day to check in that she was okay. Yet her mother had lived with that for well over thirty years?

Whatever Marcelle said, she couldn't wait to find out more. Her mother's memory might be patchy, but she'd definitely recognised Imogen. There had to be a thread that she could pull which would unravel this whole mystery. With luck, the other end of that thread would also lead her to the sister she'd longed for her whole life.

FOUR

The following morning, Erin was due in early at the hotel. Much as she'd wanted to speak to her mother about Imogen last night – and fire off an angry text message to Simon – she'd learned the wisdom of waiting until her emotions had cooled before formulating a sensible strategy. When she was getting ready for bed, though, Harriet had offered to stay home with her grandmother today. 'I want to unpack the rest of those boxes of books, anyway. I want to show Granny those pretty copies of the Brontë sisters' books that you bought me.'

Was she being particularly sweet to compensate for the bombshell she'd dropped? Even so, it was relief to know that she wouldn't have to worry about her mother while she was at work. It wasn't that she couldn't be left alone, but there were times now that she was very vague. 'Maybe you can show her some more of those photos you found, too. See if you can start to work out who everyone is.'

On purpose, she hadn't mentioned the Imogen picture in particular. It hadn't felt right to tell Harriet about her conversation with Marcelle yet. For now, she wanted to nurse the secret close to herself. Harriet would have a million questions and had a large slice of Simon's impulsive 'run with it' nature. However she investigated her missing sister, Erin knew it would have to be gently and slowly.

Jasmine was already behind the reception desk and, when she saw Erin, she clapped her hands like a child about to bestow a birthday gift. 'I have hot news.'

At least someone looked happy. 'What is it?'

'The Timster has been fired.'

Erin could almost hear her mother say, 'In England we say sacked,' as she used to when a young Harriet used her YouTube-enhanced US English. Though she had a pretty low opinion of Tim's management abilities, he hadn't been a bad man and she felt sorry for him. 'Really?'

'Yep. And we're not getting a replacement hotel manager. Apparently, they've hired some super highflyer with lots of experience who's going to oversee about five of the hotels. He's going to turn everything around apparently. He came in earlier and nearly broke my wrist shaking my hand.'

She didn't like the sound of that. This hotel ran well despite Tim. Lately, she and Jasmine ran a pretty tight ship between them. The last thing they needed was some know-it-all sweeping in and changing systems for the sake of it. 'When does he start?'

'We all have to come in to a meeting on Friday; you've probably got an email. They're paying an hour to anyone not on shift. He wants to introduce himself to "the staff".' She made air quotes and pulled a face. Anyone who used that term usually treated them as if they were half-brained droids.

Erin groaned. 'I was supposed to be off on Friday. What's he like?'

Jasmine tilted her head to the side. 'Fifty-ish, tall-ish, blond-ish.'

Erin laughed. 'Sounds memorable.'

Jasmine shrugged. 'Okay looking, I suppose, if you like that kind of thing.'

'What kind of thing?'

'The blue eyes, sharp suit, easy charm kind of thing.'

'Oh I see. Yeah, easy charm is a turn off. And blue eyes? Horrendous. You'd much rather have—'

'A limp, a lisp and a long list of baggage.' They laughed together as she reeled off her favourite triplet for the kind of man she attracted. Jasmine's weekly updates on her foray into the world of Hinge and Bumble was the most exciting part of Erin's week.

Jasmine picked up her iPad from the desk and nodded towards the door behind them. 'Are you okay here if I go into the office for a bit? I'll make you a drink.'

Reception was quiet at this time of the morning. 'Of course. No problem.'

She tilted her head to one side, her long floppy fringe swinging out from her face in stark contrast to the close-shaved other half of her head. 'Is everything okay with you? You seem a little distracted.'

Erin sighed. 'There's a lot going on at home.'

She appreciated the nod of solidarity, even if – at twenty-seven – Jasmine had no children and her parents were probably not much older than Erin. 'Do you fancy going for a drink some-time? Or maybe just a coffee? We can talk strategy for the new boss starting. These walls have ears.'

Erin remembered Macy's question about whether she had friends here. Even though Jasmine was a lot younger than her, it would be nice to talk to someone she wasn't related to about everything that was going on. 'That would be lovely.'

Jasmine looked relieved, almost as if she'd asked her out on a date. 'Great. Is tomorrow too soon?'

'Tomorrow would be lovely.'

After her shift ended at 2 p.m., Erin did a speed shop at the nearby Sainsbury's before heading home. At the moment, she didn't have to worry about her mother when Harriet was home to keep an eye on her, but she'd have to come up with a more permanent solution once Harriet started college.

Cold trickled down her spine at the thought that Harriet might not be going to the sixth form college she'd enrolled her into. That she could be going much farther afield. She'd sent a text to Simon while she was at work, asking him whether it was true about his move to California and why he hadn't let her know about it. So far, he hadn't replied.

When she pushed the front door open, Harriet's music greeted her from upstairs. After dumping the shopping onto the kitchen counter, she pushed open the door to the lounge to check on her mother. As soon as she walked in, her mother turned with a smile. 'Hello, dear. How was your day?'

Having her mother at home to welcome her was a new experience for Erin. Growing up, she'd never walked home from school alone. When she was very young, her mother had worked at the same school she'd attended – in order to keep an eye on her, she was sure. Even when she started at the secondary school, her mother would insist that Erin join her at work straight after the day ended. There was no hanging around the park with her friends or being allowed a house key to let herself in.

Now she answered her with a shrug. 'It was fine. Busy, but fine.'

The tin of photos was open on the floor; Harriet must have been looking through them. Erin sifted through to find the photo of her mother and Imogen, really looking at it this time. Her mother's clothes were ones she'd never seen before. If she had to guess, Erin would've said they looked like clothes from the sixties. What had made her sister run away from home? And why hadn't her mother gone to look for her? Or maybe she had? 'Mum? Do you remember Imogen?'

Her mother's face hardened. 'I don't want to talk about it.'

This was a face she recognised. Impenetrable, unassailable: her *Because I'm Your Mother* face. 'Why not, Mum? I know who she is. I know that she was your daughter.' Why had she used the past tense?

'I don't want to talk about her.'

She knew that her mother wasn't well, but there was no other way of finding out. 'It's okay, Mum. You can tell me. Why did she leave? Where is Imogen?'

'No!' Her voice was so loud it made Erin jump. When she was a teenager, she used to call that her mother's teacher voice.

But she wasn't a teenager any longer. 'Mum, I'm a grown woman. If I have a sister out there—'

'Stop!' Now her mother had her hands over her ears like a young child. 'You don't understand. It's trouble. She's trouble. Leave it alone.'

It was cruel to push her like this. 'Okay. Okay. I'm sorry. I'll leave it alone. It's okay, Mum.'

She reached out for her mother's arm to pat it reassuringly, but her mother grabbed her hand instead. 'Promise me, Erin. Promise you'll forget about it.'

This was also a regular refrain from childhood. Promise me you'll come straight here from school. Promise me you won't go to that party. Promise me you'll look when you cross the road, keep your purse out of sight in your pocket, won't talk to strangers. So many rules that she almost suffocated.

Ironically – like then – it was only making Erin more curious, but she'd pushed her mother hard enough for one evening. She didn't want to upset her. Instead, she crossed the fingers of her other hand, feeling stupid as she did so. 'I promise. Now let me make you a fresh cup of tea.'

That seemed to do the trick. But she had no intention whatsoever of leaving this alone. On her way to the kitchen, she picked up the biscuit tin from the arm of the sofa and took it with her.

Once the kettle was filled and switched on, she tipped out the entire contents of the tin onto the floral wipe-clean cloth on the kitchen table. When they'd first opened it, they'd only taken out the photographs. But there were other documents there, including a school report with Imogen's name on it.

The report was a small blue booklet containing thin hand-written sheets of reports. It was strange to read about this girl who was her closest relation. Most of the reports were low-level generic – must try harder, needs to focus, less chat/more work – until she got to the domestic science teacher who raved about a creative, focused student who was so different to the girl described on the other pages that Erin wondered if they'd stapled in a report belonging to another child.

It was once she'd closed the booklet that she had the idea to look up the school online. St Hilda's School for Girls. How many of them could there be?

Harriet's laptop was on the kitchen table; she must've been watching it at lunchtime. It turned out that there was more than one St Hilda's but one of them was in Stokesby, the town they'd lived in when Erin was young. It had to be the one. Now she had the school she could search for an alumni page on Facebook – there were so many of them now. She avoided her own school page like the plague. Within a few clicks she'd found it. *Memories of St Hilda's Stokesby*.

She scrolled through the usual collection of photographs and stories about old teachers. Though she scrutinised the group photographs, it was too big a leap to match the toddler in her mother's photo with one of the grinning teenagers in these black and white images. One of the recent threads was a 'Where are they now?' and people had commented with the names of fellow students that they'd like to get in touch with. For a few moments Erin scrolled through. How many of these reconnections resulted in rekindled friendship? Or extra-marital affairs? Before she could talk herself out of it, she left a comment of her own. *Does anyone remember Imogen Clarke?* She checked the date on the report card. *She would have been at the school around 1983.*

Once it had posted, she stared at it for a little longer before shaking her head. As if someone was going to reply immediately. She swiped away from Facebook and checked her messages. Simon still hadn't replied, so she called him. He answered on the fourth ring.

'Erin? Hi. Look, I know that I didn't reply to your text but I've been up to my eyes in it today. So much to get sorted out. I'm assuming Harriet told you about the potential move to the US?'

She could practically hear the swagger in his tone. 'She did. That's a bit sudden, isn't it?'

'Yes and no. Carms and I have been thinking about it for a while. Her grandmother has been unwell and she wants to be back home. Then this job came up so we decided to jump for it. It's all very last minute. The guy they had lined up for it had to bail out.'

The way he abbreviated Carmel's name put her teeth on edge. What was he, fifteen? 'Harriet also told me that you've invited her to go and live with you over there.'

At least he had the decency to sound a tiny bit contrite. 'Ah, yes.'

'Might have been nice to discuss it with me first, Simon. Or at least give me the heads up.'

His tone switched immediately to irritation. 'It's not definite yet, and she's my daughter, too, Erin. I shouldn't have to ask your permission to speak to her about something.'

He always did this. Made her out to be the unreasonable one. The old familiar rage began to bubble in her belly. 'This is not about a day trip to the beach, Simon. You're suggesting she lives a ten-hour plane ride away from me.'

'And you're suggesting she stays a ten-hour plane ride away from me.'

'But you're the one choosing to go.'

Here they were again, back and forth, tit for tat. 'Look, Erin. This is not a personal attack on you. I've had a life-changing job opportunity and I want to go for it. Let's face it, I'm nearly forty and what have I done with my life? This is my chance.'

The sting of that insult hurt; almost twenty of those years he'd been with her. She fought to keep her voice calm. 'I understand that, Simon. But why do you need to take Harriet from me?'

It was a minor victory that he was the first to lose his temper. 'Oh, for goodness' sake. Maybe because she's just as much my daughter as yours? Because I'd really like her to come and live with me and because, actually, she's old enough to make that decision for herself. She's fifteen, Erin. She's not a baby.'

Fifteen. She wasn't an adult either. And Harriet would always be her baby, no matter how old she was. *Stay calm.* 'I just think you should've talked to me about it.'

His voice got louder. 'Why? It's not up to you. It's up to Harriet. It's her life.'

It took every ounce of self-control she had not to shout back. *She is my life!* Because what was the point? It would get her nowhere. Simon had made up his mind that he wanted to take Harriet. And, after all, wasn't that what he'd always done? Put his own desires before everyone else's? But if he thought she was going to take it lying down, he had another think coming. 'Well, maybe Harriet needs some time to consider her options. Don't go booking her plane ticket yet.'

His laugh bordered on unkind. 'You go for it. You forget that I've been in your mother's house, Erin. And I know what the atmosphere is like between the two of you. I'll be surprised if *you* last it out, let alone Harriet.'

She bit on her lip rather than tell him that, surprisingly, things had been better between them recently. Having lived through her many rants about her mother's need to control her whole life, he probably wouldn't believe her. 'I'm only asking that you give Harriet a chance to think. Don't do one of your persuasive numbers on her.'

He was good at that. Piling on the charm. Hadn't that been what'd attracted her to him in the first place? 'Well, I can't promise not to show her how great her life could be in California.'

It wasn't difficult to imagine. He was going to pull out all the stops: the house was only the start. Which meant her sole option was to work on their daughter. She knew that Harriet wouldn't want to upset her. But should she use that – effectively employ emotional blackmail – to get her to stay?

FIVE

The cafe on Broad Street was large and busy. An eclectic collection of chairs arranged around square and oval tables were full of laughter and energetic conversations, leaving little room for Erin to squeeze through to where Jasmine had staked her claim on a table in the back corner. It had been a while since Erin was somewhere with such a buzzy atmosphere; she'd missed it.

'This is nice.' The opening line everywhere for the socially awkward. It was the first time she and Jasmine had met up outside work; it was as if they were taking their relationship to the next level. Though they'd only worked together for a few weeks, they'd clicked almost immediately. A quick wit, sarcasm and a kind heart: everything she looked for in a friend.

'Yes. I used to come here with my ex. The one with the twitch.'

Jasmine had had her in hysterics last week, detailing the men she'd dated in the last year. According to her, the only available men at her age were from a very thin gene pool. 'Well, he's got good taste in cafes as well as women, then.'

Jasmine winked at her. 'I see what you did there. Can you

read the blackboard menu from here or shall I grab a paper one from the counter?'

'Hey, I'm not that old.' Erin laughed. Jasmine was only about ten years younger than her, but she seemed a generation different with her cool hair and the clothes she wore. Erin felt a little frumpy in her jeans and long shirt.

'I wasn't saying that. In fact, I was going to ask if you wanted to come to a singles night with me next week.'

Erin couldn't think of anything worse. 'Thanks, but no thanks. I've got enough on my plate at the moment.'

Jasmine looked sympathetic. 'Your mum?'

Though she didn't know Jasmine that well, Erin needed to talk to someone about it. 'Simon – that's my ex-husband – might be moving to America.'

'Lucky Simon.' Jasmine tilted her head to get the lay of the emotional land. 'And that's a good thing or bad?'

'As far as he goes, I don't care either way. It's Harriet I'm worried about.'

Jasmine nodded. 'Because she'll be upset.'

If only it were just that. 'Worse. He wants her to go with him.'

Jasmine's eyes widened in surprise. 'Oh, I see. I thought she was only fifteen? Isn't she in school?'

'Between schools. She's enrolled to start at the sixth form in September.' It became clear that her mother needed care back in March, but Erin had spent almost three months doing a daily two hour round trip from her flat to her mother's house so that Harriet didn't have to move before her GCSE exams were over.

'What does your daughter want to do? Does she want to move over there?'

'We haven't properly talked about it. But she seemed pretty excited when she told me that he'd suggested it. The house he's buying or renting or whatever sounds incredible. What teenager wouldn't want to go?'

Jasmine shrugged. 'It's still a big thing to do when you're only fifteen. What about her friends here?'

Erin felt a familiar stab of guilt. It had been the main thrust of their arguments in the weeks leading up to the move here. That Erin was taking her away from all of her friends. But what could she do? Everything the doctor had said about dealing with her mother's dementia had centred on keeping her around familiar places as long as possible. And they would have had to move anyway. That was another thing she hadn't shared with Harriet: how increasingly tight their finances had become since the divorce. The cost of everything seemed to be getting higher and higher. Moving in with her mother made things a lot easier, though Erin had insisted they pay their way in terms of bills and groceries.

'Her friends are all an hour's drive away. We've found a really good sixth form, with a fantastic art department, but she's feeling understandably nervous about starting somewhere new.'

'She's an artist?'

Harriet was an amazing artist. 'Yes. I have no idea where she gets it from, but she's always been really creative. When she was tiny, if she wasn't reading or writing a story, she was wielding a paintbrush. She's into collage at the moment.'

Jasmine screwed up her nose. 'Sticking things onto paper?'

'I think there's more to it than that, but yes. The thing is, because she hasn't yet started at the new sixth form, she doesn't know what it's like. And Simon will find some amazing college over there where she can basically live her teenage dream of being a senior in high school with an American-movie life.'

It was her own fault, bringing her up on a diet of *Gilmore Girls* and *Modern Family* and *Pitch Perfect*. She'd watched so many teen movies of American proms that she'd talked about going to Yale before she'd even known it was in a different country.

'Well, of course it's going to sound amazing. It's not real, is it? Can't she go out there on a long visit and see what it's really like day to day? That might change her mind.'

It was the 'might' that was frightening. What if Harriet got there and it was exactly what she'd dreamed of? Plus, there wasn't really time for a trial run if Erin's late night google search was to be trusted. 'Schools go back earlier over there. I think she'd need to be enrolled pretty quickly if she was going to start the school year with everyone else. Meanwhile, while she's over there, she could lose her place here.'

Jasmine pulled a face. 'Crikey. It never stops, being a mum, does it? I assumed that the little kid stage was the hard part. Sounds much more complicated now.'

She wasn't wrong. As one of Erin's friends used to say, the bigger the child, the bigger the problem. 'I don't want to be one of those mothers who holds her child back, but fifteen is so young. I'm not ready to let her go yet.'

Jasmine glanced past her at a man holding shopping bags who was watching to see if they were leaving their table; she stood as she spoke. 'But if you let her go and then she comes back, it'll be her decision. It won't be you holding her back. I'd better go and order our food; there's a man over there giving me daggers for our table. I'm having a cheese toastie. What would you like?'

'I'll have the same, thanks. And a latte.'

While she was gone, Erin avoided looking at the man who wanted their table by checking her phone for messages. There was no way she could take the risk that Harriet would want to come back to her after being in that almost-mansion in California. No, she needed to make Harriet realise how nice her life could be here instead. Now she had a bit more spare money, she could take her shopping for paint and furniture for her room, make it really nice. She could arrange something for her and her friends too. They might be more persuasive than she could ever be.

On Facebook, there were quite a few replies to her question about Imogen Clarke. A couple were people saying that they recognised the name and one person used inverted commas when they said they thought she'd 'left' the school early. Were they suggesting that she'd been expelled? Then there were a couple of people with anecdotes about her. One remembered her getting caught smoking outside the school gates and another said she'd been 'really crazy' when they'd been in a science class together. Erin had been such a rule-abiding good girl at school, she was surprised to find her elder sister – it felt strange even thinking that word – had not been the same. Was this why her mother had never spoken about her? Had she been expelled from school?

Jasmine slid two large cups of coffee onto the table. 'They're going to bring the toasties over in a minute.'

'Thanks. If you wanted to find someone, where would you look?'

Jasmine tilted her head to one side. 'A man, you mean? You're asking the wrong person. I've tried everywhere bar searching under rocks.'

Erin laughed. 'No, not a man. Someone you wanted to track down. If all you had was a name.'

Erin loved that Jasmine didn't even ask her why she needed to know this. 'Online, I suppose. Facebook or a Google search. If that doesn't work, I think there are agencies you can use.'

She wasn't really at that stage yet. Both a general google and a trawl on Facebook for Imogen Clarke had brought up hundreds of results. There was also something stopping her from throwing herself into the search. First, she wanted to find out more from her mother about why they'd lost touch and why her sister's name had never been mentioned in her presence. She'd try again tonight. And if she still got nowhere, she'd step up the search.

Jasmine sipped at her tea. 'So, do you think this new manager is going to make lots of changes?'

'Probably. Otherwise, how will he justify his appointment?' Erin had worked in enough hotels where this was exactly what happened. New broom wanting to sweep away all their predecessor's plans. The problem was, the good often got swept out with the bad. She could do without hassle at work adding to her mental load at the moment.

'It would be good if he can recruit some decent people. Do you think I can request some male staff, twenty-five to thirty-five, financially solvent, fresh breath?'

Erin laughed. 'I'm not sure that dating someone at work would be the best idea.'

'Maybe not. Well, someone who isn't going to make more work rather than less. Otherwise, I think you should resurrect that dream of having a hotel and I'll come and work for you.'

'Good plan.' But that was the last thing on Erin's list. Her career would need to just tick over for now, her focus was Harriet and making her life here more attractive. The bedroom she was sleeping in was more like a glorified storeroom right now. She'd start with that.

SIX

The bedding department at John Lewis was quiet, but shopping for Harriet's room was not as easy as Erin had imagined it would be. The glint in her daughter's eye was disconcerting.

'Really? I can have *anything* I want?'

Erin clearly needed to set a few parameters. 'Within reason, yes. I mean, a water feature or a golden bed frame aren't quite possible, but other than that.'

As they wandered, they passed a room display for a little girl: princess themed bedding, a net hung from the ceiling and white cupboards with tiny crown motifs. 'You would have loved that one, once.'

Harriet took her hand and pulled her away. 'Come on, Mother. Those days are long gone.'

Everyone had told her how quickly time went when you had a child, but she was only just beginning to feel the painful truth of it. Before now, each stage had brought something new to compensate for what had been lost. Being able to watch decent films together rather than Disney on repeat, eating in nice restaurants rather than those with a kids menu, sharing funny jokes that didn't start with a *knock knock* or have a punchline that was delivered too early.

But now, it wasn't so much that Harriet was growing *up*, but that she was growing *away*. She knew it would happen – it was right that it did – but she hadn't expected it to be so soon. 'What colour scheme are you thinking of?' She pointed at the display closest to them. 'Yellow? Pale green?'

Harriet pulled a face. 'No, Mum. I was thinking navy blue. Like midnight.'

Navy blue? Heaven save her from the whims of a creative child. 'Do you remember the time you decided to paint your bedroom when I was at work and Dad was supposed to be watching you?'

She'd come home from a weekend shift and found Simon asleep in front of the television. Meanwhile, eight-year-old Harriet had taken it into her head to embellish the pale pink walls of her bedroom.

Harriet grinned. 'You mean you weren't a fan of my early work? The rainbows and unicorns were a nice touch, surely?'

Erin shook her head. 'I'd only painted it the week before. I nearly killed your father.'

After shaking him awake, she'd dragged Simon upstairs, Harriet had protested that Simon said she was allowed to do it. Apparently, there'd been some confusion between his belief she'd asked to 'paint *in* my room' and her hands-on-the-hips recount that she'd asked to paint the room itself.

Harriet held out her hands and raised an eyebrow. 'What can I say? When the muse strikes.'

Laughing together like this was one of the gifts of her being older. Though Erin missed that cute toothy eight-year-old, she loved the clever, funny almost-woman who'd taken her place. She couldn't resist pulling her into brief squeeze. 'Okay then, Frida Kahlo. What about a desk? For your college work? Something big enough for your art projects?'

Harriet squinted her eyes as if picturing it. 'And can I have a whole wall of cork, too, so that I can pin up what I'm working on?'

That sounded promising. Maybe she hadn't made her mind up yet. Erin pressed on for victory. 'Look at this bed. It's got a mattress underneath that you can pull out. That'd be great when you have a friend over. Maybe you could invite your girls from home to come for the weekend soon?'

When Harriet smiled, it lit up her face. 'Yes, that would be brilliant. I've really missed them. It's not the same when I can't meet them in the town like we used to.'

Guilt squeezed at Erin. She missed it too, the girls who would pile into their lounge to watch a film amidst mountains of cushions and popcorn. Because of her own lack of sleepovers as a child, she loved nothing more than hosting Harriet's friends whenever she wanted it. 'I'm sorry, love. About moving you all the way over here. It's just your gran...'

'I get it, Mum. I do.'

She was a good kid. She really was. 'I've been thinking. About the new sixth form? If you're really not keen on going there, maybe we could look around. At art colleges, perhaps?'

Harriet's eyes narrowed with suspicion. 'But you said that you didn't want me going to an art college. You said I should do three A levels so that I could keep my options open.'

That was before her father suggested taking her to another continent. 'Maybe I was hasty. I only want you to be happy, love.' It was true. It's just that she wanted her to be happy here, with her.

Harriet frowned at a shelf of cushions and blankets, avoiding Erin's eyes. 'I guess I need to work out what I'm doing first. With Dad and everything.'

Erin had to tread lightly, but it was like walking over cut glass. 'So you're seriously considering it? Moving over there, starting at a school there?'

Harriet smoothed a pillow with her hand, the nap of the pile becoming darker as she moved her hand against it. When she looked up, her eyes searched for Erin's approval. 'Like you said before, it's a lot to think about. I mean, I wouldn't want you to be unhappy about it.'

Even knowing that the move to California might never happen, how could she not be unhappy about the very idea of it? How could it not feel as if her heart was about to be wrenched out of her chest and carried away, leaving a huge Harriet-shaped hole. But how could Harriet possibly understand that? It was so much different for a child than a mother. The love was not equal. 'Well, it's not about me, is it? What do *you* want to do?'

With every ounce of her, she wanted Harriet to *choose* to stay.

'I don't know, Mum.'

This was too painful, too much. And what was she asking? That Harriet choose between a shabby bedroom in her grandmother's house or a walk-in wardrobe in California? Between a sixth form college without her friends or an American high school that she'd fantasised about since she was ten? Between her mother and her father?

She coughed to clear the thickness from her throat. 'Well, let's get this room decorated anyway. You'll need a bedroom here either way.'

As they wandered around the bedding department, picking up duvet covers and cushions and throws, Erin checked her phone again. There were a couple more comments on the post about Imogen. One was another memory of her being in their class, but the second was someone saying that they'd actually bumped into Imogen a couple of years ago working in a pub in Kent. The message had been posted about two minutes ago. Maybe that person was still online? Her heart beat a little faster as she clicked on their name to send a direct message.

> Hi. Would you be able to send me the name of the pub where you saw Imogen Clarke?

After hitting send, she realised that they had no idea who she was. They might be reluctant to reply in case she was a debt collector or an angry ex.

> I'm an old friend of hers and I'd love to get in touch with her again.

Three dots appeared almost immediately and she held her breath for the reply.

> It was the Dog and Partridge just outside Brabton. I don't know if she's still there. It was a couple of years ago.

After saying she was a friend, she couldn't get away with asking for a physical description. What could she ask that might help her identify Imogen among the other people who worked there?

> Has she changed much since school?

The three dots again. Then:

> Not really. Same long dark hair. Older obviously, but then aren't we all!

Erin typed a laughing emoji and a thanks, then looked up to see Harriet frowning at her. 'What's the matter, Mum?'

Erin forced a smile. 'The matter? Nothing. Just replying to a text message. Come on, we haven't made a decision about anything yet. Let's spend some money.'

After they'd bought paint and cork tiles and taken some

photos of furniture they might come back for, Harriet corralled her into an art supplies shop where she managed to spend an eye-watering amount on fresh paint and various types of glue and paper. 'I'm going to create a mood collage so that I can come up with a theme for my room.'

'That's a great idea.' What might a mood collage look like for the inside of Erin's mind? Was there enough blue paper in the world?

Once they got home, Harriet disappeared upstairs with her purchases. When Erin popped her head around the lounge door to say hello to her mother, she seemed to be looking at her hands and smiling. 'Are you okay, Mum?'

She didn't look up. 'Her dress was lemon yellow. The frill was white.'

As she came closer, Erin could see that her mother was holding the photograph in her hands. The one of her and a baby Imogen. She was remembering it. Erin tried not to sound as eager as she felt. 'That must have been pretty.'

'It was. Our neighbour made it for her. She was so clever with her needle. She tried to teach me but we decided that it was better for me to read to her as she worked. I used to read to Imogen, too.'

These were memories that her mother had never shared with her before. Erin needed to tread carefully so as not to break the spell. 'What did you read to her?'

'Stories. Poems. Whatever I was reading at the time. She didn't mind. She just liked to hear me. She was such a happy baby.'

Her finger trembled as she stroked the baby in the photograph. It was so tender, yet it was painful for Erin to watch. The look of love in her mother's face was so rare, so intimate, she felt excluded. This was the closest she'd come to finding out more, maybe she only needed to keep her mother talking. 'What was she like?'

Her mother looked up, eyes misted with memory. 'Who?'

'Imogen. What was she like?'

'She was really clever. She could have been anything she wanted to be until she met him.'

There was real vitriol in her voice. 'Who is him, Mum?'

'That boy. That boy took her away from me. He wasn't a good boy.'

They were getting close to something now. 'What happened?'

The corners of her mother's face turned down. 'She had to go. Imogen had to go.'

And she started to cry.

'It's okay, Mum. You don't need to get upset. It's okay.'

It was strange being the one to try and make her feel better, as if their roles were gradually being reversed. Yet Erin had no strong memories of her mother soothing her in this way. She'd been kind, but not tactile. Instead of hugs, she'd dispensed advice. Advice that Erin had found increasingly irritating and controlling the older she got.

Her mother wiped at her eyes and patted Erin's hand. 'You're a good girl.'

Even now, unexpected praise from her mother brought tears to Erin's eyes. She swallowed. 'I'll go and make you a cup of tea.'

It would have been cruel to push her mother further when she was so upset, but it was frustrating trying to grasp hold of the wisps of memory to make sense of them. If it was a boy who caused the rift, had Imogen run away with him? And, if so, were they still together? Why had she never come home?

Maybe the only person who could answer those questions was Imogen herself. In the kitchen, Erin found the Dog and Partridge pub website. It looked like a typical country pub – dark wooden beams, red velvet chairs, a fireplace – but there were rave reviews about the food. There was also a telephone number. Should she ring it now before she lost her nerve? Maybe she didn't even work there any longer.

There was only one way to find out. Erin's finger trembled as she pressed the number onto her phone. With each ring, though, her resolve weakened. What was she going to say? Should she explain who she was? Mention the dementia? Ask Imogen if it was true that she was her sister? As she was about to hang up, there was a metallic clatter followed by a gruff voice on the other end of the line. 'Dog and Partridge. How can I help?'

Too late to hang up, she swallowed her nerves. 'Hi. I'm looking for Imogen Clarke. Is she there?'

There was a pause on the other end, she could hear laughter and the clinking of glasses in the background. 'Er, we do have an Imogen, but she's not a Clarke. She's not in at the moment. Is it a reservation? Can I help?'

Not a Clarke? So, whether or not she was still with 'that boy', she must have married. Unless she'd wanted to distance herself from her mother so much that she'd changed her name? 'No. No. I need to speak to Imogen. I'm an old friend. Do you have a number for her?'

'I can't give out personal details, I'm afraid. But I can give her your number.'

'That would be great.'

Erin reeled off her number and then asked him to repeat it back to her to check he had taken it down correctly. 'Okay, got it. Who shall I say you are?'

'Oh. Of course. I'm Erin but she won't know that name. Could you say that I'm calling about her mother, Ava Clarke?'

She assumed he was writing all that down, too, as he repeated it back to her. 'Erin calling about your mother Ava Clarke. Okay then, I'll let her know. Take care.'

He rang off but she stayed still with the phone at her ear for a few moments more. Was this Imogen really her sister? And would she call her back?

SEVEN

Breakfast was going so well until Harriet ran downstairs waving her mobile phone.

To begin with, Erin's mother was on remarkably good form. In fact, when Erin came into the kitchen, she'd set the table for them to sit down together. What a strange unpredictable illness this was. 'Now, sit yourself down and I'll make you a proper breakfast before you leave.'

A glance at her watch confirmed that Erin had enough time. 'Thanks. Will you be okay at home today while I'm at work?'

Her mother laughed. 'Of course, I will. I've got lots of reading to catch up on. Now, how do you want your eggs?'

As a child, her mother had insisted she eat something hot – scrambled egg or porridge – before she left for school. Mornings had run with military precision as she'd had to get herself ready for work at the same time. There'd been no room for disagreement or reluctance. You ate what was put in front of you and you did it quickly and cleanly. Nowadays Erin wasn't used to eating much for breakfast. 'I don't need eggs. Just some toast will be great, thank you.'

Footsteps thudding down the stairs heralded Harriet's

breathless arrival in the kitchen. 'Mum! Look at this house that Dad and Carmel are going to rent in California.'

It'd been hard at times, but she'd always made sure that she never made Harriet feel that she couldn't speak about her father at home, so it wasn't as if she was being tactless. Still, the last thing Erin wanted to see was an online brochure for a huge white modern house that you might see a celebrity being papped outside. 'Wow. That's pretty amazing.'

Harriet turned the phone screen to herself and swiped through several pictures before turning it back to Erin. 'And this would be my bedroom.'

It did look fabulous. A gigantic double bed with a grand headboard didn't cover even a quarter of the floorspace and an expanse of wardrobes seemed to stretch indefinitely outside of the photograph. On one side, a second door had been left open to show the gleaming white tiles of an en suite bathroom. It was the kind of room you'd see in a Hollywood film and then scoff at how unrealistic it was. The paint and cork tiles she'd purchased yesterday didn't have a chance against that lot. 'Wow, again. Is that definitely the house they're going to rent? If they go, I mean.'

'I think so. Wait until my friends see this.'

Harriet was already sending it to them as she turned back out of the room. Erin snatched up her own phone from the kitchen counter and fired off an angry text to Simon. Enough was enough.

We need to meet to discuss your move and what you're saying to Harriet. It's not fair to conduct this through her.

He must have been at work already because he sent a message straight back.

I can meet you tomorrow. A drink at The King's Arms?

The King's Arms was on the A23. They used to have lunch there quite often when they visited her mum. It was only half an hour away, so she could meet him straight from work tomorrow.

Fine. 6.30 p.m.?

She jumped as the toast popped up from the toaster. Her mum pulled it out with wooden tongs and arranged it on a plate. 'Put your phone down and come and eat something.'

Most of her childhood it had been the two of them. Her dad had worked long hours and her mum – despite working full-time as a teacher – had been the one to cook all her meals and make sure she had what she needed for school. At the time, she'd taken it for granted, but now she knew what a juggling act it must have been for her. She may not have been a baking and playing mother, but she had always made sure that Erin had what she needed.

Except that sometimes Erin felt as if she'd needed more. More time, more affection. That was why, when she'd had Harriet, she'd done everything she could to make sure that she was there for anything she needed. She'd wanted her to feel wanted and needed and loved. When more children hadn't happened for her and Simon, she had felt guilt that Harriet might experience the same loneliness at home that she had done. Throwing herself into the role of entertainer and play-mate with renewed vigour to ensure that she never felt the need to wish – as Erin had done – for a brother or sister to keep her company.

Her mother waved a cup at her. 'Do you want coffee with your toast? Or tea?'

'Oh, coffee, please.'

But when her mother turned towards the kettle, she froze, staring at it. Then at the cup in her hand.

Anxiety prickled in Erin's stomach. 'What's the matter, Mum?'

She was shaking her head. 'I can't remember. I can't remember what to do.'

The confusion made her voice tremble and Erin got to her feet. 'It's okay. Sit down and have some toast. I can do it.'

'Why can't I remember?'

'You're probably tired. It's okay.'

She guided her mother to a kitchen chair. How thin and fragile her arm felt. She'd always been such a solid capable woman and Erin still hadn't acclimatised to how vulnerable she was now. The door to the kitchen swung open and Harriet's phone entered, followed by Harriet. 'Mum, look at—'

'Not now, Harriet.' She hadn't meant to sound so sharp, but the last thing she needed right now was another tour around Simon's palace.

Harriet's face darkened. 'Don't bite my head off.'

This wasn't going to help her want to stay with Erin. 'Sorry, love. I just...'

But she'd gone and it was more important that Erin focus on her mother. The dementia was so unpredictable. She'd been so active this morning that she'd almost forgotten that she needed to watch her. What if she'd scalded herself trying to work out how to pour from the kettle? The last appointment they'd had with her mother's specialist, he'd tried to explain that he couldn't tell them how quickly the illness might progress. What if she didn't manage to get hold of Imogen before her mother lost any memory of who she was? If she didn't hear from her by tonight, she'd call again.

When Erin arrived for the meeting with the new hotel manager, most of the other staff were already there. Tables from one end of the dining room had been pushed to the side and the chairs rearranged in rows of ten. Jasmine waved from the seats she'd saved at the back. As soon as Erin sat down, she slipped her a bit of paper. 'What's this?'

'One of the porters is taking bets on the speech. A quid to enter. I've already put in for yours. You need to write down how many times you think he's going to say the words *vision*, *together* or *future*. The person with the closest total gets the cash.'

Erin scribbled down a number and then glanced around. 'Is he here yet, Mr Easy Charm?'

'He's having a tour of the bedrooms. Then I think he's going to put on his satin pants and press play on "Eye of the Tiger".'

Erin stifled a giggle. It was all very well sitting next to Jasmine, but she was able to stay deadpan while Erin's face was no good for poker. Never had been. This was like school all over again.

A hush came over the room as a blondish, fifty-ish man made his way to the front. Jasmine had been right about the suit, too.

'Thank you for being here so promptly, everyone. It's great to have the opportunity to set out my vision for our future together.'

Across the room, thirty pencils scratched onto scraps of paper.

The speech was relatively short and he spoke about the refurbishment of some of the rooms, his plan to recruit more staff and some 'opportunities' for members of existing staff to take on new roles within the hotel group. Jasmine had nudged her and whispered out of the side of her mouth. 'I'm applying for CEO.'

Erin tried to disguise her laugh as a cough.

At the end of the meeting, the staff on shift disappeared quite quickly, but Jasmine insisted that she and Erin take a glass of the orange juice laid out on a white cloth on a side table. As they turned back into the room, their new boss was behind them.

'Hi. I'm Josh. We've not met.'

Erin could feel a traitorous blush travelling up her neck. 'Erin. I work on reception with Jasmine.'

'Ah yes. I noticed that you were laughing at some of my words. Was there something you wanted to talk about?'

Oh no, this really was like school. 'No, I'm so sorry, I—'

'She has a condition.' Jasmine interjected. 'A twitch.'

He frowned, clearly not believing a word. 'I see.' He paused. 'Actually, I recognise you. We've met before, haven't we?'

It took Erin a moment to realise that he wasn't talking to Jasmine. 'Me? I don't think so. I only moved back here a couple of months ago.'

'Not from here. Somewhere else. I'm sure of it.'

The way he was staring at her made the blush climb even higher. She willed Jasmine not to nudge her because she wouldn't be able to hold it together.

Thankfully, he had a whole room of staff members to mingle with. 'It'll come to me. I'll be here at different times this week, so I'll see you both around.'

He made it sound almost like a threat. As soon as he was out of hearing distance, Erin turned to Jasmine with a groan. 'You told him I had a twitch?'

'Best I could think of in the moment. You'd better start working on it for the next time you see him.'

When she got home, her mother wasn't in the chair in the lounge or in the kitchen. She checked upstairs. Not in her bedroom or the bathroom. Where was she? 'Mum?'

The back garden was empty. As was the garage and Dad's

old shed. Heart beating faster, Erin snatched up her keys and flew outside to check the street.

The road had changed a lot since Erin had lived here as a teenager. Where there'd been front gardens and children playing out, there were now dropped kerbs and paved drive-ways. The only person she knew who lived on the street was her mother's next-door neighbour, who sometimes came in for a chat in the afternoon, but her doorbell echoed in an empty house.

Erin felt sick. What should she do now? Call the police? Would they help to look for her mother when she might have only been missing a short while? When there was no reason apart from Erin's sense of foreboding to suggest that she wasn't perfectly happy wandering around the shops or visiting a friend.

Except that she'd done neither of those things for weeks. Aside from The Oasis, her mother had barely been out of the house since Erin and Harriet moved in. Whenever Erin suggested a trip to the shops or a walk to the park, she'd come up with a reason not to go. That's why she was anxious to find her gone without even leaving a note. Where should she even start to look? *Think. Think.*

Maybe she'd gone out with Harriet. Erin's phone was back inside and she fumbled with the key in the lock in her eagerness to get to it. It was a waste of time. Harriet's phone rang and rang. Dammit.

She was halfway through writing a text to ask if she'd seen Ava when there was a knock on the door. Erin threw it open with the phone still in her hand. There was her mother, looking lost and confused. 'I must have forgotten my key.'

Erin breathed out in relief as she stood back to let her mum in. 'Where have you been?'

'I went for a walk to the shop. I needed to get some milk, but I forgot to take my purse. I must have forgotten my key, too.'

Following her into the lounge, she realised that there was no bag on her shoulder, either. Had she lost it on the way? 'Did you take a bag, Mum?'

'I don't know.' Her voice was wobbly. She'd frightened herself.

It took less than a minute to locate her bag under the coats on the rack in the hall. Erin tried to make light of it. 'Oh well. We all forget things, don't we?'

Her mother's lip trembled. 'But I'm forgetting a lot, aren't I? It's like I know there's something, but I can't grasp it, I can't hold onto it.'

It must be so scary. 'I know. But it's okay. I'm here. It'll all be okay. I bought some milk on the way home, anyway. Slip your shoes off and I'll make us some tea.'

The kettle was still warm, so her mother can't have been gone too long. Erin flicked the switch to boil it again. Was it getting to the stage when her mother should never be left alone? At the moment, she went to The Oasis twice a week, as a place she could socialise. Maybe Macy had taken Erin into the office because she could see something that Erin had missed. The dementia was progressing.

At the last meeting with her mother's specialist, Erin had tried to push him for a timeline. How quickly was this going to happen? What help would her mother need? Was there anything they could do to improve her mother's chances? But he hadn't been able to give her anything concrete, except to say that – though there would be lucid moments, or hours, or even days – this was something that was going to rob her mother of her short, and then long, term memories. There was no escaping that.

When she'd gone over the doctor's prognosis in her mind, almost every night as she lay in bed trying to sleep, she couldn't have imagined that some of those memories were about someone she herself knew nothing about. Maybe Imogen had been given the message she'd left at the pub and decided not to return her call. But it was also possible that she'd never been given the message at all. And Erin didn't have time to wait and find out which it was.

She'd saved the number of the Dog and Partridge on her phone. When she rang this time, a sharp female voice answered and her heart dropped to her feet. Was this Imogen?

'Hi. I'm looking for Imogen. I left a message for her yesterday and I wondered if it has been passed on.'

'Hold on a sec.' There was muffled noise as if the receiver was being held against something, or someone. Then the voice came back. 'Darryl said he did pass it on.'

She felt a little sick. Was Imogen working up to calling her back or was she planning to ignore it? It wasn't worth taking a chance. 'Oh, great. Thank you. Would you be able to pass on another message please? Could you tell her that her mother is ill. Seriously ill and she really needs to call? She needs to call before it's too late.'

EIGHT

The new manager, Josh, was waiting for Erin when she arrived at work, leaning on the counter like he was propping up a bar. 'I've remembered.'

'Sorry?' Her head was full of her mother and Imogen.

He followed her into the office behind reception where she hung up her coat. 'I've remembered where I know you from. It was a hoteliers' conference in Brighton. About twenty years ago. I was starting out in the business. I'm assuming you were too?'

She did remember going to a conference like that, but she didn't recall him. 'Goodness, you've got a good memory.'

He held out his hands. 'Goes with the territory, right? Names, faces.'

He was right. It was a point of pride to remember a guest's name from the time you first checked them in. But that was short-term memory. She didn't keep those faces filed away in her brain. 'That was a long time ago, though.'

'I remember you because you sounded ambitious. You wanted to open your own hotel if I recall correctly.'

He really did have a good memory. She could barely

remember herself at that age. Keen, ambitious, ready to take a risk. 'Yes, that would've been me.'

'Did you do it?'

She bit back the urge to say that she had a whole chain of hotels and came in here as a receptionist for fun. She'd save that for Jasmine later. 'No. Life got in the way.'

She didn't want to tell him that she meant 'life' literally; that it was getting pregnant with Harriet that'd put paid to her pipe dream. They hadn't planned to have a baby so soon and she could still remember the disappointment on her mother's face when she gave her the news. Instead of congratulations she'd shaken her head. 'Well, that's your career over, then.'

And it had been. Having meticulously researched it for the previous two years, she'd been under no illusions how much time – and money – it would've taken to finance her own place and they just didn't have it. Plus, she'd wanted to be there for Harriet whenever she was needed. That meant that the only jobs she'd taken had been ones that could fit around her schedule.

'That's a shame. And what about here? Do you have ambitions for advancement within the group?'

So many questions. Right now, she was more in the market for some answers. 'Not at the moment, but who knows? Maybe one day.'

He tapped his nose. 'I'll keep that in mind.'

After his questions, it seemed only polite to ask the same. 'What about you? You seem to have had a pretty successful career. Overseeing all these hotels. That must take a lot of hours.'

'Yes. I suppose it does.' He put a hand to the back of his neck and frowned at the floor to the left of her. Something in his expression made him look a little... lost.

Time to make this less personal. 'And what's next for you?

Adding more to your list? Taking over the whole of the south-east? And then the world?'

She'd meant it as a joke, but he wasn't finding it funny. 'No, no. Nothing like that. Actually, can you excuse me, I need to...'

Without finishing his sentence, he strode off towards his office, leaving her wondering what the heck she'd said.

Her shift went pretty quickly. Partly because an hour of it was lost to searching for a mislaid silver locket for a Mrs Allen who'd checked out yesterday. It came to light down the back of one of the sofas in the small library. When Erin called to say it'd been found, the poor woman had broken down into sobs, because it was the last thing her late husband had bought for her. 'It's silly, I know, dear. But it has his picture in it. I don't want to lose any more of him.'

As she slipped on her coat to go home, Erin's phone began to ring in her bag. It was most likely Harriet, wanting her to pick something up on the way home. But the display showed *Number Withheld*. Probably a sales call. But her heart thudded anyway. It could be... 'Hello?'

There was a pause on the other end. 'Hello. Is that Erin?'

The hesitancy of the voice, the slight tremor, could it be her? 'Yes. This is Erin. Are you Imogen?'

Again, a pause. 'Yes, I'm Imogen. I got a message to call you. About my mother.'

Erin felt hot then cold. What was she going to say? 'So, you are Ava's daughter?'

'Yes. Is she ill? They said she was ill?'

At least she seemed concerned. That was a positive sign. 'I'm afraid it's dementia. She's losing her memory. I assumed you'd want to know, in case...'

She didn't even know how to finish that sentence. She was so afraid of saying the wrong thing, of making Imogen disconnect the call.

This time, the voice was a little firmer. 'In case of what?'

Tiptoeing around the truth wasn't going to help matters. 'In case you wanted to see her. While she was still... well, while she was still herself. She's already... changing.'

Now the voice was suspicious. 'Changing how?'

It felt disloyal to say what she felt. That her mother was nicer, kinder, gentler than she'd ever been. She changed tack. 'If you leave it too long, she might not know who you are.'

This time the pause went on so long that Erin wasn't sure that they hadn't been disconnected. Then there was a sigh at the other end of the line. 'I think that might be better. If she forgets me. It will be easier for all of us.'

This was unbearable. 'How will it be better? You're her daughter. Surely she'd want to see you? You'd want to see her?'

'It's complicated.'

Erin was sitting at the desk in the reception office and Imogen's response made her want to bang her head on the computer keyboard in frustration. 'Complicated how? What happened? I have no idea what happened between you. I didn't even know you existed until a few days ago.'

'Believe me, you're better off not knowing anything. And she doesn't need me coming back. It will just upset her. It's best to leave things as they are.'

Erin wanted to scream. How could she not want to know? What happened between them? She had to make her understand. 'It's not only about her. I want to know you, too.' She took a deep breath. 'You must know... I'm your sister.'

But it made no difference. 'I'm sorry. But I have to go. Please don't call me again.'

For the rest of the day, Erin couldn't get Imogen's voice out of her head. Even while she drove the thirty minutes to The King's Arms to meet Simon, she was still trembling. What had she expected from their call? That Imogen would break down in tears of gratitude and come rushing down to be reconciled with the family? That she would be surprised and excited to find out that she had a sister who wanted to know her? What a fool she'd been.

And she was angry on her mother's behalf. Yes, she was difficult at times and no, she wasn't the warmest of people. But she couldn't believe that she would ever have done anything so terrible as to be denied a visit from her daughter before she lost herself forever. Erin wiped away hot angry tears with the back of her hand. She needed to get a grip of herself before she sat down with Simon.

The King's Arms was more of a restaurant than a pub these days, but the bar area was still a decent size. Simon was already sitting at a table in the corner when she arrived and he waved her over. Was it thoughtful or irritating that he'd already ordered her a glass of white wine? Either way, it was precisely what she needed. 'Thanks for the drink.'

'You're welcome. Good day at work?'

She shrugged. 'The usual. Some good, some bad. I hear your career is going intergalactic. Or should I say transatlantic?'

She'd meant it as a pointed barb but he merely smiled. 'It's going very well, thank you. The promotion is a big step up the ladder. I've worked for it, though.'

This had been a constant conflict throughout their marriage. That Simon's level of work was directly proportional to the level of his salary and that he believed the same was true of her low-paid position. *Don't bite.* She raised her glass. 'Congratulations.'

'Thanks.' He took a gulp of his beer. 'So. Harriet.'

He was getting straight to it, then. 'Yes. Harriet. Or, more accurately, you trying to tempt Harriet to leave the country and not even thinking of mentioning it to me first.'

As opening gambits went, it wasn't the most subtle. Simon shook his head at her. 'I didn't mention it to you first because I knew you'd be like this. Plus it wasn't definite. There was no point getting you riled up with it all.'

But he had told Harriet. 'No point? She lives with me. I'm the one who looks after her day in, day out and you thought there was no point?'

Simon wasn't remotely put out by her anger. 'Look. Just let me show you what we'd be moving to. Wait 'til you see the house they've included in the remuneration package.'

He was scrolling through his phone and she waved it away. 'She's already shown me the links you sent to her. I don't need to see it again.'

He continued to scroll through his phone. 'Okay, then. Let me show you the school I've found for her. I haven't sent this to her yet. Look at that.'

He turned his screen towards her, then scrolled through the images. When she said nothing, he started a commentary. 'Look at that art studio. Tell me she wouldn't love it? And it's only a twenty-minute bus ride from the house. Or Carmel can take her, maybe. Until she's old enough to have a car of her own.'

Erin felt sick. It was clearly a private school that must cost a fortune. He was making long term plans. Driving? Buying her a car? 'There are good schools here, too.'

'Of course, there are. But what an experience it would be for her to study in the US. She might not stay there forever; it'd be up to her. But it'd be something she'd remember.'

It wasn't just about school. There was so much more to life than which college she went to. 'What happens if she needs me, Simon? She's a fifteen-year-old girl. There's so much she hasn't experienced yet and she'll need someone to talk to. And you'd be working long hours, I assume? Unless you're being promoted and moved to another continent in order to do less work than you already do?'

Sensibly, given that arguments about his lengthy work hours had been another chorus of their marriage, he swerved the answer to that one. 'It wouldn't just be the two of us, though. Carmel adores Harriet and the feeling is mutual. If we move to California, Carmel will be there for her whatever she needs.'

'But Carmel is not her mother. She can't possibly...'

She was so angry that she couldn't articulate it. How could Carmel know when Harriet was hiding her upset and needed nudging to open up about it? Or when she was in the middle of a tempest of emotions and had to be left alone to cool down first? And it was more than that, so much more. 'I'm her mother, Simon. I love her more than life itself. You can't talk to her about this without involving me. It's not fair.'

Now he looked cross. 'Why is it always the mother who gets to have the say? Why can't I, as her father, want to have my daughter with me?'

He was missing the point completely. 'It's got nothing to do with being a mother or a father. The point is that I would never take a job that could take me away from my daughter. I wouldn't even consider it.'

In fact, she *had* made that decision before. To not pursue a hotel manager job because she knew it would mean hours that didn't work with a small child.

'So, what's better? That she lives with you and your mother, watching you scrape by on the salary from a job you've been doing since you weren't much older than she is? Is that the life you want for her?'

Erin's cheeks burned. The reason she'd done this job for so long, rejecting promotions, working in hotels close to home was because she had always, always put her family before her career. And now he was throwing that back in her face. 'That's low, Simon.'

His tight scowl loosened and he sighed. 'I'm sorry. You're right. But you have to see how this would be a great adventure for her, Erin. And she wants to go. She's just worried about upsetting you. About leaving you alone.'

The wine tasted too strong as she took another gulp. Was it really true? Was it only concern for her that was holding Harriet back? Erin didn't want her to stay out of some kind of pity. But how could she let her go? 'She's too young to understand what she wants. You'd be moving her away from everybody and everything she knows.'

'For goodness' sake, Erin. I'm not sending her into space. It's America. They do have flights to the UK, you know. And if I get the job, I'll be earning enough to pay for a flight whenever she wants to come home.'

He was railroading her, and she wanted to put a block on the tracks. 'And what if I say no? You can't take her out of the country without my permission.'

She'd double checked this online that afternoon. But Simon wasn't put off. 'She'll be sixteen in five weeks' time. At that point, she gets to decide who she lives with. Do you really want to be the kind of mother who stands in her way?'

He knew what he was saying. Hadn't her own mother warned against marrying Simon so young? And hadn't she ignored her? She gulped another mouthful of wine. Life without Harriet was inconceivable. She was the light of Erin's life, her reason for living. Even the thought of her bedroom being empty made Erin's heart ache. She had to keep making home as attractive as possible, while hoping against hope that Simon didn't get that job.

NINE

When she got home, Erin checked on her mum before taking the stairs two at a time to see Harriet.

Harriet's bed was covered in coloured paper and pens and scraps from magazines. She was bent over a scrapbook where she was outlining a fragment from a newspaper and highlighting some of the words. Erin loved to watch her work, her face a picture of concentration. 'Having fun?'

Harriet looked up and it took a moment for her eyes to adjust back into the real world. She slipped an ear bud from one ear. 'Oh, hi Mum. I didn't realise you were back.'

'Just got in. How's your portfolio going?'

One of the summer tasks for her new sixth form was a portfolio of work for her A level art teacher. It was supposed to reflect the way she saw herself as an artist. 'It's good. I was wondering whether it would be okay to include some of Granny's photos. Not the actual ones, obviously, but if I got them photocopied? I'm thinking that a copy of a photo of an original of my grandmother might be a way of showing, you know, generations and where I've come from and,' she blushed. 'Do I sound like an idiot?'

'Not at all.' Erin stepped closer and bent to kiss her on the head. 'I think you're a genius.'

Harriet laughed. 'Yes. And that would have nothing to do with you being my mother? Also, I wanted to include some pictures of me as a baby. Where are they?'

'I've got lots on my laptop. Hold on, I'll get it.'

The laptop was still on Erin's bed from when she'd been researching dementia care last night, so it took less than a minute before she was back on the end of Harriet's bed, looking at the photographs. They were organised into folders, by year, then month, and clicking through them made Harriet grow up before their eyes.

'I was a funny looking baby, wasn't I? All that hair.'

How could she say that? Those huge round blue eyes, those cheeks you wanted to eat. 'No, you were absolutely beautiful. Look at how cute you are in this one.'

Harriet peered closer at the screen. 'Should I even ask what that is around my mouth?'

Erin could remember this day as if it'd happened last week. 'It's chocolate cake. We were driving back from Yorkshire and we thought you were content in your car seat. I'd bought a chocolate cake from a cafe and we'd left it on the seat next to you. All the time we thought you were asleep, you'd been quietly helping yourself to handfuls of chocolate sponge.'

Harriet laughed. 'Go, baby me! Great work. I have absolutely no memory of that whatsoever.'

'I'm not surprised, you were barely two years old.' Those two years had been full of so many precious moments for Erin. Memories she sometimes unwrapped slowly like chocolates. Feeding Harriet strawberries in her high chair, taking her to the beach for the first time, holding her little hand flat at the country park so that the ducks would take food straight from her palm. The days lasted forever, yet the years had passed in a flash.

'Okay, here's some I do remember.' Harriet had clicked on several years to a folder labelled *Lanzarote 2017*. Photos upon photos of Harriet and Simon on the beach, splashing in the sea, making sandcastles, flying down a waterslide, interspersed with a few of Erin and Harriet dressed up for dinner. Why hadn't she taken more of her playing with her daughter? Being self-conscious in her swimsuit had ruined that.

'Look at us in our matching beach dresses. You loved to dress the same as me in those days.'

Harriet rolled her eyes. 'I was such a weirdo.' She laughed. 'That was a really great holiday, wasn't it? We had so much fun at that waterpark. And then we found that place where you could swim with the sea lions. Do you remember? Look, there's photos of it here.'

As Harriet clicked from frame to frame, she must have been looking at their big grins and remembering happy times. But it hadn't been happy for Erin. That holiday had been the beginning of the end for her and Simon. They'd smiled all day for Harriet then, once she was asleep, Simon would disappear to the hotel bar while she'd sat reading her Kindle on the balcony, wondering how much longer they could keep their marriage going. They might as well have been on different holidays for the way they both remembered it.

'I do recall you being very brave getting into that deep cold water with the sea lions. Even Dad thought you wouldn't go through with it. You were a tough little cookie.'

Harriet grinned and curled her legs under her so that she was sitting back on her feet. 'Speaking of tough, Granny has been telling me about her being a teacher, today.'

'Has she?'

'She's got so many funny stories about the children in her class. Especially the naughty ones. Once there was a boy who brought a dead bird into class and then left it in her desk drawer for her to find.'

Erin knew this story, but she was enjoying Harriet telling it. 'What happened?'

'Granny said that the whole class was watching her, waiting for her to open the drawer. When she opened it, she didn't even react, she merely picked up her pen and carried on teaching.'

Erin laughed. If they'd thought her mother would scream or react, they'd chosen the wrong person. 'I can imagine their disappointment.'

'Do you think she was super strict?'

Erin would stake her life on it. Her mother had always been a stickler for rules and appropriate behaviour. 'Yes. I can't imagine many students got away with much in her classroom. She worked hard, too. I can remember her marking piles and piles of books at the kitchen table at the same time as she cooked dinner.'

Looking back, she couldn't remember why her father hadn't helped more. He would get in from work and sit in his armchair while her mother tried to juggle cooking, marking and minding Erin.

'She said it was really unusual in those days for teachers to have young families. She had to fight to be allowed to go back to work.'

That didn't make sense. Surely there were plenty of women teachers with children when Erin was at school. Then something occurred to her. Maybe her mother was talking about when she'd had Imogen. 'What did she say about it?'

'She said that your dad didn't want her to do it. That the school were reluctant to take her back, but they needed someone desperately and she was a good teacher. It's impressive, isn't it? I told Granny she's a feminist icon.'

That made Erin smile. 'What did she say about that?'

'I think she liked it. She said, "I suppose I am, aren't I?" and she laughed.'

The relationship between Ava and Harriet was a lovely

thing, but it made the lack of closeness between Erin and her mother even more obvious. She couldn't imagine the two of them having conversations like that when she'd been Harriet's age. Partly because her mother was always busy doing something, but mainly because she'd always been a very private woman. Finding out about Imogen was casting a new light on her own childhood. Had Imogen running away affected Ava so deeply that she'd closed herself down? Or had she always been like that and it was her lack of affection that had driven Imogen away?

'Has she talked about Imogen to you? The baby in the picture you found?'

Harriet shook her head. 'No. Why? Do you know who she is?'

Erin pushed a plastic case of fineliners out of the way and perched on the end of the bed. 'Well, apparently, Granny had another daughter. Before me. That was the baby in the photograph you found.'

Harriet's eyes were as round as dinner plates. 'Wow. So you have a sister?'

It was still strange to think about her in that way. 'Yes. But I didn't know. No one ever told me. She left before I was born.'

Harriet looked excited. 'Are you going to track her down? Like they do in *Long Lost Family*?'

'I've tried to. I spoke to her today.'

Harriet shifted herself so that she was on her knees. 'That's amazing, Mum. What did she say? Is she going to come here?'

She shook her head. 'Not at the moment. It's difficult to get to the bottom of what happened. Imogen was pretty cryptic and it's difficult to get anything out of your granny with her not being able to remember so well.'

Harriet chewed the end of a pencil, a habit from childhood. 'I'll try and talk to her about it. See what I can find out.'

She would definitely be likely to have more luck than Erin. 'Be gentle, though. I don't want to upset her.'

'Of course.'

Some of the fineliner pens were loose on the bed, and Erin picked them up and slotted them back into their case, taking care to keep to the rainbow order that Harriet preferred. 'I met up with your dad today. To talk about the America thing.'

Harriet raised both eyebrows at her. 'Did you? Does he know whether he got the job?'

It was impossible to tell from the tone of her voice what she was hoping the answer would be. 'No. He still hasn't heard. Have you thought any more about what you'd like to do if he does get it?'

Still her voice and face – that beautiful face that Erin knew so well – wasn't giving anything away. 'It's a lot to think about.'

That phrase was starting to get old. 'Of course. What about your friends? What do they think about it all?'

'They think it sounds amazing.'

'Really?' She was trying not to put pressure on her, trying to keep the disbelief from her tone.

But she hadn't been successful. 'I can tell what you mean by that, Mum. But if they're my friends, we'll stay in touch wherever I live, won't we?'

Erin reddened; her daughter was getting too clever. They were pretty much the exact words she'd used about their move here a few weeks ago.

Harriet stood up and stretched. 'I've been sitting here too long. I'm going to take a shower.'

She'd pushed too hard. The last thing she wanted was for Harriet to think she was manipulating her; she'd be getting enough of that from her father. 'Okay, love. I'm going to get the dinner on.'

As she waited for the pasta to boil, Erin scrolled through her Facebook notifications. There had been another comment on her post. Someone had added a school picture with a comment. 'If you're still looking for Imogen Clarke, she's the third in from the left on the back row. I've circled her.'

There was a clumsy red digital circle around the face of a smiling teenager. Her hair stood out from her head and it was frizzy and curly. Eighties hair. Though the picture was a little blurry when she zoomed in, she could make out a happy looking girl of around fourteen. Was there a likeness there between the two of them? It was hard to tell. She saved the complete picture to her phone, then did it again with a zoomed in version. This one she took to show her mother.

'Mum, do you know who this is?'

Her mother peered at the phone before smiling. 'Of course, I do. That's Imogen.'

This was good. 'Yes, at school. Did she like school?'

Her mother shook her head. 'She was a clever girl but I couldn't get her to focus. She had no interest in school work at all. All she wanted to do was paint her pictures and go out with her friends.'

'Paint her pictures?'

'Yes. That's what she wanted to do. She wanted to be an artist. But I kept telling her that there was no money in that. She needed to study and get her exams. Qualifications mean choices.'

It was the same phrase her mother had used on Erin two decades ago. Not that she'd needed to. Erin had been a very conscientious student. It hadn't come easily to her, but she'd got decent grades from sheer hard work. She could still remember how thrilled she'd been to show her mother her grades; how disappointed she'd been in her perfunctory 'Good. Well done.' Some of her school friends had been taken out to dinner, or been showered with gifts, in recognition of their hard work. For Erin's mother, the good results were considered their own reward.

'What did she do when she left school? Did she become an artist?'

Her mother's face clouded over and she held out the phone for Erin to take. 'Imogen's gone.'

'I know that, Mum. But why—'

'She's gone.'

From the look on her face, there was no point pushing for anything more. Her mother might be gentler these days, but that woman of steel remained in there. Still, this was another fragment, another piece of the puzzle. She'd search the house for more information or photographs. They seemed to be the way in to wherever these memories were stored.

The next morning, everyone at work was on their best behaviour, trying to impress Josh. He seemed to be everywhere, checking the rooms after housekeeping had been in, visiting the kitchen at unexpected times and – more frequently than was necessary – checking in with Erin and Jasmine on reception.

'Everything okay here?'

'Yes, fine.' Just as it had been thirty minutes ago when he asked.

He glanced along the counter at the brochures and checking-in documents in neat piles. 'You run a good reception desk, Erin. I'm impressed.'

She couldn't decide whether to be flattered or patronised. 'Well, I've been doing it a long time.'

He leaned back and called into the back office, where Jasmine was putting in an order for housekeeping supplies. 'Everything okay back there?'

Jasmine waved at him, then gave a thumbs up.

He returned to Erin. 'I'll leave you to it, then. I've got a conference call with the regional management team. If you need me, I'll be in my office.'

Once he'd gone, and despite that morning's email which had requested no staff refreshments to be visible to guests, Jasmine brought out a cup of tea for Erin. 'He's got his nose in everything today. I'm beginning to think he must have cloned himself.'

Erin took a sip then slipped it out of sight onto the shelf below the desk. 'I know. I wish he wouldn't keep checking on us. It's making me nervous.'

Jasmine pulled the second chair towards her and sat down. 'Is that all it is? You haven't been yourself this morning.'

Erin closed her eyes and sighed. 'It's all this stuff to do with Harriet and Simon. Plus, I've found out some things about my mum which have knocked me for six.'

Jasmine sipped at her tea, keeping an eye out for Josh. 'Really?'

'It turns out I've got a sister. Left home before I was born. Never spoken about.'

Once she'd recovered from spluttering her tea, Jasmine shook her head slowly from side to side. 'Wow. That's a pretty big secret.'

'I know. And I've found her.'

Her eyes widened. 'This is like a TV show. What was she like?'

'That's the problem. I don't know. I managed to find out that she works in a pub in Kent. I left her a message and when she eventually called me back, we had a really brief conversation before she hung up. She doesn't want to see my mum and she doesn't want to meet me.'

The more Erin had thought about this, the more it was starting to eat at her. She had no idea what had happened between her mother and Imogen, but whatever it was had nothing to do with her. Why would Imogen not want to – even out of curiosity – meet her?

Jasmine stared at her. 'Crikey. The plot thickens. What are you going to do now?'

'What can I do?'

'Surely you're not going to leave it like that? I'd just turn up there. At the pub where she works. Catch her before she goes in. It's a lot harder to ignore someone who is standing in front of you.'

She was right, but was it okay to do that to someone? 'Don't you think that's a bit rude?'

Jasmine shrugged. 'So is hanging up on someone. Do you want to speak to her or not?'

She really did. Maybe it was time to be more like Jasmine and make things happen. 'I'm free on Tuesday.'

Jasmine slapped her hand on the reception counter. 'Do it.'

TEN

The Dog and Partridge was on an A road towards Maidstone. A large building which had been added to over several centuries, it looked welcoming and friendly. Erin sent up a silent prayer that Imogen would also be both those things.

Erin swung her car to the back corner of the gravel car park, but made sure she had a view of the road and the entrance to the pub. All she had to go on was that Imogen had long dark hair and must be in her fifties.

It was 10.55. When she'd rung the pub earlier, they'd told her that Imogen's shift started at eleven, but she'd been here for fifteen minutes and not seen anyone arrive at all. Was she already inside? She'd hoped to catch her before she went in. Otherwise it would be too easy for Imogen to say she was too busy to talk.

The crunch of tyres on gravel caught her attention and a small red Fiesta pulled into the car park, turning hard into one of the staff spots alongside the building. Erin held onto the car door handle, waiting to jump out if the driver fit the description she was expecting.

Whoever it was took an age to get out the car. What were

they doing? Eventually, slowly, the door opened and a woman got out. Leather jacket and long dark hair. It must be her. Erin pushed open the door of her car and jumped out, walking as quickly as she could. She wasn't going to make it in time so she called out. 'Imogen.'

The woman turned towards her with a smile, which faltered when she must have realised that she didn't know who Erin was. Beneath her heavy black leather jacket, she was slim and attractive, her lipstick dark red and eyes ringed in black kohl. It was difficult not to stare, searching for a family likeness. Did she look like their mum or their dad? Would a stranger have been able to pick them out as sisters?

Imogen tilted her head to one side. 'Sorry, do I know you?'

Erin waited until she was right in front of her, slightly breathless, before she replied. 'I'm Erin. We spoke on the phone.'

Imogen's face paled beneath her make-up. 'What are you doing here? This is where I work.'

'I know. I'm sorry, but I need to know what happened. Between you and Mum. Why you haven't been in touch.'

Imogen glanced towards the pub. 'I need to get into work.'

'Please give me a few minutes. I've driven two hours to get here.'

Imogen scuffed her feet in the gravel, staring at the toes of her black leather boots. 'I don't know what you want to know.'

I want to know you. But Erin wasn't about to tell her that and scare her away. 'I'd like to know what happened. Between you and Mum. Why you haven't been in touch.'

She glanced up then. But her face wasn't revealing its secrets. 'What has she told you?'

Their falling out must have been pretty awful for her to be so defensive. 'Nothing. I don't know anything at all. Mum has dementia. Her memory is really patchy. And before we found a photograph of you, I didn't even know you existed.'

Imogen frowned in confusion. 'We?'

'My daughter Harriet and me. Well, she found it, actually. In a McVitie's Christmas biscuit tin. She was clearing out the bedroom because...' This was ridiculous. 'Please, I know you have to get into work, but can you spare me ten minutes?'

Imogen glanced at the pub entrance again, chewed on her lip, then nodded. 'Okay. We can sit on the bench here. But ten minutes and I have to go.'

At last, she was going to talk to her. 'Great. Thank you.'

The wooden bench was damp and uncomfortable. Judging by the bin full of cigarette butts, it was the smoking area. Imogen sat very neatly, her hands in her lap, not making eye contact. 'What was it you wanted to know?'

There were so many questions that Erin had to pick one at random. 'When did you leave home? How old were you?'

Imogen squinted far into the distance as if she was picturing the day she left. 'The first time, I was sixteen.'

The *first* time? 'Why did you go?'

She took a deep breath and let it out again before she spoke. 'It was too... too difficult. Living there was, well it was suffocating.'

Well, she could identify with that. Hadn't she felt the same? Her mother's need to control everything she did until she'd moved in with Simon. 'Because of Mum?'

Another deep breath. 'Partly, yes.'

A cold feeling trickled down Erin's spine. If it was only partly her mum, then... 'Was it Dad too? Something he did?'

Erin didn't have a lot of memories of her father. He was older than her mother and had died when she was barely twelve. She only remembered the smell of his tobacco and the folded newspapers that he'd leave on his chair.

Imogen was shaking her head. 'No, not Dad.' She sighed, turned in her seat and, for the first time, she looked Erin in the face. 'Has she really told you nothing?'

Erin shook her head. She could understand the confusion. It must be incredible to her that her mother hadn't even mentioned her name since she left home. Although, what had she meant by the first time? 'When you said you were sixteen when you first left home, what did you mean? Did you run away a lot?'

'Run away?' Imogen coughed a dry laugh. 'No, I didn't run away a lot. I left at sixteen, but then I tried to come back. A couple of years afterwards.' She narrowed her eyes. 'Do you not remember?'

Did *she* remember? 'Was I born by then?'

Imogen stared at her. 'Yes, you were born.'

This got more confusing. Was she trying to suggest that it was Erin's fault that she left? 'I don't remember you at all. That's what I've been trying to tell you. Mum hasn't mentioned you once. My whole life, even when I was a young child and begged to know why I couldn't have a brother or sister, she said nothing. No one told me anything. That's why I wanted to see you. I want to understand and...' she might as well get it all out, 'and I hoped that maybe we could get to know one another. I've always wanted a sister.'

It was difficult not to cry. She'd wanted a sister so much. Had always thought that her mother was so controlling because she only had Erin to focus on. If there had been the two of them growing up perhaps her mother wouldn't have been so overprotective. An older sister would have been the trailblazer, testing the waters before Erin followed behind. Even with their big age gap, it would have made all the difference, Erin was sure of it.

Imogen's face twitched, as if she was about to burst into tears. 'I'm not your sister, Erin.'

This was getting tiresome. Why was she punishing her like this? Whatever had happened between their mother and Imogen was not Erin's fault. Imogen couldn't deny that they were family. 'Look, I know that—'

'I'm not your sister.'

The edge to her voice silenced Erin. but when she spoke again, the hardness in her eyes conflicted with the tears on her face. She lowered her voice to a sharp whisper. 'I'm not your sister. I'm your mother. And believe me when I tell you that you're far better off not knowing me at all.'

ELEVEN

Imogen couldn't understand how she could be pregnant when she and Jimmy had only slept together once.

Riding the bus out of town, she kept her head down low, terrified that someone would see her; a friend of her mother's or someone from school. From overheard whispers in the girls' toilets, she had the name of a chemist who sold pregnancy tests so she'd taken some of the cash she was saving for a leather jacket and made her way there. For at least fifteen minutes, she'd pretended to be choosing a rollerball lip gloss from the limited display, waiting for the shop to be empty of other customers.

When she slid the packet across the counter, the shop assistant's expression made her face burn. Thank goodness the shop was empty, because she waved it in the air. 'Do you know what this is?'

Imogen nodded, mumbled something about picking it up for someone else. It was none of her business, the judgemental cow. Then she stuffed it into her schoolbag and practically ran out of there.

Having taken the day off school, she knew the house would

be empty. After laying the contents of the test out on the pristine bathroom windowsill, she read the instructions twice. While she waited for the results, she sat on the toilet seat, praying over and over that the test would be negative. *I'll be good. I won't get into trouble at school. I'll help out at home.*

But it wasn't. Imogen curled up in a ball on the floor and cried until she was empty.

It was another two weeks before she plucked up the courage to tell her parents, hoping all the while that she'd read the test wrong. On a Tuesday evening, before her father got home from work, she found her mother in the kitchen, frying mincemeat for a cottage pie. 'Mum, have you got a minute? I need to talk to you.'

Her mother glanced over her shoulder but continued to push the meat around the pan with a wooden spoon. 'That face looks like trouble. Please don't tell me you've got another detention, Imogen. You need to get your homework done. You've got to be better organised.'

If only it was something as simple as that. There was no easy way to say this. 'Mum. I think I'm pregnant.'

For a second, there was no sound except the sizzling of the oil. The thick meaty smell stuck to the back of Imogen's throat, making her feel sick. After an eternity, her mother turned around. 'Are you sure?'

Imogen swallowed. 'I did a test two weeks ago.'

Her mother turned off the gas and pushed the pan to the back hob, before sinking onto one of the kitchen chairs and putting her hand to her head. 'Oh, Imogen. Why?'

It wasn't as if she'd done this on purpose. 'I'm sorry, Mum. It was only once and—'

Her mother's face took the rest of the words from her. 'Why do you keep choosing the wrong path? Haven't we brought you up to know better? I suppose it's that boy.'

She spat out his name as if he was the devil incarnate, not

the affable Jimmy who loped along beside her and carried her school bag home every night. 'It's Jimmy's, yes.'

'And what does he say about it?'

That was her next hurdle. 'I haven't told him yet.'

Her mother cried then. Quiet, but devastating, her tears seemed to be never-ending. Imogen didn't know whether to stay standing, sit down, or leave altogether. When she stopped, her expression was firm. 'We'll have to tell your father tonight.' Then she softened just a little. 'I'll help you.'

They let her father get changed and drink a cup of tea before they told him. Without saying a word, he walked out of the room and she heard the front door bang. That's what he'd do every time there was any kind of argument at home. He'd go out for a walk. That's how he dealt with it for the whole of her pregnancy: just pretended it wasn't happening. One night, she overheard him speaking to her mum. 'It's your problem. I don't want anything to do with it.'

And then there was Jimmy.

Once he was over the shock, he'd really tried to be pleased that she was pregnant. He started looking for a job that he could do, talked about them getting a place together. 'It'll be alright, Immy.'

She tried to believe him, but it didn't help that her own parents were distraught and his family were full-on furious. They hated Imogen. He said that they didn't, but she could tell.

Things got worse once she started to show. Everywhere Imogen went, people's smiles froze when they looked from her sixteen-year-old face to her swollen stomach. Eventually, it was easier to not even leave the house.

Obviously, that didn't go down well with her mother. 'You have to go to school. You have your exams coming up.'

What was the point? 'It's not as if I'm going to be able to do anything with them, am I? How am I going to go to college when I've got a baby?'

Even she didn't have an answer for that. 'We'll find a way to...'

'No, we won't. How are we going to do that? My life is over.'

'You're being dramatic. Other people have babies and go to work.'

'Like you?'

When her mother blushed, Imogen felt a tinge of guilt. But hadn't her mother told her repeatedly how her dad had insisted she put her dream of being a teacher on hold until Imogen was old enough to take herself to school? How much harder it had been for her to study as an older student, juggling family, the housework and her training? 'It's different now.'

'Different how? I'll be the only one at college with a baby. Everyone will be talking about me, staring at me. I can't deal with it.'

Everyone had changed towards her. Even people who'd been Imogen's friends, who smiled sweetly to her face and asked how she was feeling, would turn and talk about her behind their hands.

And she looked monstrous. None of her clothes fit properly and there was no way she was going to wear the maternity clothes that her mum bought. She wasn't a middle-aged old woman, for goodness' sake.

And then the baby came.

TWELVE

As soon as she was back on the motorway, Erin turned off her sat nav, its tinny mechanical voice becoming intolerable. She didn't even want the radio on for the drive home. It was all she could do to concentrate on the road ahead. The battling thoughts in her brain were so loud that she needed total silence in the car.

Imogen was her mother?

After she'd hurried into work, Erin had stayed frozen to the bench. Unable to take it in. It didn't make sense. No, Imogen being her sister didn't make sense; for her to be Erin's mother was utterly unbelievable.

When she could trust her legs, she wanted to follow her into the pub, asking one of the million questions that were flooding her mind. Why had she left? Why had she lied? Why had she never come back?

But Imogen was working by then, and she'd hurried away as if she couldn't get enough distance between the two of them. What would be the point of following her inside, demanding that she speak to her? Instead, she'd walked slowly back to her car and sat staring out the windscreen for as long as it took to feel conscious enough to drive.

There were so many scenarios that could have led to this deception, and yet none of them made any sense. Imogen would have been a young mother, very young, so it made sense that having a baby would have been difficult for her. But why did she leave altogether and why had she not, in the almost four decades since, ever come back to check whether Erin was okay?

And what about Ava? She was Erin's grandmother? Why had she never told her the truth? In all the years that she'd raised her, why had she never thought to tell Erin that her mother was someone else?

By the time she got home, her initial shock had receded and left a cold anger in its wake. She stabbed her key into the lock of the front door and almost snapped it off in her frustration to get inside. The TV was blaring in the living room and she could smell the remnants of dinner from the kitchen.

Her mother turned to her with a smile when she came in. 'Hello, love. Good day at work?'

It was taking so much control to keep herself calm as she sat down on the sofa. She nodded at the television. 'Can we turn that down a minute, Mum? Or off? I need to speak to you.'

'Of course, dear.' She had the TV remote in her lap, but she stared at it as if she was waiting for the right button to make itself known.

Erin reached out for it. 'I'll do it.'

She snapped the TV off, then shifted her chair so that she was sitting almost opposite to her mother. How to begin? 'I didn't go to work today, Mum. I went to see Imogen.'

Her mother blinked a couple of times before repeating her words. 'You went to see Imogen?'

'Yes, Imogen. Your daughter.'

She watched her mother's face carefully for a reaction. It was blank. 'My Imogen? How is she? Is she well?'

Erin had no idea. 'She told me something. She said... she said that she is my mother.'

Her mother pressed a hand to her chest as if to check that her heart was still beating. 'Your mother?'

'Yes. She said that she was your daughter and my mother. But I don't understand. I thought that you were my mother.'

'I am your mother.'

'But she said you're not my mother. She said she is.'

This was getting too confusing and she couldn't help the catch in her voice as the anger brought its usual tears.

Her mother looked concerned. 'Don't get upset, dear. It's okay. It's all okay.'

'It's not okay, though, is it? Have you been lying to me my whole life? Why didn't you tell me? What happened? When did she leave? And why?'

Her mother flinched at each question as if she was throwing them at her like missiles. 'I don't understand. Where did you see Imogen? Did she come here? She said she wouldn't come here. Why did she come?'

'She didn't come. I looked for her. That photo. The one in your biscuit tin. I tracked her down.'

Now her mother began to look upset. 'Don't do that. Don't speak to Imogen. You have to stay here. You have to stay here with me.'

As angry as she was, this was beginning to feel like cruelty. How could she expect her mother to explain anything in this confused state? It was pointless. Erin reached a hand across to her mother, relenting. 'It's okay. Imogen isn't here. I only wanted to know what happened. I wanted to know...'

There was so much she wanted to know, but she wasn't going to get it out of her mother. Not right now, at least. Those memories must be in there somewhere, but they'd need to be coaxed out like timid birds, not wrung from her like this.

Now her mother was dabbing at her eyes from a tissue that she pulled from her sleeve. 'Is Imogen coming? Is she coming back?'

She looked fearful at the thought. What had happened to make Imogen leave her mother and child and never have contact with them again? And what had she done that ensured that her name had never been mentioned in this house since? 'No, Mum. She's not coming here.'

In the kitchen, she switched on the kettle to make her mother a cup of tea. How was she going to get to the truth of all this? Imogen had made it clear that she didn't want to talk about it and her mother – Ava – either wouldn't or couldn't offer up any information. Did Aunt Marcelle know anything? She must do. She would have known Imogen. Surely they couldn't have kept a pregnancy secret?

Still none of this made sense. It was a storyline from a soap opera, not something that happened to ordinary people in real life. Her mother had been so straight, so strict, so sensible. What had possessed her to keep such a huge secret all of these years?

There was something else that was creeping at the edges of Erin's thoughts. Something dark and uncomfortable. Is this why her relationship with her mother had been difficult all these years? Because she wasn't actually her daughter? Worse, she'd been the baby that had driven her beloved daughter away? As the kettle rumbled to boiling point, a heat crept over her face. Had she not been wanted by either of them?

That evening, after her mother had gone to bed, Erin watched the grandmother clock in the kitchen tick towards 9 p.m. so that she could call Marcelle in Australia. On the hard wooden kitchen chair, pulled up to the same table at which she'd done her homework as a child, it was hard not to feel as if her whole life had been torn to shreds. Her husband hadn't wanted her, her daughter might follow. And now, it seemed, her own mother hadn't wanted her either. She wasn't a woman who courted sympathy, but it was pretty difficult not to feel sorry for herself right now.

This time she sent Marcelle a text first to check that she had time for a conversation. The reply came five minutes later.

I'm at home. You can call now. Everything okay?

No. Everything was not okay. Would it ever be again?

Marcelle picked up on the first ring. 'Hello? Erin? Are you alright? Is your mum alright?'

Erin hadn't noticed it on their last call, but Marcelle was beginning to get the Australian upward lilt at the ends of her sentences. How long had she lived there? It was significant now. How much did she know? 'We're fine, Marcelle. But I need to talk to you about Imogen again. I went to see her.'

There was silence on the other end and then her aunt's voice wasn't much more than a whisper. 'How did you find her?'

'Through Facebook. It wasn't difficult.'

'I see. And you've spoken to her?'

'Yes. On the phone and then I went to where she works. I know the truth. She told me that she's my mother.'

This time there was a sharp intake of breath. 'Oh, Erin.'

Her voice was so mournful that it almost made Erin cry. 'Why didn't you tell me? Even the other day when I told you about the photograph, you said that she was my sister.'

'I didn't say that. I told you she was your mother's daughter, which is true. I've never lied to you. I always told Ava that. If she asks me outright, I'm going to tell her.'

This deception was spiralling. 'Well, I'm asking you outright now. What's the truth? What happened?'

'Oh, Erin. It's not my story to tell. Yes, Imogen is your mother. But she couldn't look after you. She left and Ava, she stepped up.'

'But why did she leave?'

'Erin, love. She was sixteen. Not much older than your Harriet. She was a child herself, it was too much for her.'

Erin could understand that, of course she could. 'But why did she leave? Couldn't Mum...' she faltered over the word, 'couldn't she have brought me up but Imogen stayed there, too?'

This was what had been going around her head on the way home. Why leave? And why had her mother – Ava – never told her the truth?

'It was so complicated. You won't remember, but we were living in Scotland at the time because of your Uncle Ted's job. By the time I knew that Imogen had gone, your mum had made her mind up. It was best for you. That's what she kept saying. It was best for you that you never know.'

This was a conspiracy. 'And do you believe that?'

There was a pause on the end of the line. 'There were... reasons. Your mother had reasons and she made a good case. And you've had a good life, haven't you? She's been a good mother to you.'

Erin didn't even know how to answer that question. Had she been a good mother? Certainly she was clothed and fed and looked after. Her education had been important. And she knew that her mother had cared. But there had been none of the cuddles in bed on a Sunday morning or film nights with popcorn or shopping trips and makeovers that she'd had with Harriet. There hadn't been a lot of affection in that house.

And as for Imogen, it wasn't only that she'd left, it was that she'd known all this time that she had a daughter and had never, ever come back for her. How could she do that?

'I know that there has to be more to this story, Marcelle. What are you not telling me?'

'I can't say any more. I *won't* say any more. Not when I am over here on the end of a phone line. I wish I hadn't said anything the other day, either. I'll be with you in just over a week. We'll talk then, I promise. Be patient a little while longer, Erin.'

Be patient? She already had the sword of Damocles over her head waiting to discover what Harriet was going to do about America. And now she had to wait for this, too? It was overwhelming. 'I can't stand it. All the uncertainty. It's too much.'

Marcelle tried to soothe her. 'It was a long time ago, love. I know you've just found out, but—'

The warmth in Marcelle's voice was all it took to have it all come tumbling out. 'It's not only this. It's Harriet. She might be going to America to live with Simon. He's going there to work and he wants her to go with him.' Though Jasmine had been a friendly ear, Erin had had no one to really talk to about this. For so long, Harriet had been her entire life. Since Simon left and she'd had to work more shifts, she let her friendships slide and now she had no friends who might understand how it felt as a mother to have to let your child walk away from you.

As she should have known, Marcelle understood straight away. 'Oh, sweetheart, that's so hard. You really do have a lot going on. When will you know for sure?'

Simon hadn't given her a timeframe, but it had sounded imminent. 'Soon, I think. Oh, Marcelle, I really don't want her to go. I don't feel as if I can tell her that, but I really don't.'

More soothing noises down the line made Erin wish that Marcelle was here with her right now. 'Of course, you don't want her to go. I can remember what it was like when my girls first came out here and I was still in England. And your Harriet is still a baby compared to them. Is she keen to go?'

Harriet's excited expression when she'd shown Erin the

house, her tentative way of answering Erin's questions, the fact she'd been nicer to live with these last couple of days, all pointed to the same thing. 'I think she might be.'

There was a big sigh at the other end. 'Then you don't really have a choice, love. You have to let her go. What else can you do?'

This wasn't what she wanted to hear. 'But I'm not ready.'

'I know, I really do. Fifteen is young. But even if she waits until she's eighteen to leave, or twenty, it won't change the way you feel. You'll never be ready. But we don't get to hold onto our children forever. I wish I could be there to give you a big hug. I'll be there soon and we can talk about all of it. Your mum, Imogen, Harriet. Hang on in there, sweetheart.'

Hang on in there. That's how she felt, like she was hanging on by her fingernails to both her mother's past and her daughter's future. What would happen if she let go?

THIRTEEN

Marcelle's words fluttered around Erin's head from the moment she woke the next day. *'We can't hold onto our children forever.'* Is that what she was doing? Trying to hold onto Harriet? Clutching onto her by her fingernails? Was she just being selfish? But what was the alternative? Encourage her to go, to leave?

No. She would stick with her original plan to make life here so good that Harriet would choose to stay of her own accord. Before she left for work, she sent a message to Harriet's closest friend, suggesting that she and the other girls in their group come to stay at the weekend, she even offered to pick them all up and take them home the following day. Swearing them to secrecy, she enjoyed the idea of it being a lovely surprise for Harriet, while simultaneously showing her what she would be giving up if she moved to the US.

Jasmine was in a particularly good mood when she got to work and commended her on the sleepover plan. 'What are they going to do?'

'What do you mean? They're coming to the house for a sleepover. They've done it lots of times before.'

'I'm sure they have. But this time you want it to be a sleep-over extraordinaire. You need to make it something special.'

She was right. Ordinarily, the girls would've been out to do something else before coming back to their flat. This time, they would only have her and her mother for company. 'What do you suggest?'

'What are they into? Makeovers? Movies? Men?' The last was accompanied with a raised eyebrow and made Erin smile for the first time that day. 'I think I'd have to decline the prospect of men in the house for a group of fifteen- and sixteen-year-olds.'

'Spoilsport.' Jasmine winked. 'Talking about men. I think our new esteemed leader fancies you.'

'Don't be ridiculous.'

'He keeps bringing up that conference you both went to. What happened there?'

'Nothing.' Once she'd racked her brains for memories of him there, she did remember that they'd got on well, but she'd already been with Simon then. She hadn't been in the market for meeting someone.

Jasmine didn't look convinced. 'I'm not sure you'd notice if someone was hitting on you. I keep telling you that you need to look out for the signs.'

It didn't matter how many times she told Jasmine that she wasn't interested in dating, she wouldn't believe her.

'Actually, I'm more observant than you think. I'm pretty sure he's not married because I checked for a wedding ring.'

Erin held out her hands for Jasmine's praise. She'd taught her that week one of knowing her. But Jasmine merely raised an eyebrow. 'Did you now?'

Erin's face warmed. 'Not like that. I just, you know, did the checks.'

'The checks' was Jasmine's list when she met someone. Wedding ring. Frequently checking phone. Needing to be gone by a certain time. All signs that your date was playing away from home apparently.

'You're learning, my young Padawan. But he does have the groove.'

This was a new one. 'The groove.'

Jasmine nodded sagely. 'Where the wedding ring usually sits. An indent in the finger. Sometimes it's paler than the rest.'

This was another level. 'How did you notice that?'

'When he signed my overtime docket earlier. He's left-handed and his signature is unnecessarily long and swirly so I had time to really check it out.'

Erin shook her head in amazement at her friend's detective work. 'So you think he might be married?' Erin was disappointed that she'd got it wrong. For no other reason than that she'd tried to impress Jasmine, obviously.

Jasmine tilted her head to one side, like a sommelier appraising a fine wine. 'My guess is divorced. Possibly in the last year or so for the groove to still be there.'

'Well, that'll mean more time for him to be here, I guess.'

'And more time for him to keep hanging around this reception desk talking to you.'

As if she'd summoned him, the lift doors opened and Josh walked out of them. He approached the reception desk with a smile. 'Hi, Erin. How's your morning been?'

She blamed the blush that started in her cheeks on the dig that Jasmine gave her in her side. 'Oh, er, fine. I just got here so I'm going to hang up my coat and have a look at the timesheets for next week.'

'Great. Can I look over them with you?'

Her face got even hotter. Behind him, Jasmine was beaming at her. 'Of course, if you want to but they're pretty standard.'

The office behind reception was small. Only two desks and then a wall of filing cabinets. While Erin was logging on, Josh pulled over a chair so that he could sit next to her. He was close enough that she could smell his aftershave and she'd be lying if she said he didn't smell good.

At another time in her life, when she had less going on, maybe she would have found him attractive. In the years since her divorce, she hadn't dated anyone else. Firstly, she'd been licking her wounds, then she'd wanted to focus on Harriet and then – just as she was putting her head above water – her mother's dementia diagnosis had taken her attention. Maybe, once Harriet was settled, she might consider dating again. But there certainly wasn't enough time in her life for that right now. All she wanted to do was get the job done and go home. Plus – if the shift was quiet – she was hoping to get a chance to talk to Jasmine about what had happened yesterday with Imogen.

A couple of clicks and the timesheet master document was on the screen. 'These are the hours for next week. We have some employees that have set hours and others who work shifts.'

'And why is it that? Why doesn't everyone have either a set time or a shift pattern?'

'It depends on the number of hours that they do. You see, here.'

She pointed at the column with the hours and Josh leaned forwards to take a look. He must have honed in on her name. 'You've done quite a lot of overtime.'

'I have done in the last couple of weeks because we've been short staffed.'

'And you're the kind of person who gets called in an emergency?'

He'd turned to look at her and the damn blush was making its way up her neck again. 'I guess so.'

'I've been thinking about that conference when I first met you. Do you remember a guy there called Luca? He was Italian, had a family restaurant business?'

Now she thought about it, she did remember him. And it made her wince. 'Did he play the piano?'

'Yes! In the hotel bar on the last night. Well, we stayed friends and I mentioned that you were here and he remembered you, too. He remembered you singing.'

That was why she'd winced. On the last night, there'd been a wine tasting session as part of the event and they'd all decamped to the bar afterwards to continue drinking. She'd never been a big drinker, which probably explained why she'd ended up sitting next to Luca on the piano stool for a duet. Unfortunately, she wasn't a singer, either. She screwed up her eyes and groaned. 'Thank you for that memory.'

'You're welcome. He was as surprised as I was that you hadn't scaled the heights of management by now. He also said to let him know if you ever needed a singing gig at one of his restaurants. He's got a whole chain of them, now.'

She had to laugh at that. 'I think my performing days are over.'

He grinned. 'Seriously, though. Everyone I've spoken to here has talked about how capable and professional you are. I'm going to need someone to—'

'Josh?' They looked up in unison at Jasmine. 'I'm sorry to interrupt, but there's a gentleman here to see you. Mark Fredericks?'

'Ah yes, thank you.' He turned to Erin. 'And thanks for showing me the timesheets. We'll pick this up again another time.'

Jasmine stood back to let him through and waited until he and Mark Fredericks were out of earshot before whipping her head around to Erin, eyes gleaming. 'He's going to need someone to *what?*'

'You totally came in at the wrong point in the conversation. We were talking about work.'

Jasmine folded her arms. 'Were you now? All cosied up in front of a warm computer monitor.'

'Now you're being delusional. You know that he wanted to see the spreadsheets with the hours.'

Jasmine laughed and shook her head. 'Oh, come on. Now who's delusional? Like he hasn't seen a timesheet before?'

Ordinarily, she enjoyed Jasmine playing around, but she didn't have the capacity for it today. 'I took your advice. I went to the pub yesterday. The one where Imogen works.'

As she recounted the events of the day before, Jasmine's mouth fell open. 'Oh, Erin. I'm so sorry I was messing around. What a shock for you.'

'Don't be silly, you weren't to know. But I'm afraid I'm not in a mood to play today.'

'Of course not. How are you feeling? Stupid question, I know. But I mean, what are you going to do?'

'At the moment, just try and take it in. I can't get anything out of my mum, except to stay away from Imogen. My aunt has clammed up and won't tell me anything over the phone. And Imogen – my biological mother apparently – couldn't get away from me quick enough.' The more she'd thought about this, the more it hurt.

'Oh, Erin. I don't know what to say. And you know that doesn't happen often.'

Erin smiled weakly at her friend's attempt to cheer her up. 'I don't know what to do next. Do I leave it alone? Carry on as if she doesn't exist?'

Much as she couldn't see herself managing to stick to that, it did feel as if she had enough on her plate without begging her sister-mother for her time.

'Are you really going to be able to do that? Without your head exploding?'

Jasmine waved her fingertips around her temples in a pretty accurate representation of the tangled thoughts in Erin's brain. She sighed. 'Maybe not. But I can't force her to talk to me, can I?'

'No. But you can try again. It must have been a shock for her, too, seeing you after all this time. Maybe she'll be more open to talking to you now that she's had time to cool off.'

There was a part of Erin that didn't want to try again. Why had Imogen not been excited – or at least curious – to meet her? 'Why should I have to be the one chasing her? She has my number.'

'Yes, but who are you spiting by not calling? You want to know the truth, don't you?'

She was right. Again. 'Okay. I'll do it.'

Jasmine nodded. 'It's quiet at the moment. Why don't you do it now?'

Erin's bag was still beside her chair, so she reached into it for her phone. 'Okay. I will.'

Jasmine glanced back through the doorway where a young couple had arrived at reception, before giving her the thumbs up. 'Good luck.'

The only number she had was the pub, so she called it, expecting to get one of the staff who'd answered last time. It rang once, twice, three times: the butterflies in her stomach becoming more intense with every ring.

'Good morning. Dog and Partridge. Can I help?'

Her stomach flipped over; she was pretty sure that it was Imogen. 'Hi, is that Imogen?'

There was a pause. 'Yes. Who's this?'

'Please don't put the phone down. It's Erin. From yesterday.'

She heard a sharp intake of breath at the other end. 'Yes?'

'Look, I'm sorry for the ambush yesterday. I'm sure it was a bit of a shock.'

The laugh on the other end was dry and hollow. 'You could say that.'

'But I'd really like to talk to you some more. I know that you don't think it's a good idea but, I need to know. I need to know what happened and Mum can't tell me. And I'd like to know you too.'

It was surreal. Her mum, Imogen's mum, Imogen was her mum. Her head really was spinning. Maybe Imogen felt the same. 'I don't know, Erin. I'm sorry but—'

'Please. Please, Imogen. One meeting. I'll come to you. You don't have to come back here. I just want to understand why you left.'

Even as she begged her, she couldn't believe that it wasn't the other way around. Shouldn't the woman who gave her up be the one to beg her for a chance? Nevertheless, she held her breath in the silence from the other end of the line, until Imogen spoke. 'Okay. We can meet halfway. Do you know The King's Arms on the A23?'

Erin almost laughed. Was that place destined to be the scene of every drama in her life? 'Yes, I know it. I can meet you there.'

As she put down the phone, Jasmine's head popped around the doorframe and she nodded at the question in her face. 'I'm going to meet her. We're going to talk.'

FOURTEEN

Erin had taken the box room at her mother's so that Harriet could have the room she herself had grown up in. By the looks of the walls in here, it hadn't been decorated since she'd moved out to live with Simon. There were still patches of white where the Blu Tack that had held up her posters had been torn down. Last night, she'd rubbed them down to prepare for painting; the exertion of scratching at the plaster with sandpaper had been good for her and she'd fallen into bed exhausted.

Jasmine took in the room with her hands on her hips. 'Remind me again why I am painting your daughter's bedroom wall when it's my day off and I should be swiping right on Tinder with abandon?'

Shortly after Erin had finished speaking to Imogen yesterday, Harriet had called. She was going to Simon's for the next couple of nights and Erin took it into her head that she'd paint her room as a surprise for her return.

'Partly because you were in the wrong place at the wrong time yesterday and partly because it was your idea that I put on some kind of extravaganza for her and her pals at the weekend.

They are hardly going to be impressed with a room that looks like a storage cupboard.'

Jasmine turned to dip the roller in the paint and glanced at the boxes in the middle of the room, all the unpacked belongings that Erin and Harriet had brought from the flat. 'Don't we need to move those?'

'Yes, I'm going to move them to my room for now. I'll do it once we've got the first coat done. If you're good, I'll even make coffee and butter a toasted teacake or two.'

'You're too good to me.'

Erin loaded up her roller with more of the dark blue paint. Though Harriet had picked it out, she hoped she would be pleased with the end result. It was much darker than Erin had anticipated, but she would have let her paint the whole place black if it would keep her here.

With the sun warming them through the window and the radio playing songs from the nineties, it was the most relaxed Erin had felt in days. Even the smooth swish of the roller was therapeutic. 'I've been thinking about Josh.'

Judging by the high level of interest on Jasmine's face, she should have worded that differently. 'Have you, indeed?'

She shook her head. 'Easy tiger. Not like that. I mean I was thinking about what he said about the conference we both went to. I was so different then.'

Jasmine held the roller at a dangerously drippy angle. 'Different how?'

'Focused. Ambitious. I really wanted to get into one of the big hotel chains, work my way up. Once I'd learned the business, and had some experience, I planned to open my own hotel.'

She hadn't been hugely academic at school, but – when she was interested in something – she could learn fast. Her mother had wanted her to go to university and do an English or history degree, but that had never been her dream. At eighteen, she'd taken a course in hotel management and never looked back.

'Is that what the conference was for? High flyers?'

That phrase made Erin think of power suits and briefcases. 'It wasn't a conference, it was a training week for the Bjorn Group of hotels. A fast-track programme.'

From memory, there had been about thirty of them, all staying in the same hotel in Brighton. For the first time, she'd been surrounded by people who liked doing what she liked doing. Wasn't that a wonderful thing, to be with people who were just like you?

Jasmine rolled her eyes. 'Sounds riveting.'

'Actually, it was great. There were sessions on everything from the latest computer booking systems to purchasing to managing people to get the best out of them.'

Jasmine waved her paint roller again. 'Like getting them to decorate your daughter's bedroom for free?'

'Exactly that.' Erin nudged her. 'The thing is, I keep wondering what I'd have been doing now if I'd stayed with the company. I suppose I'd be doing what Josh is doing. Or I might even be at head office making big group-wide decisions.'

'So why did you leave?'

'I got pregnant with Harriet. Part of the fast-track programme was that you would move around the country, working at a different hotel every six months. It was supposed to be a baptism of fire, I suppose. But it would've been impossible with a husband and a young baby. I couldn't keep uprooting them and I couldn't stay away all week.'

This was part of why she was so upset with Simon. She'd sacrificed her career to be there for the two of them. And now he wasn't even thinking about the impact of his decision to relocate to California.

'Did you give up work?'

'No, but I asked to drop out of the fast-track programme and work at the hotel nearest to me. Even then, the management shifts required me to work odd hours which wouldn't work around Simon's career when we had a young child, so I ended up on reception.'

At the time, she hadn't expected it to be forever. When Harriet went to school. Or when she was a little older. Or when she didn't need her to be running her around to clubs and events. Somehow, she never picked it up again. And Simon had been more than happy to have her manage the vast majority of Harriet's school and social life. Maybe he was right that it wasn't fair that mothers were given precedence over fathers, but – for them at least – she'd been the one who'd gladly put in the hours. Surely that counted for something?

Jasmine slapped another full roller of paint onto the wall. 'And what about now? Harriet is older. She doesn't need you around so much. Why don't you start now?'

She ran her roller through the pot and slopped it against the wall. 'Because now I have to worry about my own mother.'

Wasn't that the irony? There was such a small window between caring for young children and caring for ageing parents. If you missed it, it was gone.

For a few moments they painted in companionable silence before Jasmine changed the subject. 'How are you feeling about meeting up with Imogen? Have you got your questions ready for her?'

While she'd sanded the walls yesterday, she'd thought about that. 'I want to know why she left. But I also want to know why she's never come back. I mean, if I really am her daughter, wasn't she curious?'

'Have you told your mum that you're going? Sorry, I mean your mum here. Blimey, it's confusing.'

It really was. 'It's okay. She's still my mum. I mean, she's the one who brought me up, isn't she? Even if she wasn't that keen on the idea.'

'What do you mean?'

It was difficult to put into words. 'Sometimes it felt as if she was keeping me at arm's length. Like she didn't really want me there. Once, I had a nightmare and I came downstairs to see her and she was busy at the kitchen table doing something for school. All she did was send me straight back to bed. I can remember her exact words. *It's just your imagination, Erin. You need to control it.* No hug, no reassurance. Nothing.'

Simon might have criticised her over the years for pandering to Harriet, but she knew that her own daughter had always felt loved and supported. That was another reason that she hadn't looked for promotion; she wanted Harriet to always know that she came first.

Not that Harriet seemed to need her at all now. She couldn't dwell too long on how hurt she felt that Harriet would even consider leaving her already. Maybe it was a good thing that she was so adventurous, but it felt like a betrayal.

Changing her roller for a brush, Jasmine knelt on the carpet to paint above the skirting board. 'I wonder what she was like with Imogen? Maybe that's why she left?'

It was possible, but Erin didn't think so. 'I don't know. The way she looked at the photograph we found, there was a real sense of affection. The way she talked about Imogen... I think it's more likely that she was devastated that she lost her.'

She didn't tell Jasmine how jealous that made her feel. She hadn't been able to shake off the impression that her mother had loved Imogen more than she'd ever loved her. But then that didn't explain why she'd let her go and not tried to track her down.

Jasmine must have been thinking along similar lines. 'Do you think she ever tried to find her? I mean, they didn't have all the social media back then, but there must have been ways?'

Something Imogen had said came back to her. 'Imogen made it sound as if she'd run away more than once. Maybe she got tired of chasing after her?'

Not that she could understand that, either. Had Harriet run away, she would've spent every waking moment looking for her.

'Well, at least you should find out when you meet again.'

'I hope so.'

Jasmine had made it to the corner, three more brush strokes and the first coat was done. She stood back to survey her work. 'Not bad for an amateur.'

'Not bad at all. I'll get the kettle on.'

'Good plan. Also, did you say that Harriet was away for two nights?'

'Yes, so you'd better get working. I want this done for when she comes back.' She grinned and winked at Jasmine.

'Well, if you're free, some of us from the hotel are going for a drink after work tomorrow night. You should come.'

As if she had the time for that. 'Thanks, but I've got too much going on right now, Jasmine. I'm sorry.'

'It's only a few people. Nothing full on. Josh is going to be there.'

She knew what that eyebrow was suggesting. 'That makes no difference at all.'

Now she was all mock innocence. 'I just meant that you can talk to him about your career.'

'Of course you did. I appreciate you inviting me, but really, between looking out for my mum, worrying about Harriet and trying to get my head around the Imogen situation, I'm really not in the right place for a work drink.'

Jasmine dropped her brush onto the lid of the paint tin and held out her hands. 'But that's exactly why you *should* come. What are you going to do? Lay down and think about it all until your head explodes? You deserve a night out and it'll do you good to be distracted for a while.'

When she put it like that, it was quite tempting. 'Maybe I could come for one drink. If Mum's neighbour is free to keep her company.'

Jasmine clapped her hands together. 'Perfect.'

FIFTEEN

The pub was pretty quiet. Aside from a few men at the bar who looked like they were on the way home from the golf course, there were only a few pairs and trios dotted around.

Jasmine was like a flash towards the back corner, pulling tables together and rearranging chairs. 'Okay everyone, let's put a tenner into the whip and then I'll make a list of what everyone wants.'

Josh coughed. 'I'll get the first round. To thank you all for making me so welcome.'

A murmur of approval rippled through the eight people who'd come, followed by a few 'cheers mate', followed by everyone ordering doubles.

There were so many detailed orders that Josh took out his phone to write them down. 'Takes me back to my time as a waiter.'

Erin had had a waitressing job when she was at college, too. 'I don't miss those days.'

Jasmine shoved her off the bench they were sitting on. 'Well why don't you go and help Josh carry all the drinks and you can both show off your skills?'

Hopefully no one else saw the wink she was giving Erin. There was more to this plan than helping to carry drinks. But Josh was smiling at her. 'That would be great. Thanks, Erin.'

The barmaid was also all smiles as she took their lengthy order. Erin was always impressed with their ability to hold all the drinks in their head and get it right. Maybe it was her mother's dementia, but she found herself thinking about this more and more. Where did those facts live in your brain? How long did they last?

Josh looked relieved to have got through the list. 'I hope I got those right. The correct combination of mixers and low calorie and no calorie.'

Erin picked up a beer mat from the bar and turned it around in her fingers. 'It's alcohol and you're paying. I think they'll let you off.'

He looked younger when he laughed. 'I hope you're right. Everyone seems pretty nice.'

Erin glanced back at her colleagues. Jasmine was telling a story, probably another dating horror show, to two of the girls from the kitchen. Three of the chambermaids, one of whom was getting married next summer, were gathered around a mobile phone. The guys from the kitchen were staring at the football match on the corner TV. 'Yes, they're a good bunch. We make a pretty good team, I think.'

Josh nodded. 'I've noticed how good you are with people, Erin. There's a management opportunity coming up soon. I think you'd be perfect for it if you'd like me to put your name forward?'

Wow. He didn't beat around the bush, did he? They'd all been wondering when and if there'd be a new hotel manager. Was he really offering it to her? 'Oh. Thanks. Yes. I mean, I'd need to know more about it, but, yes, I'm interested. I've got lots of ideas about how we could make the hotel more efficient and profitable.'

Josh frowned at the beer mat that she was still twirling. 'The hotel took quite a hit over Covid, I've heard.'

That sounded less positive. 'It was like that for everyone, though, wasn't it? It'll get back up again.'

Josh still wasn't looking at her. 'Yes, but... head office will have a lot of difficult decisions to make in the next few months.'

She was prevented from asking what he meant by the barmaid pushing two trays of drinks in their direction. 'There you go, all done. Are you paying by card?'

Erin slid the first tray from the bar and left Josh to pay. When she got back to the table, Jasmine had engineered it so that there were only two spare seats and they were next to each other. She could only hope that Josh wasn't as alert to her machinations as Erin was.

After the drinks had been distributed to a chorus of thank yous, everyone returned to their huddles, leaving Josh and Erin on chairs like two satellites outside of the main cluster. Josh sipped at his beer and smiled at her. 'So what have you got planned for the weekend?'

She had the sudden urge to shock him by inventing an all-night rave. Were they still called that? 'My daughter has a sleep-over for three of her friends. I'm going to pick them up in the morning, from back where we used to live in Sutton. It's a surprise for her.'

He pulled a face. 'Rather you than me. Four teenage girls? Sounds like a world of pain.'

She smiled and shrugged. 'It's not so bad. They're good kids.'

She'd always been grateful for that. It was all very well hoping that 'like attracts like' but she was still relieved that Harriet had always chosen sensible, kind girls to be her friends.

He nodded as he sipped his beer. 'I've got a couple of years before the teens hit and I'm not looking forward to it.'

So he did have children. 'How old are yours?'

'My son is eleven and my daughter is nine. Nine going on nineteen.'

Erin smiled. She remembered those days. 'She knows more than you'll ever know, right?'

'Yes. Exactly that.' Josh laughed. 'Most of the time she rolls her eyes at me. Lorna says it's karma because she was the same at that age.'

And a wife, too? Or was Jasmine on the right track with divorce? 'It must be tricky finding time with them with the hours you're working at the moment? You're with us a lot and then you must be putting in similar hours at the other hotels. How many are you overseeing?'

'Six. But the others don't take up as much time because they have their own manager. I can usually check in on them with a daily phone call and then visit once a week. It's difficult, but I can work my hours around the children sometimes. I get to take them to school or collect them. I'm home for dinner at least three nights a week.'

Home. That didn't sound like divorce. So why wasn't he wearing his wedding ring? 'And does Lorna work?'

'She's worked from home since the pandemic which has made everything a lot easier. It's not been easy since the children were born because my hours have been pretty unsocial over the years. The hospitality sector is a jealous mistress, isn't it?'

She joined in his laughter, even though she didn't feel it. Why did she feel strangely disappointed when she didn't even really know him?

Jasmine nudged her. 'I'm going up to get some drinks. Do you want to put into the whip? Ten pounds each?'

'Yes, I'll come up and help you.'

She silenced Jasmine's protest with a look and followed her up to the bar.

'How's it going with old blue eyes?'

'He's married with kids. So you can stop with the winks and the pushing us together.'

Jasmine stuck out her bottom lip. 'That's a bummer. Are you sure? What's with the lack of wedding ring, then?'

'I don't know. But he definitely has a wife and a home and kids. Maybe he just doesn't wear the ring when he's at work?'

'That doesn't make any sense. It's not like he's working with his hands or anything.'

Erin didn't tell Jasmine about her feelings of disappointment; it would only encourage her to start setting her up with someone else. Plus, there was something else bothering her. 'He was also a bit shifty about the hotel. He mentioned the fact that bookings are down and said that head office are going to have to make some difficult decisions.'

'That doesn't sound good. What does that mean?'

Erin didn't know, but with everything else in her life up in the air, she hoped that it wasn't going to be bad news. Jasmine had worked there a lot longer than she had. She didn't want to ruin their friendship by accepting a promotion if other members of staff were going to be made redundant. Was yet another storey in her house of cards about to come tumbling down?

SIXTEEN

The excitement of the three girls she collected for Harriet's sleepover was infectious. Initially, they made polite conversation with her, asking how the move had gone and whether she was settled into the house yet. Their parents should be proud of them.

Then, after about twenty minutes, they started to have a conversation about the teachers they'd met at their new college induction week. Funny and forthright, they made her laugh with their impressions of some of their tutors. She felt a tinge of guilt, though. If they hadn't moved, Harriet would have been with them, talking about the same people and the same classes. If they hadn't moved, maybe Harriet wouldn't even be considering going to America with her father.

As they got closer, she tried to formulate a plan. 'Harriet's dad is dropping her home in about half an hour. Just before she comes, I was thinking you could all hide in her bedroom and surprise her?'

'Sounds great.'

. . .

She left the girls in the bedroom with a tray of snacks, unpacking their things. On her way back down the stairs, Harriet's key scraped in the lock. 'Hey, Mum.'

'Hi, love. Good to have you home. Why don't you take your bag straight upstairs?'

She'd wanted to follow her up and watch her reaction to seeing her friends all there, but Simon hung around the front door. 'Can I come in?'

Trust him to spoil the moment. She wanted to enjoy Harriet's surprise as much as she did. But she could hardly turn him away. 'Of course, come in.'

He was stepping over the threshold when the screams came from upstairs. He looked terrified. 'What the heck is that?'

Erin grinned at his confusion. 'The greeting call of the lesser-spotted teenage girl.'

They were interrupted by Harriet flying down the stairs and throwing her arms around Erin's neck. 'Thank you, Mum! Thank you. Thank you. And my room looks incredible. You're amazing. I love you.' And then she was gone again.

'What did you do?'

'Decorated her room and invited her friends for a sleepover. It was a surprise.'

'Oh. Nice.'

Never had Simon been involved in any of those kinds of arrangements. Even when they were together, it was Erin who'd dealt with kids' parties and sleepovers and anything to do with Harriet's friends. It was a side of parenting that he'd have no clue about. She nodded in the direction of the kitchen. 'Do you want a drink?'

'No, I'm fine thanks. I just wanted a quick chat with you about everything. Our plans.'

Upstairs. Erin could hear the squeals and laughter of Harriet and her friends. Hopefully, being with her friends this weekend would make her realise what she'd be giving up and this would put paid to these 'plans' of Simon's. 'Mum's having a nap in the front room. Or at least she was. Come into the kitchen.'

It was the first time Simon had been in her mother's house since their divorce, so she could understand why he looked so uncomfortable, shuffling from one foot to the other. She pointed at the kitchen chairs. 'You can sit down.'

He looked around at the kitchen units which hadn't changed since he'd brought her home here after their first date, sat drinking tea and whispering so as not to wake her mother. 'Well, this is a blast from the past.'

'Your past. My present and probably future.'

He tilted his head. 'How is your mum?'

It was difficult to explain. Sometimes she was fine, others Erin worried about leaving her alone. 'She's okay. It varies. What did you want to talk to me about? Have you got the job?'

He shook his head. 'Still waiting to hear. But I'm pretty confident. That's why we need to talk about it. Like grown-ups.'

He knew exactly how to push her buttons. 'Okay. Talk.'

If he got out his phone to show her another picture of paradise, she might throw it in the washing up. But he leaned forwards and rested his elbows on the plastic tablecloth. 'Look, we've been talking for the last couple of days. Harriet's pretty keen on coming with us to the States. But she doesn't want to let you down. She's got it into her head that you need her. She thinks that you've got a lot to deal with right now. With your mum, I mean.'

Had Harriet really said that? 'I've not asked her to help.'

He held up his hands in surrender. 'I didn't mean that. I meant that... she's loyal to you, Erin. She loves you. She won't go if she thinks you want her to stay.'

Of course, she was loyal, she was her daughter. What did he expect? 'What are you saying exactly? You want me to tell her to go?'

He looked her dead in the eye. It was his signature *I really need this* move. 'This could be really great for her.'

She wasn't about to let him 'manage' her like one of his office juniors. 'It could also be really awful. She could hate it over there.'

He shrugged. 'And if she does, she can come back, can't she?'

He made it seem so easy. On one level it was. But the most she'd ever been apart from Harriet was a week when she went on holiday with Simon and Carmel. Even that was intolerable. By the end of the week, she was almost nauseous with the strength of the yearning to see her. Her absences were a physical loss. If she moved away, she wasn't sure that she would be able to breathe freely.

And that was without the worry about what might happen to her out there. Simon was a good father, but his rules were not the same as hers. On their holiday to Zante last year, he had let her spend the evening with a group of kids she'd only just met. Going to a nightclub that was, admittedly, adjacent to the hotel, but not necessarily suitable for a girl who might look eighteen but was really a rather naive fifteen.

'Why can't she come later? Once she's finished her A levels? Why does it have to be now, Simon?'

He shifted from one foot to the other, there was something else going on here. 'Okay, I'm not supposed to tell anyone. But Carmel's pregnant.'

For a moment, Erin froze. There it was. Hadn't she called it from the word go? It was hard not to think about the years that the two of them had tried for a second child. And now it was only Simon who'd been successful. She wasn't about to show how much that hurt. 'I see. Congratulations.'

He had the decency not to rub it in her face. 'Yeah, thanks. It's really early days and Carmel is superstitious about saying anything to anyone. Please don't tell Harriet yet.'

It was a pretty big secret to keep when Harriet was making such a life-changing decision. This wasn't something that should be kept from her for long. 'It's your news to tell. But it needs to be soon. Before she makes her mind up about coming. It's only fair on her.'

He nodded. 'You're right. I'll talk to Carmel. But this is why I want her to come with us. There's already going to be a huge age gap between them. I want her to know her new brother or sister. I want us to be a family.'

Each word punched her bruised heart a little harder. Did he have any idea how she felt? She'd made her peace with the end of their marriage a long time ago. But the idea of the three of them – four of them – living a picture-perfect family life while she was demoted to weekly FaceTime calls made her want to bend double with pain. Harriet wasn't just a big sister that he could slot into his shiny brand-new family. She was Erin's family, the centre of her world. Without her, Erin's life didn't even make sense.

But she didn't want to say anything she might regret. After a rocky start, she and Simon had managed to co-parent pretty successfully, resolving sticky issues like Christmas and birthdays and finances without too much conflict. It was better for all of them that way. Especially Harriet. She had to be the grown-up here. 'I understand, Simon. I really do. But I don't agree that this is the best thing for her. Listen to her upstairs with her pals. She'll lose out on all of that if she goes.'

'She'll make new friends.'

He made it sound easy. That's because he hadn't been the parent she'd clung to for the first five weeks of primary school, who'd lived through her desolation when she'd fallen out with her best friend in Year 6, who'd had to live with the fear and trepidation of the first week of secondary school. Harriet had lovely friends now, but it didn't happen easily for her. Still, what could she do? 'I'll make sure that she knows that this is her decision. That she doesn't have to feel bad about me. But I'm not persuading her to go. I can't do that.'

He took a deep breath and nodded. 'Okay. Well, I guess that's something. I'd better be off.'

The girls emerged from the bedroom thirty minutes later, looking as if they were headed out to a nightclub. 'We're going to walk to the shops.'

'The shops' consisted of a Budgens, a hairdresser, a tile shop and a couple of takeaways. Whatever were they going to do there? 'Okay, love. I was thinking of ordering in pizza tonight unless there was something you'd prefer?'

'Pizza would be great, thanks Mum.'

They passed though the hall, leaving a trail of strong perfume behind them. She'd lived in this house at their age, knew how little there was to do around here. She could remember her mother's frustration when they were leaving the house and she would want to make herself look nice before they went. 'We're going to the shops, it's not a fashion show.' She'd said the same words to Harriet not two months ago.

As she shut the front door, her mother appeared at the sitting room door. 'Hello, love. I was about to make some tea. Do you want one?'

'I'll make it.'

'No, it'll do me good to get up. Has Harriet gone out with her friends?'

This must be a good day. Her mum was keeping up with what was going on. Maybe she could venture some more questions before going to visit Imogen tomorrow?

She followed her out to the kitchen and resisted the urge to take over while her mum filled the kettle. Only enough water for two cups, obviously. 'I can't remember having any sleepovers here when I was Harriet's age. Did I?'

Her mother frowned. 'I don't think so.'

She knew she hadn't. Her mother had barely wanted her friends to come over in the evenings, let alone stay the night. Quite early on, she realised it was more enjoyable to go to her friends' houses which were full of noise and mothers who made snacks and thought of fun things to do.

'Did Imogen have friends to stay?'

Her mother jumped as if she'd thrown something at her. 'I don't want to talk about Imogen.'

'I know, Mum. But I don't understand why. Why don't you want to talk about her?'

'She's gone.'

They kept coming back to this. 'I know that. But why did she go? Did you have an argument?'

Her mother was twisting her wedding ring in the way she'd always done when she was anxious. 'Imogen needed to go. It wasn't safe.'

This was new. Safe? For whom? 'What do you mean, Mum?'

'I needed to look after you. I needed to keep you safe.'

Her mother was getting more agitated. Maybe this was cruel, if Harriet had been here she definitely would've stopped Erin pressing for more, but there had to be a way to get to the truth of the story. 'Why wasn't I safe? Did she not look after me?'

Her mother shook her head. 'Imogen. I had to keep Imogen safe. I had to keep you both safe. I did the best I could.'

Both of them safe? What danger had they been in? Her mother started to cry. 'I'm sorry, Erin. I'm sorry. I did my best.'

'It's okay, Mum. It's okay. I just want to know what happened. And why you didn't tell me. Why didn't you tell me that she was my mother?'

The pain in her mother's eyes made her want to kick

herself. She should have worded that differently. 'I had to do what I had to do, Erin. At the time...'

She looked helpless as she trailed off. How much was the dementia and how much was it the habit of a lifetime of keeping secrets? 'But Mum—'

'No, Erin.' Her tone of voice was the same as it'd been when Erin was a teenager pressing to be allowed to stay out later or buy something to wear that her mother deemed inappropriate. 'I don't want to discuss this any longer.'

The girls were full of giggles when they came home; it was a pleasure to hear them. When the pizza came for their dinner, she laid it out in the kitchen for them and took the stairs two at a time to let them know it was ready.

At the door to Harriet's room, she hadn't intended to eavesdrop; she enjoyed hearing their laughter, the joy they had in being together. But she did pause with her knuckles about to knock on the door when she heard Harriet telling them all about the house in America.

'That looks amazing. I'm so jealous.'

'But what about your mum? Wouldn't you miss her if you go?'

'Of course I would. But I'd be able to call her whenever I want and Dad said he'd pay for her to come and visit if she can't afford it.'

Erin's cheeks burned with the embarrassment of Simon making it sound as if she couldn't pay for herself and the fact that he was being Mr Bountiful and throwing his largesse around.

She could have kissed the friend – was it Charlotte? – who said, 'I don't think I could leave my mum. What if I needed her?'

There were some mumbles of agreement, before Harriet's

confident tone rang harsh in her ears. 'If I don't like it, I'll come home again. Anyway, it's not definite yet. It might come to nothing.'

On the other side of the door, Erin closed her eyes. *Please, God, let it come to nothing.* Because, if Harriet chose Simon, she wouldn't be able to cope.

SEVENTEEN

The King's Arms was a little busier than when she met Simon here last week. Ironic that Imogen should choose the same place. Erin had thought she might sit outside, but the sunshine of the morning had been overshadowed by a rather threatening cloud that was hopefully not a portent for the outcome of this meeting.

As she shuffled towards an empty table, hands full of car keys and a glass of juice, Erin had to press her mouth into her shoulder to stifle the yawn that escaped. With their chatting and giggling, the girls had kept her awake most of last night. Ordinarily, around 2 a.m., she would have asked them to quieten down, for Ava's sake if not hers, but that didn't fit with the mandate to show Harriet how wonderful her life was here. She'd dropped them all home an hour ago.

There was a table in the corner which was small but out of the way. Erin took the bench seat facing the entrance so that she could watch for Imogen's arrival. As she was fifteen minutes early, she wasn't expecting her yet. But three minutes later, the outside door opened and in she came.

Imogen scanned the bar with the confidence of someone

who'd spent years working in pubs and, when she spotted Erin, she gave her a tentative little wave and made her way over.

'Hi.'

'Hello.'

The first time they'd met had been impromptu, for Imogen at least. This time, it was like an excruciatingly awkward first date. 'You're early, too. Must be a family trait.'

Imogen glanced at her watch and raised an eyebrow. 'You know what Mum says. On time is late.'

Ava always had been a stickler for timekeeping, among other rules she thought were important. Funny that she'd always been like that. And even funnier hearing someone else refer to her as *Mum*. 'Ah, yes, of course. Look, sit down and I'll go and get you a drink. What would you like?'

Imogen held up her hands to stop Erin from standing and backed towards the bar. 'Stay where you are. I can get it.'

This was painful. Now Erin had to sit and wait while Imogen was served at the busy bar. Why hadn't she bought two drinks? Everyone liked orange juice, didn't they?

But Imogen was served almost immediately and back in her seat surprisingly quickly. 'Wow. That was impressive.'

Imogen smiled. 'Not my first rodeo. I've worked in pubs for years. You have to know how to catch the barman's eye.'

'You'll have to teach me how to do that.'

Was that too much? Had she sounded too eager? Assuming that Imogen would stick around long enough to teach her anything? But Imogen smiled. 'I will.'

She tried to get a good look at her this time. Last time was too much of a shock to take anything in. There was something so familiar about her. It wasn't the long dark hair, although Erin's had looked very similar until she'd decided to cut it into a short bob two years ago. It wasn't her skin, which was much more tanned than Erin could ever achieve. Then she realised what it was.

'You look like Dad.'

Imogen grimaced. 'I know. It's the nose, isn't it?'

Their shared laugh lessened the tension. 'I didn't like to say that, but yes. Not that I remember him that well, to be honest.' Something occurred to her. 'You did know that he passed away?'

She was relieved when Imogen nodded. Erin had been twelve when her dad died. Old enough, people assumed, for her to have a lot of memories of him. But he'd not been the most attentive or hands-on of fathers. Had spent most of her childhood at the office or away on business. He'd been fifteen years older than Erin's mother and her memories of him were more like those of a distant grandfather than a parent. The irony of that was only just hitting her now.

'I heard that he had a heart attack. We weren't close.'

Another thought occurred. 'Did you not want to come to the funeral?'

Imogen blushed as she shook her head. 'Like I said. We weren't close.'

A thousand questions were bubbling under Erin's tongue. *But didn't you want to see Mum? Or me?* She wasn't going to release them and risk scaring Imogen away. After the disaster of their first meeting, she planned to approach her as if she were a timid wild animal. 'I wasn't close to him, either. He worked a lot.'

Imogen's laugh was hollow. 'Oh yes. His precious job. Poor Mum.'

This was surprising. 'What do you mean?'

'He wouldn't let her work when I was young. You know how much she wanted to be a teacher? But he said she had to stay home and raise the children. Even though the children turned out to be just me.'

This was news to Erin. It wasn't quite the story she'd been told. Although, hadn't her mother been telling Harriet how difficult it had been for her to work when Erin was young? 'But she was at home with you when you were young?'

She couldn't quite keep the note of envy from her voice. She wouldn't imagine Imogen had to come straight home and peel potatoes for dinner every night.

'Yes. She didn't train to be a teacher until I was about fourteen.' Imogen took a sip of her Coke. 'I often wondered if the reason that I was an only child was that she'd have had to wait even longer if there'd been more children.'

Erin was about to interject that she was a younger sibling before she realised that she wasn't. She wasn't Ava's daughter. It was still so difficult to get her head around this.

Imogen filled the awkward silence, though she looked down into her drink as she spoke. 'You said on the phone that Mum isn't well?'

Her lack of eye contact showed how even the question made her uncomfortable. Erin nodded. 'It's dementia. We got the diagnosis a year ago, but it's getting worse. She still has lots of good days, but we don't know how long that will last.'

Imogen's expression was difficult to read. 'I see.'

Did she? 'It's what makes it so tricky. It's hard to press her for information about the past.'

She didn't want to press Imogen too hard. The last thing she wanted was her disappearing again. But she seemed to be processing the news. 'What about Auntie Marcelle? Have you asked her?'

'I've tried. But she's in Australia and it's difficult over the phone. She's coming to visit soon, though. Would you like to see her?'

Again, she wondered if she was pushing too hard, but Imogen gave a little nod. 'Maybe. I like Auntie Marcelle. She was always very kind.'

That's what Erin had always thought, too. But how kind

was it to keep a family secret that was now blowing her world apart? 'I'll let you know when she confirms dates for her visit.'

A few more awkward seconds passed before Imogen put down her drink and picked up her bag. 'I brought something for you.'

Erin wasn't sure what she was expecting, but it wasn't what she got. A photograph of the two of them.

Imogen handed it over as if it were a holy relic. 'It's a copy of the one I have at home.'

Even though the fresh copy was smooth, the lines across it suggested the original had been handled many times. A younger version of Imogen was unmistakable. She looked so young. In fact, she reminded Erin of Harriet in many ways. The shy smile, the self-conscious way that she sat with her left foot hooked behind her right. In her arms, a bundled-up baby who must have been Erin.

Imogen leaned forwards to look at the photo, too. 'You were a very beautiful baby. I remember the midwife in the hospital remarking on that. You had all that dark hair. And blue eyes.' She sat back and waited for Erin to look up at her. She smiled. 'You've still got them.'

'We all have. Mum. And Harriet. That's my daughter.'

Imogen nodded. 'When you were first born, they put you next to me in a little cot. I kept looking at you. It's a strange feeling, isn't it? Realising that you've made an actual baby?'

That made Erin smile. She remembered the feeling well. After Simon had gone home at the end of visiting time and she had lain in bed in the ward, watching Harriet sleep. 'I'm your mummy.' She'd whispered to her. One of the most surreal nights of her life. 'It is strange. You kind of wake up the next morning and it's like you should feel really different. But you don't. You're still the same person and yet, you're not.'

She knew this made very little sense, but Imogen was chewing her lip and nodding. 'Yes. That's exactly what it is.'

Erin looked at the photo again. The young Imogen appeared nervous, but there was a smile on her face. How had this woman left her baby behind and disappeared for over thirty years? 'Why did you go? Did you not want to be a mother?'

Imogen frowned. 'It's so complicated, Erin. But I want you to know that I did love you. I left because I love you. And it's meant that I have lived without a part of myself for the last thirty-eight years.'

'Tell me. Please tell me what happened.'

'Okay. I'll need to start from the beginning.'

Erin shuffled back into her seat. 'I'm listening.'

EIGHTEEN

The birth was so much harder than she'd thought it would be.

Her mum had offered to be in the room and support her, but things had been so strained between them that Imogen had lied and said she didn't want her there. Instead, Jimmy came, but he was no help at all. They were two kids; how did they know what to expect?

Labour was agony. Nothing like she'd expected. And the midwife was harsh and unhelpful. 'Stop making such a fuss. You're wasting energy with that racket.'

All she wanted was her mum to come and make it okay. When she was younger and off school with a stomach ache, her mum used to make up a bed on the sofa for her, switch on the TV, bring toast or soup. That's what she'd needed in that delivery room, her mum's cool hand on her head, her soft voice telling her it'd all be okay. But it was too late. She'd left it too late. She was on her own.

When Erin was born, she was this tiny red screwed up ball of flesh. Even though Imogen had had months to get used to being pregnant, she hadn't ever got her mind around the fact that she was having an actual baby. Once she'd been weighed and cleaned up, the midwife put Erin into Imogen's arms. She was so tiny, so vulnerable. Imogen hadn't realised that she was crying until Jimmy tried to press a tissue into her hand. 'It'll be alright, Immy.' She'd begun to wonder if he had anything to back up that mantra.

Back on the maternity ward, the nurses tried to encourage her to breastfeed, but it was so painful and difficult. She cried; the baby cried. Eventually, she'd begged them to give her a bottle of formula. It was her mum who brought them in in the end, showed her how to warm the milk and how much the baby would need. From the word go, her mum was so much better at it than she was. Erin was so much happier in her arms than Imogen's. She tried to reassure her. 'It'll be easier when you get her home.'

But it wasn't.

To begin with, Erin didn't sleep. Not for more than two hours together anyway. Imogen had never known exhaustion like it. Even her bones were tired. Every time Erin cried in the night, she dragged herself out of bed like she was stuck in a swamp and had to pull her limbs free. Even after Erin was fed, it took forever to settle her. Sometimes she would beg. 'Please, Erin, please just sleep.' Her tears would mix with the baby's until finally, finally she would give in.

Sometimes, she got so desperate that she begged her mother to help. 'Please. Could you get up with her for one night?'

But she refused. 'I have to work tomorrow, Imogen. I'm sorry. I can't be up in the night.'

That wasn't the real reason. They were punishing her, both of them. Making her do this on her own. During the day – when her parents were both at work – she would shuffle around the house as if she was wearing a heavy blanket. Her world had become so small. The bedroom. The kitchen. The bathroom. She didn't even make it as far as the tiny back garden.

Jimmy would try to persuade her out of the house. 'Let's take Erin for a walk. I can push the pram.'

But she told him to take the baby on his own. She couldn't cope with the stares, the muttering, the eyes on them all the time. At least she was safe from judgement at home. Other than her mother's and father's, of course. And her own.

She was failing as a mother. It wasn't only the sleep; Erin was such an unhappy baby. Aside from the pretty constant crying, she would squirm in Imogen's arms as if she was trying to escape. Eventually, a midwife at the clinic said it was colic, and prescribed something to add to her milk. It helped. A lot. But then Imogen felt guilty that the baby had been in pain and she hadn't done anything about it until now. And she was angry at her mother, too. Why hadn't she known that Imogen needed to get help?

As the spring brightened the days, Imogen's moods only got darker and she couldn't see a route out of the way she was feeling. Had she done the wrong thing in having a baby? Should she have had the baby adopted? Her father – through her mother – had made it absolutely clear that she would have to take full responsibility for the baby, but was her mother really not going to help at all?

And then Jimmy had to go.

His uncle had got him a job on an oil rig off the coast of Scotland. It was really good money and he didn't think he could turn it down.

'This might be the only chance we have to get a deposit together for a house.' He was so eager, so persuasive, that of course she let him go. To be honest, it was a relief; he wouldn't be pressuring her to leave the house, eat dinner downstairs, wash her hair. She couldn't help but suspect that he was also relieved. Who would want to be around a depressed girlfriend and a screaming baby?

With Jimmy gone, her world became even smaller. When

Erin was first born, a few of the girls from school came to visit, bringing gifts for the baby, wanting to hold her and telling Imogen how cute she was. But they didn't come again. Imogen was different now. She was one side of a river and they were still on the other: motherhood was a bridge that, once crossed, she couldn't come back from.

At some point, her mother must have realised that she would have to intervene. She would take Erin for an hour or two, bathe her, feed her, soothe her. Imogen would watch her mother walk the baby up and down the hall, rocking her to sleep. Did Erin feel safer in her arms? Is that why she let her eyelids flutter closed in a way that didn't happen when she was with Imogen? The only way she would fall asleep on her was if she'd screamed herself to utter exhaustion. Was it because she didn't trust Imogen to keep her safe while she slept?

If so, she was right. Imogen couldn't be trusted. She didn't know how to keep a baby safe.

NINETEEN

'I was a terrible mother, Erin. And you deserved so much more. Looking back now, the signs were there from the beginning. But things were different then. And by the time anyone realised, it'd gone too far. It was too late.' Imogen started to cry. 'I don't know how to tell you the next part. I don't know how to put it into words.'

As Imogen had poured her story forth, Erin had stayed very still and quiet, frightened that, if she interrupted or asked a question, Imogen might stop speaking. It wasn't easy to listen to this version of the first weeks of her life. That she hadn't been planned, or wanted, and that her birth had brought so much misery to the people around her.

'I'm sorry.' Imogen pulled her handbag onto her lap and rummaged around in it, probably for a tissue that she couldn't find. 'It's just that, I haven't spoken about it in such a long time.'

'It's okay. Of course, you must be upset. I'm sorry for making you live through it all again.'

It was a pleasantry, a reflex, to say sorry. She wasn't sorry at all. She was angry. Upset. Confused. But not sorry. Someone should have told her this story a long time ago. Not left it until now. It was hard to feel sorry for the person who had known where you were for over thirty years and never come back to look for you.

Imogen gave up looking in her handbag. 'I'm going to go to the ladies and sort my face out. Blow my nose.'

'Of course. I'll get us another drink while you're gone.'

Imogen pushed the chair back as she stood and it scraped on the floor. 'I won't be long. Sorry.'

It wasn't until she'd gone that Erin realised that neither of them had touched their drinks. There was no point going to the bar. She sipped at her drink, her throat so tight that it was difficult to swallow.

She'd known that Imogen must have been a young mother but hadn't realised how young. Sixteen. Only a few months older than Harriet and Harriet was a *child*. It must have been incredibly difficult for her to have a baby at that age. She had sympathy with her for that. Maybe even had some sympathy for her running away. Hadn't every mother fantasised about running away on a bad day with a newborn? The lack of sleep and relentlessness of the bathing and changing and feeding was certainly a lot to get used to. And Imogen had been so young.

No, it wasn't that that made her angry. It wasn't even the fact that she wasn't wanted, although that hurt. It was that no one had told her anything.

'Hi, Erin.' She looked up into the smiling face of Carmel, Simon's wife. 'Fancy seeing you here.'

Why had she agreed to meet at this pub? The same one she'd come to with Simon. 'Oh, hi, Carmel. Are you with Simon?'

She shook her head. 'No, with some friends for lunch. I was on my way to the bar. How about you?'

She wasn't about to tell her who Imogen was. 'Same. Just one friend. She's gone to the bathroom.'

Carmel looked as if she was making her mind up about

something. Then she pointed to the chair that Imogen had vacated. 'Do you mind if I sit for a minute? I want to say a quick something.'

Erin's heart plummeted. This was obviously going to be about California. She liked Carmel, but this really wasn't a conversation that she wanted to have. 'Look, Carmel, I—'

Her beautiful face looked pained. 'Please, Erin. One minute, I promise.'

'Okay. But when my friend comes back...'

'I will get straight up.'

She slipped herself onto the chair. Erin tried not to look at her midriff; she wasn't supposed to know that Carmel was pregnant.

Due to the tight time limit, she got straight to it. 'Look, I know that Simon should not have spoken to Harriet about California before he told you about it. I was really cross with him about that.'

She couldn't imagine the serene Carmel getting cross but appreciated the support. 'Thank you.'

'But please don't hold that against him. It was excitement. About the job. It's a really good move for him.'

Though she didn't want to be rude, Erin really didn't give a stuff about the career prospects of her ex-husband. 'I see.'

'And it's my fault, too. I miss home. My grandmother hasn't been in the best of health and I'd like to be closer to her. Like you've done for your mother.'

She might be gentle, but she was also clever. 'I understand that. But I don't see why he had to ask Harriet to come.'

'Because he's her father and because he thinks she'd love it out there. She really would, Erin. I grew up out there. The weather, the waves, the outdoor life. She would thrive.'

Erin didn't need anyone telling her what was best for her daughter. 'She's too young to up and leave the life she has. She's not even sixteen yet, Carmel.'

Carmel leaned forwards and Erin caught a breath of her light fresh perfume. 'I'm not her mother, Erin, I know that, but I promise that I'd be there for her. I love her, too. And she's pretty much a grown-up now, anyway.'

Fifteen wasn't grown-up. It might be grown-up on the outside. It might be *I can cook my own dinner and walk to the shops and decide what I want to study at college.* But it was also *I'm scared and I don't know what to do and can I sleep in your bed with you tonight, Mum?* Simon and Carmel only saw one side of Harriet. It wasn't their fault. She stayed with them. She didn't live with them. And there was a big difference between the two.

'I appreciate what you're trying to do, Carmel. But this is between Simon and me. And, anyway, this might all be for nothing. The move might not happen anyway.'

She knew by the downward glance and blush of her cheek that Carmel was keeping something. She barely met Erin's eye as she stood up to leave. 'Okay, well, it was nice seeing you. I'd better get back to my friends.'

Erin knew before she asked. 'What is it, Carmel? What are you not saying?'

The blush got deeper. 'It's not my place. Like you said, it's between Simon and you.'

She'd had enough of enigmatic ends to conversations. Her voice had a bite to it, 'Tell me, Carmel.'

'He's going to call you later. Simon found out this morning that he got the job. We're going in two weeks' time.'

Erin opened her mouth but nothing came out. Then Imogen stepped up to the table, her make-up back to normal. 'Oh, great. You've found someone you know. I need to go.'

Carmel held up her hands. 'No, it's me that needs to leave. My friends are going to think I got lost on the way to the bar. I'll see you soon, Erin.' She smiled gently as she left.

Erin barely acknowledged Carmel's departure. Imogen was

going? But she hadn't even finished her story. 'You can't leave yet.'

'I have to. I'm sorry. This was a bad idea. Take care of yourself.'

Erin quickly shuffled out from the bench to follow her. There was no way she could leave it like this. Every time she got close to finding out what had happened, her mother would clam up or Imogen would run away. Not again, this time she wanted answers. She was *owed* answers.

As the bar was empty, it took Imogen no time to get across it and out of the door, leaving Erin in her wake. By the time Erin got to the door, Imogen was already at her car. Terrified she might not get to her in time, Erin shouted across the car park as she ran towards her. 'Imogen. Wait!'

When she turned round, Imogen's face was full of tears. 'I can't do this. It's too much. You don't want to know.'

'I do want to know. Why do you think I've tracked you down? What did you mean about what happened next? I need to know what happened.'

'But it could change things. For you and Mum, I mean. It could ruin everything.'

Erin felt a roar in her belly. Everything was already changing. Her mother was changing. She needed to know. 'Please. Stay.'

Imogen shook her head. 'I can't. Please. Let me go.'

This was ridiculous. Every time she'd spoken to her, they'd got so close to finding out what had happened and then she just shut down. Imogen struggled with her car key in the lock, but eventually she turned it and, as she wrestled the door open, Erin reached out to grab her arm. 'This isn't fair, Imogen. You can't leave me hanging like this. I deserve to know what happened.'

When she turned to Erin, Imogen's face was ravaged with fear and guilt. 'Do you? Do you want to know the truth? I tried to kill you, Erin. Is that the truth you want to hear? I was your mother and I tried to kill you.'

Her words were like a slap across her face. Erin dropped her arm, numb with disbelief, and watched Imogen drive away.

TWENTY

'Excuse me, love.'

Erin hadn't realised that she was standing in the way of the exit until the voice was directly behind her. She shuffled out of the way. 'Sorry.'

'No problem.' A large man with a red shiny face peered at her. 'Are you okay? You look like you've seen a ghost.'

Maybe she had. 'I'm fine, thanks. Just trying to remember where I parked the car.'

To prove the lie, she strode off towards the back of the car park, leaving him behind.

I tried to kill you, Erin. Is that the truth you want to hear?

Imogen's words had slapped the breath out of her. She'd understood the depression Imogen had described; anyone would expect the realities of motherhood to be a challenge for a sixteen-year-old girl. But trying to kill her baby? Surely, she hadn't meant that literally? Had she abandoned her, maybe? Neglected her?

But she'd looked as if she meant every word the way it sounded. Looked as if she had actually tried to...

Erin shook a terrible image from her mind, clicked the car

door open with her key fob and got in. If her life was tearing apart before, now Imogen had thrown a lit match that threatened to burn it down.

She'd had to concentrate on pulling out of the car park and getting back onto the main road before she could even begin to process what had just happened, but it was almost impossible to stop the questions whirling around her brain. For the second time in the last two weeks, her world had shifted on its axis. She'd just begun to get her head around Imogen being her birth mother. That she'd left her and Ava had picked up the pieces, stepped into the breach, done what she had to do. But today's speech had put a very different spin on things. What had happened? And had Ava been the one to tell Imogen to go?

Thankfully, there wasn't too much traffic and she was back onto the motorway within ten minutes. Rather than trying to beat the traffic, she stayed in the left-hand lane behind a large lorry driving a steady sixty miles per hour. Then she allowed herself to unpick some of the thoughts.

Now Ava's fear about her contacting Imogen made sense. Of course, she wouldn't want Erin hearing that bombshell. It also explained why she'd never mentioned Imogen. It would be a terrible thing to have to tell a small child. Even as an adult, it was pretty difficult to shoulder. The depression must have overtaken her somehow, made it difficult to carry on.

It made her look at Ava differently, too. At what point had she stepped up? According to Imogen's version of events, she'd been pretty much left alone to learn about motherhood. But this didn't fit with Erin's experience of being raised by Ava. If anything, she had felt under the microscope, not trusted to make her own decisions about anything.

Was that why? Having had one daughter slip spectacularly

through the net, had Ava been determined to keep Erin well and truly on the hook?

She jumped when her phone rang through the hands-free. Harriet.

'Hi, love.'

'Hey, Mum.' Over the phone, her voice was still that of a young girl and its chirpy tone brought a lump to Erin's throat. 'When will you be home?'

Erin didn't know how far down the motorway she was. 'Not sure. About forty-five minutes?'

'Okay. Well, Dad wants me to go over there tonight. He said I can get the train and he'll meet me at the other end.'

Panic rose in Erin. After the revelation from Imogen, she'd forgotten about the conversation with Carmel. Simon's job had been confirmed. They were definitely moving to America. Which meant that Harriet had to make a decision about whether she was going to go, too. Was he going to tell her tonight? But Carmel had promised he would speak to Erin first. 'Uh, do you have to go over tonight, love? I was hoping we could watch a film or something together.'

There was a pause at the other end. 'Dad said they were going to order in from that Turkish restaurant. You know the one I like near him?' Another pause. 'I think he has some news he wants to tell me. It sounded important.'

Your father thinks everything he has to say is important. Was it okay to speak her thoughts aloud now that Harriet was fifteen? No. She'd never been that kind of parent and she wasn't about to start now. 'Okay, love. What time do you need to go?'

'I was going to get the train in about an hour. If you're not back to drop me to the station, I'll have to leave a bit earlier so that I can walk there. It doesn't matter. If it gets to half past, I'll start walking.'

'I'll do my best to get to you.'

Erin pulled out into the overtaking lane. If Harriet was

going to hear what she thought she was, Erin wanted to see her first. Hold her tight, imprint her love on her in a way that would convince her not to go. When the phone rang a second time, she pulled back into the left-hand lane.

'Hello, Simon.'

'Erin? Is this a good time to talk?'

'Not really. I'm driving.'

He didn't acknowledge that. 'Well, I kind of need to talk to you now anyway. I got that job. In America.'

She gripped the steering wheel tightly. 'I know. I saw Carmel this afternoon.'

'Yes. She called me. Sorry about that. I had intended to call you and tell you first.'

Only because your new wife told you to. 'Well, I know now. Can we talk about this later? I'm on the motorway.'

Again, he ignored her. Had he always only heard what he wanted to hear? 'Well, the thing is, I want to tell Harriet tonight. I've invited her over here.'

'I know that, too. She just called me.' Did it not bother him that he was always a step behind the women in his life?

'Oh. Well, that's okay then. We all know. I didn't need to call.'

She could imagine the face he was pulling at Carmel right now. He loved to be proved right. 'I wouldn't say that. I think we have a lot to talk about, just not when I'm trying to drive at the same time.'

This time – when it was convenient for him – he acknowledged her. 'Right, of course, well, I'll speak to Harriet and then you and I can maybe have a conversation about logistics tomorrow?'

Logistics. As far as he was concerned, this was already a done deal. 'Goodbye, Simon.'

She pressed 'End Call' before he had a chance to reply.

Pulling back into the overtaking lane for the second time,

she pressed her foot to the pedal. Coughing back angry sobs, she opened the window for cold air; there was no time to pull over and give in to tears. Even ten minutes with Harriet at the station would be worth it. Every minute with her had taken on a new significance. Though what could she say in those 600 seconds that would make any difference at all to the outcome of her decision?

And, after that, she had her own mother to deal with. She'd allowed Ava's dementia to keep her from asking the difficult questions which might upset her. But the time for that was over. She needed proper answers, however upset Ava got. She might be forgetting more and more about the past, but Erin didn't believe for a second that she would have forgotten something as serious as Imogen had described.

Once she'd said goodbye to Harriet and got her safely on the train, she would sit down with her mother and find out the truth. What had Imogen done to her as a baby? Why had Ava sent her away? And why had Ava chosen to keep the truth from her for the whole of Erin's life?

TWENTY-ONE

Crawling traffic onto the slip road meant that Erin had no chance at all of getting to the station before Harriet's train left.

Maybe it was for the best. In her current emotional state, she'd probably have erupted into tears and hung onto her legs like a tragic heroine in a terrible B-movie. Harriet had been excited at the pictures of the house and pool in California, but Erin had to hope that – when the reality of moving away from everything she knew was presented to her – she'd make the right decision. The decision that Erin wanted.

It also meant that she could focus on her mother.

For the last ten minutes, she'd felt herself getting more and more agitated at the prospect of the conversation they needed to have. If she'd watched the scene between her and Imogen on a soap opera, she'd have laughed at the unbelievable storyline. How had she not known that she had a different mother? How had the secret been kept for so long?

As soon at the front door was open, she called out to let Ava know that she was there. 'Mum?'

'In the front room, love. Have you had a good day?'

Before pushing open the door to the front room, she took a

deep breath. She couldn't launch straight into this. She would have to go softly.

Her mother was sitting with a magazine open on her lap, thumbing through without really reading it. 'I'm looking at these magazines that Harriet gave me. But they've all got holes in them.'

'They're her collage magazines. She buys them for the pictures so that she can use them in her collage. She uses the faces or sometimes cuts out outfits or other objects. It's clever the ways she does it. She showed you one, didn't she?'

'Oh yes. I'd forgotten. I remember now. Silly me.'

Did she remember, or was she masking her memory problems? It was so difficult to tell.

'Mum. I need to show you another picture. I got it today.'

She slipped the photograph of her and Imogen from the envelope and passed it over. 'Do you recognise who that is?'

Her mother stared at it for a while then looked up at her. 'It's Imogen. It's my daughter.'

At least she wasn't going to go back to denying who Imogen was. 'Yes. And the baby? It's me, isn't it? Imogen is holding me as a baby.'

Her mother swallowed, then nodded. 'Yes.'

'Why didn't you tell me, Mum? Why didn't you tell me about Imogen?'

Mists swirled in her mother's eyes. One of the dementia nurses had explained it like this. At this stage, her mother's memory was moments of clarity that were sometimes covered by clouds. As it progressed, those clouds would thicken and the moments of sunshine would become rare, then cease to exist.

'You don't understand. I had to keep her safe. I had to keep my baby safe.'

Then Imogen must have been telling the truth. She *had* tried to hurt Erin. It was a very strange thing to imagine. It went against a mother's fundamental instinct to protect. 'I understand, Mum.'

Her mother's lips were trembling. 'I didn't want to send her away, but I had to. I had to do it.'

Erin took her mother's hand, the skin papery and fragile. 'But why, Mum?'

'Frank wouldn't help. He wouldn't have anything to do with it. "It's your problem. You wanted it. It's your problem now."'

She could hear her father's gruff voice saying that. 'What was the problem? What exactly happened?'

But she might have been talking to the wall for all the response she got. It was like Ava was in another dimension. Speaking to someone over Erin's shoulder. Or even speaking to herself?

'It was my fault. I should have seen it coming. It was dangerous. I didn't realise.'

Erin's heart thudded in her chest. Was she about to get to the truth? 'What was dangerous?'

'It was dangerous. I had to keep Imogen safe.'

Clearly she was starting to get confused. 'Do you mean Erin? You had to keep baby Erin safe?'

Her mother was shaking her head. 'No. Imogen. Imogen was in danger. I had to protect her. She had to go. I had to call them to take her away. It was awful. My own daughter. But I had to keep her safe.'

All of this was such a muddle and Erin wasn't sure that her mother wasn't confusing the two of them. She laid a hand over her mother's to stop her from twisting at her fingers. 'It's okay, Mum. Take it slowly. Imogen was at home with her baby? In the bedroom?'

Her mother's eyes were full of fear. 'Yes. In her old bedroom. We got her a cot for the baby. Just a second-hand one. But I rubbed it down and painted it and it was lovely.'

This was better. 'Okay. And then she was depressed? She found it difficult?'

'She was only young. But Frank said she had to get on with it. Said I couldn't interfere. So I left her to find her own way. And I was out at work during the day.'

'But she didn't cope?'

'No. She found it really hard. I tried to help. I tried to offer her advice but she got so angry with me. She said I didn't know what I was talking about.'

This hadn't been part of the story Imogen had told. She made it sound as if she'd been completely abandoned. 'She wouldn't let you help?'

'No. But sometimes when the baby cried, I would creep up and hold her for a while, so that she didn't wake Imogen. She needed her sleep. Sleep cures everything.'

This had been another of her mother's mantras throughout her childhood, so she could imagine her thinking this at the time. It was more difficult to imagine that she was the baby her mother was talking about. The crying child that had needed to be soothed in the middle of the night. 'But she didn't get better?'

'No. She got worse. And she didn't want me holding the baby any longer. *"Put it down."* She'd yell at me. *"It's not yours. Put it down."*'

The 'it' stung more than the rest of it. When she'd had Harriet, Erin hadn't wanted to let go of her for a moment. In fact, her mother had been the one to tell her that she needed to lay her in her cot. 'You'll spoil her,' she used to say.

But she hadn't cared about that. She'd wanted Harriet to feel spoiled and loved and cared for; couldn't bear to hear that lamb's bleat of a cry without rushing to scoop her up and keep her close.

'So, what did you do?'

'I did what she asked. I left her to look after the baby. But then... then...'

Her mother's fingers trembled as she brought them up to her lips. Whatever she was about to tell Erin was causing her a lot of pain. Erin tried to keep the eagerness from her voice, to stay calm and gentle. 'Then what, Mum?'

'I was bringing some washing up to the room. Nightclothes and towels and muslins for the baby. I had to sneak Imogen's dirty clothes out when she was asleep. She kept telling me that she'd do it herself, I should leave her alone, but she never did. And they needed clean clothes, both of them. I would take the clothes and wash them and then sneak them back into her drawers. I had to do that, didn't I?'

Her mother was looking at her for reassurance, as if she was the child and Erin was her mother. Again, this didn't tally with Imogen's version of events. 'Of course, you did, Mum. You were looking after her.'

Erin couldn't tell from her mother's expression whether that made her feel better or worse. But at least she continued with the story. 'It was so quiet in the room that I thought she must be sleeping. So I pushed the door open a little bit, tried to see whether she was in bed. And that's when I saw it. I saw what she was going to do.'

Erin could barely breathe. She was frozen in place. 'What did you see?'

'She was standing over the cot with a pillow in her hand. And her face, oh her face, I've never seen anything so frightening in my life. It was terrifying.'

Her mother started to tremble and her eyes filled with tears. Looking closely at her now, Erin could see how much her face had changed in recent years; edges softened, lines deepened. She reached for her mother's hand again and this time she gripped it as if for dear life. 'I had to call them, Erin. They had to take her away.'

'Who did you call, Mum?'

'I called the police. They took her away. But she was safe. I had to keep her safe.'

After recounting this awful story, her mother was in such a state that Erin persuaded her to go for a lie down. She tucked her into bed, so exhausted herself that she could've happily lay down beside her and closed her eyes on the world.

Layer upon layer of lies. Her whole childhood covered and hidden and papered over. Now those layers were peeling and tearing apart and what was she going to find underneath? Why was her mother's version of events so different from Imogen's? Who was telling the truth? Her mother had repeated like a mantra, even as she was going upstairs to bed, that all she'd ever wanted was to keep them safe. Imogen and the baby. Was she even making the connection that the baby she wanted to protect was Erin? That she was here, now, in front of her, begging to be told the truth?

Erin sank down onto the bottom step, rested her head against her left hand where it held the last spindle in the banister. How many times had she sat here as a belligerent hormonal teen? Angry and upset at the woman she'd thought was her mother because of the restrictions and rules she'd imposed. Picking at the edge of the carpet that – even then – had been old and worn enough that the edges had started to fray. She felt the same. Coming apart. Unstuck. Untethered. Who did she belong to? Who had wanted her? Who had ever really cared?

At the same time, she was beginning to understand why her mother had been so determined that Erin should stay close to home. Why she hadn't been allowed on school trips, or sleep-overs at people's houses. Having lost one daughter, she must've been desperate not to let the child she was left with out of her sight. That was a feeling that Erin understood too well. Her own heart was sore and exposed with the fear of the exact same thing.

As if on cue, her phone dinged with a message from Harriet.

Dad says can I stay over here tonight.

Erin bent over her knees; hands pressed to her aching chest. Every scrap of her wanted Harriet home. Close beside her, wrapped up tight, never to be let go. *Stay with me. Please stay with me.*

But wasn't that what her mother had tried to do with her? Hold her too tightly. Not tell her the truth. Keep her safe. Was it selfishness? Holding Harriet back? She'd told Simon and Carmel that Harriet wasn't old enough to be away from her, but was she actually thinking about herself? That she was the one who couldn't handle the pain of being separated from her daughter?

She took a deep breath, forced herself to add a smile to her response.

Of course, see you tomorrow :)

She knew what was coming. Tomorrow, she would have to be brave and listen as Harriet tore her apart by telling her she was moving to the other side of the world.

TWENTY-TWO

'She tried to kill you?'

Erin wasn't sure which was bigger and rounder, Jasmine's eyes or her open mouth.

'Shh. You'll give poor Mr Reid a heart attack.' She smiled reassuringly at the elderly gentleman making his way towards the breakfast room. From his check-in details, she knew that he was in his early nineties and, even though he looked possibly a couple of decades younger, she didn't want the story of her upbringing to be the thing that finished him off.

'Sorry.' Jasmine lowered her voice but she looked no less shocked. 'That's what she actually said? That she'd tried to kill you? How? I mean, what...'

Had her face looked the same when Imogen had told her? 'Where, why, when? Yes, I've been through the whole list of questions, too. I don't know. She dropped the bombshell and she left.'

'And have you spoken to your mother, I mean...'

She couldn't blame Jasmine for being confused. 'To Ava? Yes, I've tried, but to be honest, I'm even more confused than I was. Also, as I was on my way back, I got a call from Simon to confirm that he is definitely going to America. Harriet went over to his last night. He's going to ask her to make up her mind to go with them.'

Jasmine reached over and rubbed her arm. 'Oh, Erin. And what has she said? Is she definitely going to go?'

'I haven't seen her yet. She ended up staying over. I guess I'll hear all about it when she comes home later.'

'How are you feeling about her leaving?'

How was she feeling? Like someone had wrapped a rope around her heart and they were just waiting for the signal to pull it from her chest. 'Totally heartbroken, if I'm honest. But I can't let her know that, can I? It wouldn't be fair.'

Jasmine shook her head slowly. 'No, it wouldn't.'

'I have to smile and let her know that whatever she chooses is okay with me.'

Jasmine nodded. 'Yes, you do.' She reached out to squeeze her arm. 'You're a good mum.'

'Everything alright on reception this morning?'

Josh made them jump. Jasmine was the first to react. 'Yep. All fine. No one's checked out yet, so there'll probably be a mad rush in about half an hour.'

He raised an eyebrow. 'A mad rush? When we're only half full?' He frowned at Erin. 'Are you okay, Erin? You look a bit pale.'

Out of sight, below the reception desk, Jasmine pressed her foot onto Erin's toes. She didn't react. 'I'm fine. Thanks. Just didn't sleep well last night.'

He rolled his eyes. 'I know how that feels. My little boy wasn't well last week, so I was up and down with him in the night. Poor little thing was so hot and he couldn't breathe properly, so I ended up propping him up on pillows and sleeping next to him to make sure he was okay. I was wiped the next day.'

Further confirmation that he lived at home with his children. Clearly, they'd got it wrong about the divorce. How could they ask without sounding inappropriate? 'Did you dose him up on Calpol? That was a lifesaver when Harriet was young.'

'His mum had already given him a dose before he went to bed but it didn't seem to help.'

This was an opportunity to confirm for sure that he was married, but neither of them got the chance to ask because they were interrupted by Caitlin, one of the chambermaids, strolling down the stairs with one hand behind her back. 'There you are, Josh. Can I have a quick word? I've got something for you.'

There was something about the expression on her face that made Erin assume it wasn't an overtime docket. And was Josh blushing?

'Sorry, Erin, Jasmine. We'll catch up later.'

He hurried over to where Caitlin was now walking backwards towards the dining room, her hand still behind her back. As he reached her, she turned around and flicked whatever it was into his hands. He scrunched it up and stuffed it into his pocket and she collapsed into giggles before he opened the door to the dining room and bundled her inside.

From the reception desk, all she had seen was a flash of coloured fabric, but it hadn't been so long since she'd lived with a man that she didn't know what it was.

Jasmine turned to her with her eyebrows almost at her hairline. 'Was that what I think it was?'

'It did look like it.'

'Why would Caitlin have Josh's underwear?'

Erin shrugged. 'No idea apart from the obvious. But that can't be right because it seems as if we were wrong on the divorce front. It sounds as if he's living at home with his wife.'

'I know. Did you notice that he was wearing his wedding ring again?'

She hadn't noticed. Why would he have taken it off for work one day and not another? That didn't make sense. 'He doesn't seem the type to be sleeping with someone at work if he's married.'

Jasmine laughed. 'You are naive. There's no type for that kind of thing. There's only opportunity.'

Erin didn't believe that. And Caitlin had a boyfriend. She'd been living with him for years. 'Caitlin wouldn't cheat on Sam.'

'Well.' Jasmine leaned forwards and lowered her voice. 'When we went for that drink the other night, she was complaining that he won't make plans to get married. Apparently, he's a guitarist in a band and he doesn't want the whole marriage and kids thing for a while. Meanwhile, all her friends are getting hitched and she's fed up of being the bridesmaid all the time.'

Erin remembered her as one of the three transfixed around the phone full of wedding plans the other night. 'But she's only about twenty-five. She's got plenty of time for all that.'

Jasmine held out her hands. 'That's what I told her. But she's a woman on a mission. She already has a dress picked out.'

Erin was hardly one to judge, seeing as she'd had Harriet at twenty-three. But that hadn't been planned. And she was acutely aware of all she'd given up by starting a family and putting her career on hold.

Jasmine squinted at her. 'Has Josh talked to you about the hotel and head office again? At the pub, you said something about difficult decisions.'

He hadn't, but she wanted to be honest about what he *had* said. 'No. But he did float the idea of me going for a promotion.'

She wasn't sure how Jasmine was going to react but was relieved when she grinned her approval. 'You should definitely go for it. If Harriet does go to America, you'll have more time on your hands. It'll be the perfect distraction managing this place.'

She hadn't really considered that. It had been so long since she'd only had herself to think about. 'He didn't actually say it was the hotel manager's position. Are you trying to work break-up with me?'

Jasmine laughed. 'No, but they're going to have to appoint someone and I'd much rather it was you. Right, I'm off to make tea before the rush starts.'

Alone at the desk, Erin checked they had all the paperwork ready for the guests checking out today. Josh was right, there were fewer reservations these days, but it would pick up again. It looked as if room fifty-seven had been hitting the minibar hard in the last couple of days, but the rest of the invoices were pretty standard. She loved working in the hotel business, but she could do this job with her eyes closed; there wasn't much she hadn't seen and dealt with in the last fifteen years. Maybe it was time to think about a step up?

Although now was possibly not the right time, either. Not only because of Harriet but because of this business with her mum. Whatever she'd said to Jasmine, she still had questions about what'd happened all those years ago. But she couldn't get anything from her mother and she wasn't sure that she wanted to see Imogen again, or if she would even talk to her about it if she did. At least she'd had a text message from Marcelle with her flight details this morning. Hopefully, she'd fulfil her promise to answer all Erin's questions when she was here in person. Erin's past, her childhood memories, everything had shifted on its axis. Her life had been nothing like she thought it was. Everything was up for scrutiny. Who even was she?

The lift door pinged and rolled open to reveal a large suit-case and a young couple about to check out. She pasted on her professional smile. All she needed to do was get through this shift and go home to talk to Harriet about America. Everything else would have to wait.

TWENTY-THREE

Simon was true to his, or Carmel's, word and he called Erin halfway through the morning after he'd put Harriet on the train home.

'I haven't mentioned this to Harriet until I'd spoken to you, but I'm flying over to California on Wednesday to meet the team I'll be working with and go to see the house. I'll only be there a few days, but Carmel is coming and we thought it might be nice for Harriet to come, too. Help her to make her mind up about staying.'

For a second, Erin perked up at the suggestion that Harriet hadn't given Simon a firm yes, but surely she would very quickly be saying that once she'd seen the amazing life he'd be offering her on a plate. She swallowed, tried to remember what she'd said to Jasmine an hour before. 'That sounds great. Can you get her a flight that quickly?'

'The company will sort it out.' Though he sounded nonchalant, she knew how much he enjoyed saying those words. He'd always been ambitious and, to be fair, he'd always worked hard. The only problem with that was that, with him at work all hours, she couldn't be. Her career hadn't so much been in the back seat as in the boot.

'Okay. That's fine, then. What will she need? Clothes wise I mean. Just casual or...'

She tailed off at his laughter. 'She's not a baby, Erin. I think she can pack her own clothes.'

Tears pricked the corners of her eyes. On top of everything right now, she didn't want to listen to his mockery. 'Okay, then. I'll speak to her tonight about it and if she's happy to go, that's fine with me.'

The rest of her shift went backwards; she was so desperate to see Harriet. About an hour before she left, Josh came to see her on reception. She hadn't even realised that he was in the build-ing. Didn't he need to check on the other hotels sometimes?

He smiled at her, but there was a tiredness in his face. 'How's your shift been? Quiet?'

It had been slow. 'Yes, but at least I've had a chance to tidy up everything back here.'

'Don't you get bored?'

'A little. But it's okay when Jasmine's here.'

He looked at her as if he was reading something in her face, deciding whether to speak. 'Look, this job I mentioned. It's not the hotel manager job here. It's an area management position. I'll get the details and email them to you.'

He hadn't actually detailed what he'd meant, but she'd assumed it would be something here. 'I see.'

'The thing is. There might not be a hotel here much longer. There are cuts that need to be made.'

No hotel here? They were going to close the hotel completely? He couldn't have made her feel more unsettled if he'd pulled at the literal rug beneath her feet. This place was the one area of her life that was working.

He seemed to be studying her for a reaction. What could she say except to repeat herself? 'I see.'

'That's why I'm here. To see if there's anything worth saving.' He paused and looked at her. 'Or anyone.'

She knew that he was talking on a professional level so she could really do without the traitorous blush that was making its way up her neck. 'There are a lot of good people here.'

He nodded. 'I know that. And I'm going to do my best. Can you keep this to yourself for now?'

She wasn't sure if she could keep it from Jasmine, but she didn't want to stir up a lot of bad feeling before any decisions were made. It seemed to be the story of her life right now. 'Okay.'

When she got home, Harriet was waiting for her and she pulled her into a tight hug, breathing her in. She still had the traces of vanilla and coconut from Simon and Carmel's. 'It's good to have you back, love. Did you have a nice time at your dad's?'

Her mother was at The Oasis for the day and she didn't need to pick her up until five. They settled onto the sofa together. Erin tried not to think of all the times they'd cuddled up like this to watch a film from under a blanket.

Harriet was all smiles. 'Yes, it was great. Did he tell you? He got the job.'

'Yes, he called me.'

Now she looked at her hands. 'Which means I need to make my mind up.'

Erin's heart was being pulled in two directions. She wanted to make this as easy as possible for her daughter, but it would tear her apart to let her go. It was a physical effort to keep her voice calm and controlled. 'Well, he also told me that he's going out there for a quick visit. Leaving in a couple of days. He wondered if you wanted to go? You can see what it's like out there. Might help you decide.'

Harriet twisted to look at her, the hope in her voice was like salt on an open wound. 'And you'd be okay with that? Mum, I really do love you, I don't want to do anything that would make you sad.'

Erin had to dig her fingernails into her palms to stop her from clutching Harriet close. She had to do this. There wasn't a choice. 'Of course. I only want you to do what makes you happy. It's a big decision. It's a good idea to go and check it out, isn't it?'

A smile unfurled itself on Harriet's face. 'Really? That would be great. When is he going?'

That was the other problem. 'Tomorrow.'

Harriet's face fell. 'Tomorrow? I have to pack. I don't even know what to take.'

This was the easy part. 'I can help you with that. Why don't we go shopping and get some things for you to take?'

Harriet was practically hopping with excitement. 'When?'

'How about now? Bluewater is open until 9 p.m. I can collect Granny early and give her some dinner and then we'll go.'

'Really? Okay. I'll go and get ready right now.'

Erin knew to her cost how long that could take. She wouldn't need to rush for her shoes and coat. 'Don't take forever.'

'I won't.' Harriet skidded to a halt at the door to the bedroom. 'I'm going to need a suitcase. Where did we put the suitcases?'

Erin closed her eyes and tried to picture where they'd stashed them. 'I think they're up in the loft. You go and get ready. And have a quick flick through your wardrobe, work out what clothes you might be able to take and what you'll need and I'll go up into the loft and find a case for you.'

'Thanks, Mum.' Harriet skipped back towards her and threw her arms around Erin's shoulders. 'I love you so much.'

'I love you too, baby.'

She jumped as Harriet gasped. 'I don't even know what the weather is like in California right now. I have to check.'

And she was gone.

The loft hatch was on the landing. One tug and the end of the wooden ladder landed with a thud onto the carpet. Erin took a deep breath; even the twelve rungs was a height she didn't like. Nothing else for it: Harriet needed that suitcase.

When they'd moved in, Erin had only climbed four or five steps and then kind of launched the suitcases up here so now they weren't quite within reaching distance. This time she needed, not only to climb to the very top, but she'd have to sit on the edge of the hatch, then pull herself across the beam to get to it. It was for Harriet. She could do this.

It was dusty up here, of course it was. She couldn't imagine that her mother had been up here for years. The suitcase had wedged itself between two cardboard boxes. Erin tried to hook her finger into the loop on the end and pull it towards her, but she couldn't get any purchase. She shuffled further along the beam, picking up another layer of dust on her jeans. 'Dammit.'

The suitcase really had wedged itself in there, but she managed to wrench it free. Unfortunately, it pulled one of the boxes – and its contents – with it.

Papers spilled out between the beams of the loft. More photographs, by the looks of things, and lots of envelopes of different sizes. Erin swore under her breath as she tried to scoop them back into the box without leaving the safety of the wide wooden beam she was on. It wasn't until the third handful that she realised that all of the envelopes had been addressed to Imogen.

She frowned as she looked through them. They were different sizes and colours, but the name and the handwriting were the same on every single one. Imogen. Written in Ava's distinctive loops. Tempting though it was, Erin wasn't about to open a letter that hadn't been meant for her eyes: it would be like reading Harriet's journal when she found it tucked beneath her mattress. It wouldn't be right. But she would take the box down with her – somehow – and ask her mother if she remembered writing them.

It was an act of some contortion to inch herself back towards the hatch, pushing the suitcase in front of her and dragging the box of letters behind. When she got to the opening, she gritted her teeth and dropped the suitcase through the hole, where it slid down the ladder and clattered onto the floor.

The noise brought Harriet to the door of her bedroom. 'What are you doing, Mum?'

Her tone was so much like her own when she would tell Harriet off as a child that Erin had to laugh. 'Sorry. I thought it would kind of, drop. Although, while you're here, can you give me a hand?'

The box was too heavy to risk pulling it down the ladder – she didn't want it pushing her down with the same thud as the suitcase – so Erin reached inside it for handfuls of letters and photographs and passed them down into Harriet's waiting arms.

'Wow. Where have all these come from? Have you seen these photographs before?'

'Not that I know of.' Erin sneezed. 'Judging by the amount of dust, no one has seen them for a while.'

After four handfuls, the box was light enough for her to grab the top of it with her right hand while holding onto the ladder for dear life with her left. Keeping her face turned away from the dust, she pulled it out of the loft and lowered it towards Harriet.

By the time she'd inched back down the ladder, Harriet had already pulled out a fistful of photographs and was leafing through them. 'These are amazing. I think this must be Imogen. And she's holding you. It's not a good one, though. I'm surprised they printed it out.'

Erin took the photograph and looked at it. A young woman sat in a chair with a tiny baby in a bundle in her arms. She must have been in the process of leaning down when the photograph was taken, because the top of her head was blurred. 'We didn't get to see the photos before we printed them out back then.' She realised how old she sounded. 'You took the roll of film to the chemist and hoped for the best.'

Harriet screwed up her face in disbelief. 'So you had no idea how they would turn out when you took them?'

'Nope.' She nudged Harriet. 'A bit like daughters.'

'Ha ha. Very funny, Mum. Look here's another one.'

She passed a photo with the same person in the same pose, but this time it was clearer. It was definitely Imogen. But the Imogen in this photo didn't smile like in the one she'd given Erin in the pub. Whether or not she'd known her photo was being taken wasn't clear, but the corners of her mouth were turned down, her eyes dark pools and her posture was so awkward that it was hard to believe that the child she was holding was her own.

It was none of those things that struck Erin, though. Looking at this photograph with Harriet sitting beside her, it was difficult not to acknowledge how young Imogen was. It was like imagining Harriet with a baby. Unthinkable. What was it Imogen had said? The woman that had mumbled 'children having children' at her? Looking at this picture, the sentiment – if not the rudeness with which she'd expressed her opinion aloud – was understandable.

'She was really beautiful, Mum.'

Yes, Erin supposed she was.

'Have you seen all of these letters? The ones addressed to Imogen? What do you suppose they are?'

'I don't know, love. But maybe your granny will be able to tell us.'

TWENTY-FOUR

The shopping trip had been expensive. Mainly because Erin hadn't wanted to say no to a single thing that Harriet wanted. That wasn't completely true. She *had* drawn the line at a bikini that looked smaller than the cloth she used to clean her sunglasses.

Back home, once she'd packed her case, and chosen the outfit she wanted to travel in and selected the books she was going to take for the flight and made sure she'd downloaded several favourite *Modern Family* episodes from Disney+, she was good to go. Almost. 'Snacks! I need to get some snacks for the plane.'

'Do you want me to take you to the shop?' She was more than capable of walking there herself, but Erin didn't want to waste a minute apart. 'I was going to call Josh to see if he could sort out someone to take my shift until I get back from the airport.'

Harriet frowned. 'You don't need to come to the airport, Mum. Dad said he'd pick me up in the morning. The flight isn't until four o'clock.'

That was the first time she'd mentioned that. 'Don't you want me to come and see you off?'

Harriet laughed, but it was gentle rather than mocking. 'I'm only going for five days, Mum. I'll be back before you even get a chance to miss me.'

Erin felt like she was missing her already and she hadn't even left. 'I know. But I thought you might like me waving you off.'

'I'll be fine. Honestly. And I'll bring you back some Hershey's Kisses.'

Simon did actually call Erin to arrange the pick-up and he agreed with Harriet. 'This is only a quick trip, Erin. You don't need to make a big deal out of it. If she decides to come for good, you can come and do the whole emotional send-off thing then.'

She didn't think he meant to be cruel, but that's how it felt. 'Come for good' looped around her brain long after he'd collected Harriet and she'd held her close for a squeeze before watching her run down the path to the car, trailing a bouncing suitcase behind her.

Harriet had been away from home before, of course she had. She'd been away on holiday with the school and with Simon. But this felt different. This was a dress rehearsal for a bigger leaving and Erin wasn't ready for that at all.

She was still only one misjudged comment away from tears when she arrived at work and, unfortunately, that comment came from Josh.

'Hi, Erin. Sorry to jump on you as soon as you get in. But there's a problem with the rota this week. We don't have enough kitchen staff and those that are in are plotting my death as we speak. Do you know how it happened?'

She never made a mistake with rotas. She triple checked everything usually. But her mind had been on other things this week. Had she made a mistake? 'Are you sure it's the rota? Not just that someone hasn't turned up?'

'No. I checked. It's okay because I've managed to call someone in, but I'll have to pay them double rate which is obviously not great for the staffing budget. You need to make sure that we're covered.'

Tears stung the back of Erin's eyes. She prided herself on her efficiency. And now, only a couple of weeks into the job, Josh would think she was incompetent. The weight of everything was crushing her: something had to give. 'I'm very sorry, I... I...'

The last thing she wanted to do was cry at work, but all the sadness she'd pushed down this morning when she'd said goodbye to Harriet came tumbling out. Josh's face fell. 'Hey. It's okay, You don't need to... let's go into the office.'

He sat her on the easy chair in the corner with a box of tissues while he tracked someone down to cover the reception. When he returned, he closed the office door quietly behind him. 'I'm sorry if I upset you.'

She waved away his apology, feeling like an absolute fool. 'No. You didn't. It's me. I have a lot going on. My mother is unwell and my daughter left for America this morning.'

Those two phrases didn't even touch what was going on right now, but Josh looked sympathetic. 'I'm sorry, that must be hard. Are you okay to be in work? I could call someone in?'

She was going to make a joke about the staffing budget, but she wasn't really in a comical mood. 'No, it's fine. I'm better off working. I'll miss her more if I'm rattling around at home.'

He nodded his understanding. 'It's tough being a parent, isn't it? They drive you crazy when they're there, but it kills you to be away from them.'

That was exactly it. 'It must be difficult for you working the hours you do.'

He nodded again. 'Yes. When they were small, they'd often be in bed before I got home. Still asleep when I had to leave.

I've worked in a few different places and the commute is a killer. My car is like my second home.'

This was exactly why she hadn't wanted to climb the ladder of hotel management. She was glad she'd been there for Harriet's childhood, glad that she'd kept her job manageable around her day. But it made it feel even more unfair that Simon, who had worked every hour he could in the pursuit of his career goals, had now seemed to 'win' Harriet at the end of it all. While she was left with absolutely nothing. 'It's hard being the mum, too.'

He frowned and ran his hand through his hair. 'Yeah. She's pretty much had to do everything for them. Sometimes, when they're ill or upset and all they want is their mum, it really hurts. But I can only blame myself, really. I should have been around more.'

Erin couldn't even imagine having a conversation like this with Simon. She and Jasmine must have been mistaken about the chambermaid. Josh was a good guy. 'Well, I'd better get out there and get started on the day. Jasmine's due in shortly and there'll be hell to pay if I haven't cleared the in tray.'

She and Josh stood at the same time and, in that small office space, they were close enough that she could smell the citrus of his aftershave. For all of Jasmine's teasing, she wasn't wrong that Josh was an attractive man. But, if he was to be believed, he was also a family man. There was nothing here to be concerned about. And she was too old for a crush on someone unavailable.

Jasmine was early for her shift, so Erin was approaching the last of the invoices when she plonked her large bag on the counter. 'I have just had the worst breakfast date in the entire world.'

Breakfast date? Was that a thing? 'Why did you meet him for breakfast?'

Jasmine rolled her eyes. 'Well, I thought I was meeting him

for breakfast because it was a fun and quirky idea and because he suggested that new cafe that's opened on the high street. But it turns out that it was merely an opportunity for him to turn up in his running gear, bore me about his marathon training and then take call after call on his mobile from the office because clearly the universe can't run without him at the helm.'

'I'm sorry.'

'Don't be. I ordered fifteen quid's worth of eggs Benedict and he offered to pay the bill on his company card so I let him. I'm normally very *split the bill*, as you know, but I figured he owed me for wasting my time. Tea?'

'Yes please. Harriet left first thing this morning.'

Jasmine mouth dropped open. 'Oh, I'm sorry, I had no idea she was going so soon. How are you?'

That was the million-dollar question. 'I'm okay. I had a bit of a meltdown when I got here. But Josh was very kind.'

Jasmine's eyebrows shot up to her fringe. 'Really?'

'Not like that. I think we've misjudged him. I don't think he's flirting with the chambermaids.'

'What about the boxer shorts?'

She'd thought about this, too. 'We don't know they were his. And, to be honest, we don't even know for sure that's what they were.'

Jasmine didn't look convinced. 'If you say so. I'm reserving judgement. Speaking of reserving judgement, have you heard from Imogen?'

'No. But I did find some letters in the loft with her name on.' Erin had meant to ask her mother about them but, with everything going on with Harriet since, there hadn't been an opportune moment.

'Really? What were they?'

'I don't know. They were from my mum to her. I'm guessing they were letters she wanted to send and couldn't. Maybe about me?'

'You haven't opened any?'

She'd be lying if she said she hadn't been tempted. But it felt immoral. 'I was wondering whether I should send them to her. If my mum says it's okay.'

'You could deliver them to her yourself?'

And put herself out there to be rejected again? 'I don't know. If she wanted to see me, she'd get in contact, wouldn't she?'

'What do you want? Don't you want answers?'

Initially, shock had made her recoil from wanting to know any more about the whole situation. But now curiosity was nibbling at her again. 'Maybe.'

'Why don't you call her about the letters and see what she says?'

There couldn't be any harm in that, could there? Ask if she wanted Erin to send them on? She would need to talk to her mother about them first, because they might have been some kind of therapy for her rather than something she ever intended to send. Who knew if she'd even remember writing them? 'Okay. I'll talk to Mum tonight and then I'll message her.'

'Good. Now I'm going to make us a drink and you can tell me more about Josh's sympathy.'

She had to smile. Jasmine was incorrigible, but she lifted the spirits like a sunny day. Should she tell her about the conversation with Josh about the hotel? Or would that just stir up trouble before anything was decided? Her brain was so addled after this morning's goodbye that she didn't know what was best. She glanced at her mobile. Harriet would still be in the air right now, making her way through the party bag of sherbet lemons and *Modern Family* episodes. When the phone rang in her hand, she jumped. Imogen's name flashed onto the screen.

They weren't supposed to take personal calls when they were on the reception desk and Erin wasn't sure she was ready to hear whatever Imogen had to say. She rejected the call but prayed that Imogen would leave a voicemail. What did she want?

When Jasmine appeared with the mugs of tea. She waved the phone at her. 'Are you okay for two minutes if I go and listen to this voicemail? It's from Imogen.'

Jasmine's eyes widened. 'Of course.'

The message was short and Imogen sounded breathless. 'Hi, Erin. It's me. Imogen. I'm sorry that I ran away the other day. It's just... it's hard for me. But I do think you're right. You deserve an explanation. If you'd like to, maybe you could come to my flat? I'd rather we talk somewhere privately. It might take a while, but I want to tell you it all. Let me know what you think. I'm sorry.'

TWENTY-FIVE

Imogen's flat was on the top floor of a small block not far from the pub she worked in. When she opened the door, it was obvious how nervous she was. 'Thank you for coming.'

'That's okay. I'm off until this evening, so it was no trouble.'

She led Erin through a door to the right into a sitting room which was clean but bare. Aside from a sofa and a TV, there was a long sideboard and a tiny square table with two chairs. Erin hovered at one end of the sofa; it was a three-seater, but even so, they would be pretty close together if they sat at either end.

'Can I get you anything to drink? Tea?'

She sounded so much like her mother that Erin almost smiled. 'That would be lovely, thank you. Milk no sugar.'

While she was gone, Erin scanned the room for evidence of Imogen's interests, her personality. There were a few framed pictures propped against the wall which looked as if they'd been painted by the same artist. Were they hers? On the sideboard, there was one frame. It contained the photo of Imogen holding Erin that Imogen had copied to give to her at the pub. She must have carefully removed it to copy, then placed it back in its frame. Did she look at it every day of her life? Erin thought of the letters from the loft. She'd decided not to bring them because she still hadn't asked her mother about them.

Imogen appeared with two mugs of tea which she slid onto the coffee table. 'Sit yourself down, I'll get the biscuits.'

She was clearly trying hard to be welcoming. The biscuits were laid out on a blue china plate. Erin pushed down her discomfort and sat at the other end of the sofa, keeping herself as close to the arm as she could.

Imogen took the other end of the sofa and angled herself towards Erin. 'Before you ask me anything, I need to tell you what happened. Well, as best as I can remember it. It's all pretty hazy.'

Erin wanted to be encouraging. 'It was over thirty years ago.'

Imogen twisted at a ring on her right hand. 'It's not my memory. I mean, it is, but it's not that I've forgotten over the years. I didn't ever really know. I mean...' She sighed deeply as if to reset herself. 'I had post-partum psychosis.'

Erin had heard of this but didn't know much about it. 'Is that an extreme form of postnatal depression?'

'To begin with it was similar to that. I had no energy and I couldn't eat, but then I couldn't sleep at night either. I felt so anxious all the time. You'd cry and I couldn't remember if I'd fed you. I was terrified that I'd starved you. Or that I'd fed you too much and made you sick. I was just so confused all the time.'

She'd told her this when they met at the pub. 'And then?'

Imogen swallowed. 'Then I started to see things. And hear things. I didn't know what was real and what wasn't.'

'What kinds of things?'

'I thought that my mum and dad were talking about me outside my bedroom door. I mean, sometimes they probably were. Dad would tell Mum I had to get up and she would say something like, 'What do you want me to do? Pull her out of bed?' and then he would mumble something else and leave. But then I started to think that they were plotting something. That they were going to have to take the baby. That there was something wrong with the baby. That I had done something to the baby.'

She faltered at the end of each sentence. She must've been thinking, as Erin was, that she was the baby in this story. 'Did you talk to them about it?'

She shook her head. 'No. I became more and more paranoid that they were going to do something. I thought, I began to think, that they were going to try and kill me. I wouldn't eat the food that Mum brought to the room because I thought that she'd poisoned it. The only time I would eat was in the middle of the night when they were asleep. I would open a fresh packet or can of something from their cupboard because I knew that they wouldn't have been able to tamper with it.'

Imogen was so matter of fact in the way she described this memory that it was hard to believe that she was speaking about herself, that this had been her reality. 'That must have been awful for you. I'm so sorry.'

Imogen waved her hand. 'Please don't feel sorry for me. Let me tell you everything first.'

This time Erin kept quiet and nodded.

'The voices were still there, but they started to change. They told me it wasn't me that needed to die. That everything had been fine until...'

Erin's cheeks burned. 'Until I was born?'

Imogen nodded. 'You have to understand. I was really, really ill, and I didn't know it.'

'I know. Keep going.'

'They, the voices, said that I had to... to kill you. That that would be the only way for everything to be back to normal. And then the hallucinations started. Every time that I looked into your face you were… it's difficult to explain… there was so much hate in your eyes.'

Hate? That was such a strong word to use for a baby. When Harriet had been small, all that Erin had seen in her eyes was the love she felt reflected back at her. 'I don't understand.'

'There's nothing to understand. It was the illness. I know that now. But at the time, it was so real. So very real. And I couldn't make them stop. Couldn't stop them telling me that I had to do it and then…'

'You were standing over me with a pillow in your hands?'

Imogen had been staring at her hands and her head snapped up. 'Did my mother tell you that?'

'That's all she told me. I didn't know what had led up to it.'

'Yes. That's what happened. And I thank God daily that she came in when she did. I can't even think about whether I would've actually done it.'

How many stories had Erin seen in the news about mothers who had killed their child, killed themselves? There had been one in particular that had always stayed with her. Harriet had been around two at the time and there'd been a story in the local news about a woman jumping off a bridge into the river holding her newborn baby. She'd held Harriet extra close that night. She had no idea how a mother could get to that point without someone realising what was happening. But now? 'What did she do? Mum? When she came in.'

'It all happened so fast. She took you away and then there were people – doctors? Police officers? I'm really not sure. They took me to a secure unit. Later, I found out that they usually take mothers and babies in together, but there were no places at the mother and baby unit. So they took me in and told my mother that they would move me and the baby to a unit as soon as they could.'

Erin had noticed that Imogen always referred to Ava as 'my

mother' rather than 'Mum'. It seemed to distance her somehow. Maybe that was the point.

'What was it like? The hospital?'

Imogen shrugged. 'I had a small room. There wasn't anything in it. To begin with I slept or paced. Until they got the drugs right, I think. And then I just felt empty. Alone. But it wasn't a bad feeling. It was almost as if I was on the outside looking in on myself.'

'What were the other patients like?'

'Varied. Some were quiet and would sit in corners or close to walls. Others were scary and tough. Some of them had been there before.'

'Really?'

'Yes. That was scary. Apparently, if you've suffered with psychosis with your first pregnancy, it increases your risk of having it with a subsequent pregnancy.' She shuddered. 'It's why I knew that I would never have another child.'

'How long were you there for?'

'A few weeks. I thought it was going to be forever. I couldn't understand why they would ever let me out. Not after what I'd tried to do. When I told them that – told my therapist that – she said that it was a sign that I was getting better.'

Erin was trying to understand what it had been like, she really was. 'Did you get to see me at all? Did they move you to a mother and baby unit?'

'I didn't want to go. I didn't want you in there with me. I wanted to know that you were safe. My mother called every day. She wanted to tell me how you were doing, but I couldn't feel anything. Not the things a mother should be feeling. When I came home from the hospital, I was numb. Looking back, it was the medication I was on, but I had no feelings. No feelings for you at all.'

Even bearing in mind that she hadn't known of Imogen's

existence until a few weeks ago, this was difficult to hear. 'What about when you came off the medication?'

'By then, you'd changed so much. You'd got so much bigger and you looked healthy. And you didn't cry all the time. I watched my mother with you and she was so confident. She could hold you in one arm as she tidied the house or wrote a shopping list. She tried to give you to me, tried to make me hold you, but every time I took you, you would cry.'

'I must have been confused. Babies tend to prefer one person, don't they?' Again, she thought of the first few months with Harriet. She hadn't wanted anyone apart from Erin. Even Simon could only hold her a short while before she was crying to be back in Erin's arms. Secretly, she'd enjoyed it.

'Yes. But that person is supposed to be their mother. You were supposed to prefer me. But I ruined it. I destroyed that bond.'

This sounded like guilt talking. 'I would have been too young to be affected by any of that.'

'That's what my mother said. But how she acted was different. She wouldn't leave me alone with you, she would hover every time I said I was going to check on you in your cot. I was being watched all the time. And then I was anxious. Was she really watching me or was it happening again? And then I got the letter from Jimmy. Your father.'

There were times in these conversations with Imogen when Erin felt as if she was having an out-of-body experience. That they were talking about someone else completely. 'My father?'

'Yes. I told you that he was working on a rig off the coast of Scotland. That he was getting some money together. I thought he was coming back. But it turned out that he'd met someone. I have no idea how. Do they get on-shore leave like sailors? Who knows. But he'd met someone, and he wasn't coming back.'

Erin was appalled. 'Just like that? Cutting you – us – out of his life?'

'He offered money. Said he would help out. But I didn't even bother to reply. Never have.'

Erin couldn't help but think of Simon. Who – despite her anger in the way he'd gone about it – wanted nothing more than to have his daughter with him. 'I can understand how you felt.'

'It was the final straw. I knew then that you were better off without me. That's why I left. One day, when my mother had taken you to the doctor for your inoculations, I packed up a bag and left. But it wasn't abandonment, Erin. It was sacrifice. And she kept you safe, didn't she?'

The tea on the table had gone cold while Imogen was speaking; Erin felt much the same. She should have felt sympathy for this woman. She did feel sorry for all that she'd been through. But that wasn't the end of the story, was it?

Imogen made a big fuss of clearing away the tea cups and making fresh drinks. Did she need a break from telling her story? How many times had she told this before? Clearly she lived alone. Did she have friends she could speak to about this or had she carried it alone all these years?

Unable to sit still with her thoughts, Erin picked up the plate of biscuits that neither of them were likely to eat and carried them out to the kitchen. It was a tiny space with the sink on the right and the cooker straight ahead. The kettle looked ancient and it rumbled and clacked in the corner of the work-top. Despite everything she'd heard in the last half an hour, there was still something bugging her and she couldn't leave until she'd asked it. 'I think I can understand why you left. You were ill and you probably weren't looking at things rationally. But why did you never come back? Why didn't you try again?'

Imogen jumped at the sound of her voice, but she didn't turn around. 'I did, Erin. I did try again.'

TWENTY-SIX

Imogen had spent at least two weeks' wages in the toy shop on the high street. What do two-year-olds play with? *You should know*, her guilt reminded her, *you're her mother*.

At the clinic, they'd told her that most women make a full recovery after post-partum psychosis. It was the 'most' that had played on her mind for the last few months. Was she well? Would she be able to be a mother to the little girl she barely knew?

Maybe she should have called her mother in advance and warned her that she was coming. But she was scared that, if she'd done that, she might have lost her nerve and put it off even longer. She should have come six months ago, five months ago, four. Each time she'd planned to come, though, the old anxiety had made a reappearance. *Most people recover fully*.

Now, standing at the familiar doorstep, she stood with her hand raised, about to knock. Willing herself to knock. Just do it.

The choice was made for her when the door opened and she was nearly knocked out of the way by her father leaving the house. He started as if he'd seen a ghost. 'What are you doing here?'

It wasn't the reaction she'd expected. 'I've come to visit. To see you and Mum. And the baby.'

He looked at her as if she was a dirty stain on the step. 'Your mother is inside. I'm on my way out.'

They'd never been close, but she had expected him to ask where she'd been at the very least. Was she well? Did she need anything? Her throat tightened and she almost turned around and walked away, but then she heard her mother singing.

In the hall, the words of the song were more distinct. A lullaby she remembered from her own childhood. Then she heard the lisp of a young child. 'More. More thing.' And her legs nearly buckled beneath her.

With the tips of her fingers, she leaned against the wall until she could trust herself to creep up the corridor to the open door to the sitting room. When she looked inside, her mother was knelt on the floor, her back towards the door, changing Erin's nappy.

'You're a big girl now, Erin. You can start to use the potty soon.'

'No potty.' Her voice was so sweet yet so stubborn; it pulled at Imogen's heart to hear it.

Her mother laughed. 'You'll have to learn to use the potty soon. You'll be a big girl.'

Imogen watched from the doorway as Erin pushed herself up from the floor. She looked as if she was about to run, but then she spied Imogen and stopped dead in her tracks and reached out to Ava. 'Mama.'

It was like someone had stuck a knife into Imogen and she couldn't stop the sharp gasp of breath which sent her mother spinning round to look at her. 'Imogen?'

She stepped just inside the room, saw Erin push herself so tightly into her mother's side that she was only looking at her out of one eye. 'Hi, Mum.'

Her mother stood and scooped Erin up into her arms in one swift movement. 'I didn't know you were coming.'

'Nor did I until this morning. I've been trying to pluck up the courage for weeks.'

Initial shock over, her mother stepped towards her, then paused, as if Imogen were a wild animal and she didn't want to scare her away. 'How are you? Where are you living?'

'I'm okay. I live in Ipswich. A flat. It's okay.'

'How are you doing for money?'

'I've got a job. Two actually. They pay the bills.'

She could imagine her mother's thoughts about the bars she was working in. It was hardly the kind of career she had wanted for her. Although, maybe that was the last thing on her mind right now. 'Are you staying?'

'I don't know. I just wanted to come. I wanted to see her. I wanted to see Erin.'

It was as if Ava had only then remembered the child in her arms, who was trying to burrow into her neck while eyeing this stranger in front of them. Ava tried to move her body so that Imogen could see Erin better. 'Say hello, Erin. This is Imogen.'

A jealousy she hadn't expected to feel so strongly gripped at Imogen. 'I'm your mummy. I've come to see you.'

She reached out a hand towards her small, beautiful daughter but she snapped her face away from her. 'No!'

Her mother's face was almost apologetic. 'It's time for her nap. She's not normally this grumpy. She's tired. Let me put her down and then we can talk.'

Imogen pushed her fingernails into the palms of her hands as her mother took a frowning Erin into the hall. She heard her on the stairs 'no nap' and her mother soothing her with soft words of encouragement.

What had she expected? That she would come home and they would all be overjoyed to see her? That Erin would run towards her with arms outstretched? She was a fool to think that this would be easy, but now she was here, she had to try. She had to try and be the mother she should have been for the last two years.

For the fifteen minutes it took her mother to settle Erin into her cot, sing her another lullaby and return downstairs, Imogen paced the floor like a caged animal, unable to settle for long enough to sit down on the familiar sofa.

'So how have you been?'

She turned to see her mother in the doorway, twisting a muslin in her hands. Why did she look so nervous? 'I'm okay. I've been well. Mostly.'

'Mostly?'

It was difficult to explain the ups and downs of the last eighteen months. The medication worked, but she didn't feel like herself. Then she'd try to come off it and be fine for a while and then... then she wasn't. 'I'm learning how to live with it.'

Her mother nodded. 'Your doctor said that most people make a full recovery. As long as they don't—'

'Have another child?' Her laugh sounded bitter even to her. 'No chance of that, Mum. Don't worry.'

Her mother took a step closer, came into the room. 'But I do worry about you, Imogen. Where are you living?'

It was suffocating. And this wasn't what she wanted to talk about it. 'Erin looks well.'

Something lifted in her mother's face. 'She's very well. She's bright and healthy and such a good baby.'

Why did this feel like criticism? The baby she'd left had been fractious and difficult. What magic had her mother been able to weave? 'Why did she call you Mama?'

At least she had the decency to blush. 'She didn't. It's the way she says it. It's Nana, but she finds it difficult to say her Ns.'

Was she telling the truth? Did it even matter? She had, after all, been looking after Imogen's child. She'd sworn to herself that she wouldn't be like this. Wouldn't act like a spoilt child.

She needed to focus on what she'd come for. 'I'd like to take her back.'

Her mother reached out for the back of the sofa as if she needed to steady herself. 'Back where?'

'With me. I have a job and a place to stay.'

Her face paled. 'But how will you work if you have a baby to look after? It's not easy to do both on your own. Why don't you come back here? This is your home, Imogen.'

She thought of her father as he'd left. '*What are you doing here?*' This felt nothing like home any longer. 'I can't live in this house.'

Her mother stepped around the arm of the sofa, sat down, smoothed her skirt. 'Sit down, Imogen. Please. We need to talk about this properly. Like adults.'

There was something in her tone that made Imogen so angry. Like adults. She was an adult. She was eighteen. 'Erin is my baby.'

'I know that. Of course I do. But you need to think about what's best for you both. How are you going to manage a job and a baby and your own health? If you come and live here, I can help you. She has a nursery that she goes to and you can work and be her mother. I mean, what job do you have?'

She knew before she said it what her mother's reaction would be. 'I work in a bar.'

To be fair, the grimace may have been imperceptible to someone who didn't know her mother as well as she did. 'There you are, then. You can do that anywhere. Why don't you get a bar job here?'

'Would Dad like that? Me coming back?'

There was a deep sigh at that. Coupled with her mother's expression, it told Imogen everything she needed to know. 'Your father is very busy at work.'

In many ways, it would be a relief to try it that way. Live here, share the care of Erin with her mother. But she could already feel a prickle of anxiety at the pit of her stomach at just being back here. 'I don't think I can. I need to do this myself.'

Her mother's face hardened. 'I can't let you walk out of here with her, Imogen.'

The shock knocked the breath from her. 'She's my baby. You can't just keep her.'

Now her mother folded her arms in the way she had throughout Imogen's teens. It always meant no. 'I can if it's what's best for her. Best for you.'

'How can it be best for me if you keep my child away from me?' She'd been determined not to raise her voice, but it was impossible not to when faced with her mother's obstinate cruelty.

'Erin is still a baby. She needs consistency, she needs—'

'Her mother! That's what she needs, And that's me. It's not you.'

She practically shrieked the last part and the shrill notes carried upstairs where they were met with their counterpart. She'd woken the baby.

This time she wasn't about to let her mother take control. Before she'd moved, she was around her and past her and on her way to the sound of her daughter crying. It pulled at her insides in a way she hadn't felt in months. 'I'm coming, Erin. I'm coming.'

She had no idea if her mother was following her, she just wanted to make it to the small bedroom at the back of the house. The door was ajar and, when she pushed it open, Erin was standing up in her cot, her face red and wet with angry tears.

Imogen's heart hurt to look at her. 'Hey, baby. What's up? Don't cry. It's okay.'

She tried to keep her voice sweet and soothing, but – if anything – Erin's cries grew louder and her face took on the fear of a trapped animal. 'No. Want Mama. Want Mama.'

Now Imogen started to cry, she tried to reach for her in her cot. 'I am your Mama. I'm here, baby, I'm here.'

But Erin held out her arms to push her away. 'No.' She screamed. 'No. Go.'

Another pair of arms reached beyond Imogen's and Erin practically leaped into them. Imogen reached out and squeezed the bar of the cot before turning to face her mother. 'I was getting her.'

In her mother's arms, Erin's sobs receded into hiccups as her mother rocked her gently and wiped her face with a cloth. 'You need to give her some time, Imogen. You can't expect her to understand straight away.'

So Imogen had stayed. She promised to give it a couple of weeks, to let Erin get used to her again. It was so hard. All she wanted was for her daughter to forgive her, to let her love her again. But Erin would look at her as if she knew the guilt that ran through her veins, knew that she had abandoned her, left her. 'I couldn't do it.' She would whisper to her as she watched her sleep, chubby faced and pink in the cot her mother had painted. 'I couldn't look after you, I was ill.'

But how could she expect a baby to understand? Especially when her mother was there all the time. Watching. Hovering. Judging. 'She doesn't like to be held like that' or 'she prefers to do that herself' or 'let me show you'.

The worst times were when she'd scrutinise Imogen herself. 'You look tired, let me do it' or 'why don't you have a rest?'

Sometimes Imogen would lose her temper and then she would retreat to her bedroom like a scolded child. She stayed there when her father came home from work, unable to stomach the heavy weight of his disgust in her, the way he spoke only to her mother as if she, and Erin, were invisible.

It was at the beginning of the third week that the old feelings came creeping back.

It had been a particularly trying day. Erin was a fussy eater and Imogen had tried to cook a meal that she would like, spending hours cutting the vegetables into interesting shapes and blending a tomato sauce full of healthy ingredients. Erin had refused every spoonful, wouldn't even try a tiny taste. 'No.'

It was her favourite word whenever Imogen was around. 'Come on, baby. Just try it. Look it's nice.' She turned the spoon and tasted a little of the sauce; it really was delicious. She just needed to get her to try it.

Erin's hands shot out in front of her, she caught the end of the spoon and sent it straight to the back of Imogen's throat which made her gag. Her reaction was instinctive. 'Erin. That hurts!'

Within seconds of Erin's screams her mother swooped in and took her up from the high chair. 'You can't shout at her, Imogen.'

Suddenly, it was all too much. She threw down the spoon and took the stairs to her room, two at a time. Closing the door behind her, she slid down it onto the scratchy carpet and let her face fall into her empty palms, tears slipping between her fingers. She felt it then. The stranger in the room, the darkness that had been her companion all those months ago. It was being here, in this room, that was the problem. She needed to get out of here. She needed to take Erin and leave. It was clear that she could never do it here. They wouldn't let her.

She couldn't tell her mother what she'd planned. Clearly she would try and stop her, make her stay. But if she could take Erin away, it would all be okay.

Without stopping to plan where or how she was going to take Erin, she started to throw things into her bag. In Erin's room, she found some sleepsuits and other clothes, just enough to get her through the next few days before she could buy her some more things. Things that Imogen had chosen for her.

Her mood lifted by the second as she imagined the two of them, on their own. She'd go back to the flat with her. Find a nursery. Get a new job. It would all be fine. It would all be fine. It would all be fine.

It was all she could do to sit quietly at dinner with her mother that evening, knowing that – as soon as she was asleep that night – Imogen would be creeping into Erin's room and softly, gently, quietly slipping her out of bed and then out, out, out of the house and free. They would be free!

'Are you okay?' Her mother's frown looked her up and down. 'You look hot. Feverish. Are you coming down with something?'

She wasn't about to tell her that it was excitement about her plans. Instead, she focused on the peas on her plate. One, two, three of them on the tines of her fork. 'I'm fine.'

Her father pushed his plate away. 'I'm off to the pub, Ava.'

A thought so strong it almost made her gasp. *I hope you die.*

Had she said it aloud? She focused on the plate again, ignored the scrape of his chair, the slam of the front door.

Her mother cleared the table and she paused before taking Imogen's plate. 'Are you sure you're okay? You're not... I mean you don't feel...?'

She didn't need to finish those sentences; they both knew what they meant. *Most people make a full recovery.* That's what her doctor had said. *Most people. Most.*

She pushed her chair backwards so quickly that it clattered to the floor. She bent down to right it, trying to avoid her mother's eyes. *Don't let her see. She will know. She will know.*

She made it up to her bedroom. She needed to wait. To wait. *They know. They know what you're going to do. Go now. Go now.*

Should she do it? Erin was asleep. Her mother was in the

kitchen with the radio on. Maybe she could make it to the door. No. No. Later. Later.

They know. They're watching. They know.

By the time she heard her father return from the pub and the two of them climb the stairs, clean their teeth, get in bed, she was trembling with anticipation, pacing the floor like a caged dog. It was this place. If they could get out of here, everything would be okay.

She waited twenty minutes, thirty, then picked up her bag and made for Erin's bedroom.

She was deeply asleep. All Imogen needed to do was pick her up without waking her. She untucked the flannel sheet from under the cot mattress and wrapped it around her daughter gently. *Don't wake her up. Don't wake her up.*

Once she was wrapped in the sheet, Imogen slid her hands underneath her warm body and tried to roll her towards her. Gently, slowly, carefully.

Erin's eyes snapped open and the shock of their darkness hit Imogen like a punch to the gut. Her face changed before her eyes, twisted in disgust. *She hates you. They all hate you.*

'No.' Her voice came out in a sob. 'No. I'm your mummy.'

When the scream came, it sliced through the darkness like a knife. Was it from Erin or from her? The door to the bedroom crashed open and her mother was there. 'What are you doing?! What's going on?'

She ran then, from the room, from the house, from the street. She had to get away. She had to leave. She couldn't do it. She couldn't. She had to get away. Why did she even think she could do this? She was a terrible mother. A terrible person. Terrible. Terrible. Terrible.

TWENTY-SEVEN

'I'm so sorry.'

What else could Erin say? Imogen's face begged her to understand and she did, of course she did, but it wasn't the end of the story.

'So it had come back? The... the psychosis?'

'I lost a few weeks after that. I'm not really sure where I went or what I did. I know that I slept rough that night. Maybe the next one. There was a woman, she found me. Took me to a hospital. It wasn't until much later that I realised that I hadn't been taking my medication. They sorted me out again. I moved again. Found a job.'

'Did you try again? With me, I mean.'

Imogen shredded the tissue in her hands. 'You have to understand how terrified I was. About it coming back. I was terrified about what might have happened if my mother hadn't interrupted me that night. Again.'

'I understand. I do.' But she also knew that, if it had been Harriet, she would have found a way. With Harriet out of the country, she felt the physical pangs of her absence. Had Imogen not felt the same about her?

Imogen picked up a cushion from the couch and held it in front of her, stroking it like a child with a comfort blanket. 'About six months after I left, I started waiting outside the house in the hope of catching sight of you. You were in your pushchair and I'd watch you chattering away, pointing at everything around you, kicking your legs and waving. You were so tiny but full of life. Healthy and happy. I knew I'd done the right thing.'

Erin wasn't ready to agree with that. 'Is that what you really believed?'

Twisting the corner of the cushion, Imogen took a while to reply. 'I did. But that doesn't mean it was easy. I missed you all the time, Erin. Every day. It was there all the time, something in the background that I could never totally ignore. Like the kind of dull ache you get after a bad injury. After a visit, though, after I'd seen you, the pain was intense again, like a wound that had been exposed to the air, and I could barely function for thinking about you.'

Had she really done this? Had she really managed to spy on them without being seen? 'Did Mum know you were there? Did she know that you were watching us?'

She wasn't even sure if she wanted the answer to be yes or no. Because, if her mother had known that Imogen wanted to see her, wouldn't it make it much worse that she hadn't allowed it? It was almost a relief that Imogen wasn't sure. 'I don't know if she knew. But there was one time when I'd followed you to the park and I got too close. Do you remember the little park near our old house? The one with the yellow slide? I took you there myself a few times.'

There was so much hope in Imogen's eyes that Erin didn't like to say that she had no memory of it at all. 'I think I've seen a photograph of me on a swing there.'

That seemed to please her. 'Well, I was watching you there with Mum one time, and you fell. You were running to get to the slide and I heard Mum tell you to slow down, but you kept going. It made me smile. You were so determined. But then you tripped and scraped your knee. Your screams sliced through me like a knife, down to the very depths of me. I had to hold onto the side of the bench to stop myself from running to you, scooping you up, kissing it better. What help would you be, I kept telling myself, you're a stranger to her.'

Erin's heart ached so much at the very thought that she had to press the heel of her hand to her breastbone. 'What did Mum do?'

She was twisting the edge of the cushion again. 'She picked you up and dusted you down. Then she sat you on her knee and sang to you until your tears were gone.'

Now Erin felt sad that she couldn't remember this park, couldn't remember this moment when her mother had soothed her pain. 'You said you got too close. Did Mum see you?'

'I couldn't be sure, but she might have. It scared me. I didn't come to see you again for about twelve months after that. Then the urge got too strong to ignore. I was more careful, though. I kept my distance. But I was able to find out where your playschool was. Discovered that I could see you from the wire fence at the bottom of its garden. I came several times and walked slowly down that path, hungry for a glimpse of you. I couldn't stand and watch, the staff would have been suspicious. I had to walk and hope. Twice I managed to see you, once you were playing in a sandpit, another time you were banging two pans together and laughing. The sound of your laugh was... oh, it was quite something, Erin.'

Erin's throat tightened. She remembered Harriet's laugh as a baby, how it made her smile. 'I'm so sorry you had to go through this.'

Imogen shook her head. 'I was happy to know that you were happy. I thought, maybe, when she's older, I can try again. When I can explain. When I can tell her that I didn't stop loving her. Not for a moment. Because I didn't, Erin. When I was well, I loved you so very much.'

Was this what she'd been waiting for Imogen to say? Maybe it was, but her own heart was so sore with missing Harriet, it made it even more difficult to understand. 'You could have tried to live with us. You didn't have to do it on your own.'

Imogen's laugh was dry and bitter. 'With my mother? And my father? It was impossible. They made it impossible. She wanted you for herself.'

This didn't sound right. Her mother had been overprotective to the point of controlling, yes. But she was beginning to see why. Surely, she wouldn't have stood in the way of her own daughter and granddaughter getting to know one another? Heartbreaking as these stories were, Imogen hadn't actually tried to get her back, had she?

There was quite a lot of traffic on the way home and Erin kept playing Imogen's words over and over in her head. She couldn't believe that her mother would do this to either of them. She'd seen the way her mother had looked at that photograph of Imogen, how she'd stroked her face and talked about what a beautiful girl she was. There was no way she'd seen Imogen following them. Because, if she had, why wouldn't she have tried to involve Imogen in their life?

She'd tried to persuade Imogen to come to the house, to see Ava. 'You need to talk to one another. You'll never know what she was thinking unless you ask her. Give her a chance to explain.'

But Imogen had been adamant. 'There's nothing to explain. She didn't want me, and I don't want her. She has you. She doesn't need another daughter.'

Eventually, she'd had to leave. She had a shift at the hotel that evening. When they'd said goodbye at the door, they'd hovered for a few moments as if one was waiting for the other to move in for a hug. But they hadn't. And Imogen's last words seemed to close the door on the possibility of getting her and Ava in the same room. 'You are welcome here whenever you want. I would really like to know you, now, if you'd like that too. But I can't go to her, Erin. I'm sorry.'

Erin hit the steering wheel with her hand when the traffic slowed to a standstill. How was she going to get her mother's side of this story? Would it be cruel to even try? To take her back down a path she clearly didn't want to go? How could this have happened? If only she had someone to share this with, a sister, a partner, a friend. But there was no one who could help her, no one she could even talk to who would understand.

She had an overwhelming longing to see Harriet, to hold her close and breathe in the life of her. Knowing that she was so far away was so hard. And yet *her* mother – it was still strange to think of Imogen that way – had been less than two hours away and hadn't tried to be in her life. Should she trust the version of events of someone like that?

For the first time, she began to wonder whether there was more to the story. But how was she going to find out? Was there a way to unlock these memories in her mother's mind so she could get to the truth?

As soon as she was home, she sent Harriet a text and was overjoyed when she responded almost immediately with a Face-Time call.

'Hey, Mom!'

She smiled at the over-exaggerated American accent, her body flooding with love for this bright, funny girl. 'Hello, sweetheart. It's so lovely to see you. How are you?'

'I'm great. It's so amazing here. The house is incredible. Those pictures don't do it justice.'

Erin swallowed down her jealousy. 'That's great. They let you visit it?'

'Yeah. I mean, Carmel has been moving their stuff in already. She said I might as well leave my things in the wardrobes in my room rather than take them all home again.'

Did she now? 'That's nice.'

'And my room is incredible. There's a balcony that you can sit out on and it looks out on the pool. It's like being on holiday.'

Like? 'Well, you are on holiday, aren't you?'

'You know what I mean. When I come and live here. It'll be like being on holiday every day.'

Tears stung the back of Erin's eyes. If she'd hoped that being away was going to make Harriet realise what she'd be giving up, make her actually miss her, then she was clearly much mistaken. She didn't trust her voice for much longer. 'Well, that's great. Look, I have to go, your gran needs me and then I need to get to work.'

'Say hi to Granny for me. Tell her I'm taking more pictures for her tin.'

She squeezed her eyes closed. She mustn't cry. Not yet. 'Will do. Stay safe. I love you.'

'Love you, too, Mum.'

And she vanished.

As soon as the screen went blank, Erin doubled over and let go. Tears spilled from her eyes; sobs convulsed through her body. Was this really happening? Had Harriet been swept away by the promise of this sparkly new life so swiftly? Was she gone for good?

Pressing her hands to her mouth, she tried to deaden the volume of her pain before it reached her mother's ears. If Harriet stayed with Simon, then this is all they would have. Snatched conversations that would leave her as raw as an open wound. How can you be a parent from a distance? When you're too far to reach for your child and pull them close?

But what option did she have? She couldn't make Harriet stay with her, couldn't force her to choose a life here over a life in America with her father. All she could do was hope and pray that Harriet would change her mind.

Once she could trust her mouth not to betray her pain, she wrapped her arms around herself and rocked gently until the storm had passed.

Downstairs, Ava sat in her chair with a book open on her lap. There were times when Erin had envied her this, the ability to lose herself in a book. As a child, she could remember her mother stirring a pot on the hob with her right hand while holding a book open in her left. Harriet was the same; when she'd banned her from reading at the dinner table, the child had read the labels on the condiments instead.

Erin had washed away any evidence of her tears and replaced them with a smile. 'Are you ready to go out soon, Mum? To The Oasis?'

Ava pulled her eyes away from the pages, they were unfocused for a moment, as if they were still in the story they'd just left. Then they cleared and wrinkled into a smile to match Erin's. 'Yes, love. Whenever you're ready.'

These affectionate names still sounded odd coming from her mouth. Maybe she was merely repeating them after hearing Erin speak to Harriet. She wanted so badly to talk to her mother about the things Imogen had told her today. But she didn't know where to begin. They had an hour before she needed to be at work. Maybe she'd hang round for a while when she dropped her mother off and ask Macy to help.

TWENTY-EIGHT

The centre was quiet that afternoon, subdued even. It was as if someone had dimmed the lights. Even Macy was less than her usual bright positive self when she met them at the door.

'Are you okay?'

Macy smiled, but there was sadness at the corners of her mouth. 'We lost someone yesterday. Got the call from the relatives today. Bill. One of our regulars.'

Erin had never really considered what it must be like for the staff here when someone passed on. For some of these people, the care workers were like their family, they certainly saw them more than the sons or daughters who lived too far away, or were too busy, to be in their lives. 'I'm sorry.'

Macy's eyes were bright. 'It's okay. Goes with the territory. Bill was an old charmer, though. We'll miss him and his terrible jokes.' She turned her attention onto Erin's mother. 'How are you today, Ava? Enjoying this weather? It's good for the flowers.'

Ava shook her head. 'Only you could find something positive in this rain. Imogen is going to get all wet now, aren't you, love?'

For a beat, Erin froze, but Macy carried on as if the name slip hadn't happened; it must be usual for her. 'Well, if you get your coat off, I think Beryl is about to do another round of teas.'

As soon as she was out of hearing distance, Macy put a hand on Erin's arm. 'Are you okay? Is that the first time she's done that?'

Her mother had slipped between her and Harriet's names several times, but everyone did that sometimes, didn't they? Using Imogen's name was more significant. Looking at Macy's kind, unjudgemental face, Erin pulled the string that was holding all her mother's secrets bound up inside her. 'It's just, Imogen. That name. It was the name of her other daughter. The one in the photograph.' She sighed. 'More than that. I've discovered that she was actually my mother.'

Macy blinked twice, but other than that, she didn't react. 'Well, that's a lot for you to take in. How are you holding up?'

'I'm okay. It's just that I want to ask her about her, find out what happened, but I haven't been able to.'

Macy nodded slowly. 'Maybe I can help. What did you want to know?'

The list was so long that Erin didn't know where to begin. 'I want to know why she sent Imogen away. Why she didn't try harder to help her. What she thinks has happened to her, maybe? I don't know. Anything really.'

As always, Macy was ready to help. 'If you don't have to rush off yet, why don't you come and play a round of cards with us? Sometimes the memory works better when the brain is focused on something else. Like the security guard is occupied and the vault's open.'

That sounded good. 'That would be great, thank you.'

Beryl might be a volunteer with a heart of gold but her tea-making skills left a lot to be desired. Erin almost laughed at the look on her mother's face as she peered at the watery-grey liquid and pushed it aside. 'What shall we play, Mum? Gin Rummy?'

Shuffling and dealing the seven cards each for the two of
them and Macy brought back memories of caravan holidays in
Clacton with her mother and her Aunt Marcelle and cousins.
Five of them crammed into a four-berth van, the three girls
sharing the sofas in the lounge area, the two sisters in the one
bedroom. Maybe Macy was onto something with this trick to
release memories from the depths of your mind. 'Do you
remember playing this with Auntie Marcelle, Mum?'

'Of course, I do. She was a terrible cheat.'

Erin laughed, her aunt *had* been a terrible – in both senses
of the word – cheat, ostentatiously making a show of needing to
use the tiny bathroom so that she could get a good look at your
cards as she walked past. 'You always won, though.'

Her mother tapped the side of her nose. 'It's all about
knowing what to keep and what to discard.'

This was going well. 'Maybe Auntie Marcelle will play
some cards with us when she comes to visit soon. Did you used
to play cards with Imogen? Did she go to the caravan with you?'

She held her breath and waited for her mother to shut
down, but instead, she continued to arrange the cards in her
hand. 'Not to the caravan. Marcelle didn't get the caravan until
later.'

'After Imogen had gone?'

Her mother nodded. 'Are we going to play cards, then? You
first.'

Erin took a card from the top of the pack. A seven of clubs
which didn't fit with anything in her hand, so she discarded it.

'Thank you very much. Precisely what I wanted.' Macy's
chuckle was rich and deep.

Her mother narrowed her eyes. 'Do I have competition?'

Part of Erin didn't want to interrupt this pleasant game by
pushing for information, but it was too good an opportunity to
miss. 'I met her again, Mum. I visited Imogen.'

Behind her cards, her mother's face paled. 'Why did you do

that?'

'Because I wanted to know what happened. And you won't tell me anything. She said that you wouldn't let her look after me. Is that true?'

'She couldn't. She couldn't do it.'

This was further than they got last time. 'She was depressed?'

Her mother tapped her cards on the table. 'She was so young. It was too much. She needed help. I told Frank. I said she needed help.'

'Dad didn't want you to help her?'

'He said she had to do it. But she couldn't do it. She couldn't.' This time her mother's voice was loud enough to attract the attention of the people at the next table. She started plucking at the cards in her hand.

She had no desire to put her mother through the trauma of Imogen's illness again. 'I know that she left, but she came back, didn't she? Why couldn't she come and see her baby?'

'Frank said no. Frank said she was going to hurt the baby. He said she couldn't come back. Make your choice, Ava. Make your choice. That's what he said. That baby stays here or goes with her. Make your choice.'

Anger towards the father she barely remembered rose in Erin's chest. 'Why did you listen to him? Why did you not stick up for Imogen?'

She hadn't realised how loudly she was speaking until she saw the fear in her mother's eyes. 'I didn't... I couldn't... Where's the baby? Who's got the baby?'

'It's okay, Ava. It's okay.' Macy's voice was soothing as she laid a hand on her arm. 'The baby is fine. She's asleep now. You can relax. The baby is asleep.'

The childlike trust in her mother's eyes as she looked at Macy brought tears to Erin's. 'She's right, Mum. The baby's fine.'

Within a few minutes, her mother seemed to have forgotten that they'd even had the conversation. Macy took the opportunity to speak to Erin alone. 'Actually, Ava, Beryl wants to join in this game. Can you play with her because I've remembered that I need to speak to Erin in the office for a moment?'

Still shocked by her mother's words, Erin followed Macy towards her office like a schoolchild in trouble. When they got there, Macy pushed open the door to her office and held it open for Erin. 'Make yourself comfortable.'

Macy was a cross between the calm authority of a head-teacher and the gentle warmth of a grandmother. Her smooth open face made it impossible to guess her age, but Erin wouldn't mind betting that she was older than she looked. 'Sorry, I didn't mean to cause such an upset.'

She slid herself behind her desk. 'No need to apologise. I know how frustrating it can be when you don't get an answer to your questions.'

'I want to know what happened. Imogen made it sound as if my mother had chased her away, cut her out. But that doesn't make sense to me. If she'd wanted me all to herself, how come she hasn't been more... loving to me?'

She hadn't known she was about to cry when she walked in here, but she couldn't control the tears that spilled from her eyes. Imogen had described a mother that she hadn't known, one who picked her up and held her close. But, for all of her overprotective control during Erin's teenage years, she couldn't remember a time when her mother had put her arms around her or kissed her.

Macy was looking at her, as if waiting for the right moment to speak. 'Do you know how old I was when I came to England? Seven. My mother dressed me in the best clothes she could afford and gave me to my Auntie Mae to bring with her. Mae was only twenty, no more than a child herself. Apparently, I cried so much during the trip over here, she was tempted to turn around and take me home. I was so angry that my mother had sent me away, I felt so rejected. But you know why she did it? Because she believed it would be a better life for me here.' Macy raised an eyebrow. 'Now, whether that was true or not is a subject for a longer discussion, but she did it because she loved me. It was a huge sacrifice for her, I know that now. Now that I have my own children, I can feel it here, in my heart, what that must have been like for her. Parents don't always get it right, Erin, but you have to look at why they made those choices. Your mother wouldn't have sent Imogen away lightly. Look at the way she's holding onto that photograph of her and Imogen that Harriet found. She loved the girl. She must have believed it was the right thing to do.'

In light of this story, Erin felt ashamed of her outburst. 'I know you're right, I do. I just want to know why she didn't let Imogen see me. And why she never told me that she existed. I can't understand that.'

Macy sighed and pulled two more tissues from the box, pressing them into Erin's hand. 'You might need to make your peace with never getting a definite answer. Your mother... she might not remember it as clearly any longer.'

This was what Erin was afraid of. 'This is why I want them to speak to one another. If I can get them in the same room, maybe I can find out the truth.'

'Maybe. But your mother loves you, Erin. I can see that. And if she made the sacrifice of sending Imogen away, I'm sure that she believed it was the right thing to do. For both of you.'

Erin nodded even though she didn't know whether she agreed. Maybe it had been a sacrifice for her mother. Didn't she know how that felt right now? She was making a sacrifice herself by letting Harriet go to America with Simon.

The problem was, what if that sacrifice was the wrong thing to do? What if it ruined everything?

TWENTY-NINE

After saying goodbye to her mother, who seemed to have forgotten all about their conversation, Erin headed into work.

Jasmine was waiting for her with a huge packet of biscuits and a foot in plaster.

'What have you done?'

Jasmine rolled her eyes. 'It's a long story involving a date at an ice skating rink. Normally I steal one of those penguins from a small child but I didn't think that'd be too sexy so I tried to skate unaided.' She motioned towards the plaster with the chocolate digestives. 'Turns out that wasn't such a good idea. Neither was my date, who dropped me at the hospital and then remembered a very important prior engagement.'

'Oh you poor thing. Is it broken?'

'Yep. According to Anthony, the very handsome doctor who looked after me.' She winked at Erin. 'That's why I bought the biscuits. I can do nothing but sit, so you'll need to do all the running around. These are bribery for all the extra work you're going to have to do.'

'You didn't need to do that. Not that I won't take them, obviously. Do you want a drink to go with them?'

'Yes, please. But I need you to do an invoice run if you don't mind?'

They always slid the invoices under the door of anyone checking out the next day. 'I'll make the tea and then I'll go.'

Even though it had brought her date to a disastrous conclusion, Jasmine's story about sliding through the legs of an unsuspecting man before crashing into the barrier did make Erin laugh. She was clearly quite taken with Dr Anthony, too, and had given him her number. Once she'd got the full description of how funny he was – and how intelligent his eyes were – Erin left Jasmine on the front desk, smiling like a lovestruck teen, while she delivered the invoices.

She had one left when it happened. The lift had opened on the second floor and she'd turned right towards room 212 – Mr and Mrs Thompson, both keen golfers – when a door opened at the end of the corridor and Josh came out into the hall in a manner which could only be described as furtive. This would have been strange enough, but then he was followed out by Caitlin, the chambermaid, who was laughing at him.

She froze on the dark purple stripe that ran along the middle of the carpet. Josh turned and froze too. 'Erin. Hi.'

Caitlin's hand shot up to her mouth and she hurried past Erin towards the stairwell. The door clattered closed behind her, leaving Josh and Erin looking at each other.

He was the first to get over the shock. 'There was a complaint about the cleaning in that room. I was just, er, going over it with Caitlin.'

The excuse was weak even without the fact that she knew that that room wasn't occupied. 'Okay. Well, I need to slip this invoice under a door and I'll be on my way back to Jasmine.'

'Jasmine. Oh, yes. Her foot. Look, you haven't told her, have you? About the hotel?'

'That it might be closing? No. I haven't said anything.' Right now, she was wondering whether her loyalty was misplaced.

'Good. Good. No point upsetting anyone until we know for sure what's happening.'

He was back in professional mode and – considering what she thought she'd seen – she wasn't sure she could stomach that. 'I need to get on.'

He moved to the side to let her past and, once she'd bent to post the invoice under the door of room 212, she turned back towards the stairs to find that he'd gone.

Back in the office, her phone vibrated in the pocket of her blazer. Harriet.

Her face on the screen practically glowed with health and happiness. 'Hi, Mum.'

'How's things?'

'Brilliant. Tell me about you first. How's work? And Granny?'

Being able to see Harriet's face on the screen, Erin was under no illusion that she had something to tell her. Despite her attempts at polite conversation, the twitch in her eye was a tell that she'd had since she was really small. 'We're fine. What's new with you?'

Harriet laughed. That was a phrase she'd used when she was about eleven, gleaned from one of those American teen shows she'd loved. Again, Erin realised she had only herself to blame for her daughter's love affair with the United States.

'What's new with me is that I went to see a school out here.'

Erin was conscious of her heart thumping in her chest. 'Really?'

'Yes. Oh, Mum, it was so cool. It was *exactly* how I thought it would be. No uniforms or anything. Everyone was really casual and there was a huge library and the art rooms were incredible. They had a pottery wheel and everything.'

Usually, Harriet's excitement was infectious. When she'd

been passionate about anything in her life – hockey, art, One Direction – Erin had gone along for the ride: encouraging, listening, enjoying her passion for something new. But this time was different. The more enthusiastic Harriet sounded, the more terrified Erin became. 'That sounds great, sweetheart. Definitely gives you something to think about.'

There was a pause at the other end that was so deep it gave Erin vertigo. 'Well, that's the biggest news of all. Dad spoke to the principal and explained about the move and he's managed to enrol me for the new year, after the summer break.'

She was falling, falling and there seemed to be nothing to hold on to. This had not been the deal. Harriet was only supposed to be there on holiday. To check out the area. To – hopefully – realise that it wasn't all as glamorous and perfect as she'd made it in her mind.

'Dad wants to speak to you.' She lowered her voice. 'I wasn't supposed to tell you about the school yet. He said he should speak to you first. But I couldn't wait.'

He was expecting Harriet to keep secrets from her now, too? 'Of course you couldn't. Don't worry, love. I'll tell him that I squeezed it out of you.'

Harriet giggled. She was practically drunk on the excitement of her new life. 'Thanks, Mum. I'll talk to you tomorrow.'

There was a scratchy exchange at the other end and then Simon's confident clipped tone. 'Hi, Erin.'

'Simon.'

'I understand our daughter has sprung the news on you. About the school. Sorry, I wanted to speak to you about it first.'

This was ridiculous. What did it matter who told her, if the deed was already done? 'You said you were just taking her out there for a look around. You said nothing to me about a school.'

'Yeah, well, I hadn't really intended to look into it yet but one of the other directors at the US office mentioned that his daughter was going to the school near the house we're renting and he suggested we take a look at it. I couldn't see the harm in it, so we went to look and it was great.'

She had no idea how far she could believe him at this stage. 'And, of course, it was perfect and Harriet begged to be allowed to go there?'

He laughed as if her sarcasm had been lost halfway across the Atlantic. 'Something like that.'

Erin had to take three breaths before she spoke again. 'You've enrolled her in a school even though I haven't agreed that she can come. I trusted you, Simon, and, as usual, you have gone and done exactly what you wanted to do.'

Before he spoke, Simon leaned backwards and closed a door behind him. 'This is not either of our decisions, Erin. It is Harriet's decision. If she wants to come and live with me—'

'Because you've basically made it seem like she'd going to be living some kind of movie star life. How can I possibly compete with that, Simon?!'

His tone was so irritatingly calm that she wanted to reach into that phone screen and punch his smug face. 'It's not a competition, either.'

The familiar tightness in her throat was about to betray her; this conversation needed to end before he could see her cry. 'You agreed that we would talk about this.'

'We are talking about this. And it doesn't matter, Erin. Harriet will be sixteen before school starts. She can make her own decision.'

'And you really think she'd leave if I begged her not to go?'

He sighed. 'Are you really going to be the parent that stops her from taking the biggest adventure of her life so far?'

She cut the call – unable to look at his face for one second longer – bent over and rested her head on her knees to stop the world from swimming in front of her. Wave after wave of disappointment and grief crashed from her heart through her throat to the hands she'd pressed to her mouth. This was real. She wasn't coming back. Harriet – her baby, her beautiful girl – wasn't coming home.

In the last three months, her entire world had turned upside down. Her daughter was leaving her, her mother was forgetting who she was and she had another mother who she'd never even known existed. What had her life become? Who was she? Everything she'd known about herself as a daughter and as a mother was about to change. Where did she go from here?

THIRTY

Fallen leaves crunched beneath their feet as Imogen and Erin walked the path through the trees. Instead of meeting in the pub again, Imogen had suggested walking together. She'd got in the habit of walking, she said, as a way to help her mental health. Erin couldn't help wondering if it was also so that she didn't have to look at her as they spoke.

The more Erin had thought about her plan to have Imogen and her mother in the same room together, the more it seemed like the most obvious thing to do. Last night, she'd called to suggest it. But Imogen hadn't been keen. 'I don't think it's a good idea.'

'Why not? It's been over thirty years. Surely its worth trying?'

Imogen had sighed. 'Some things don't change in a hundred years. I doubt she's changed. I doubt she ever wants to see me again.'

She couldn't reconcile the mother that Imogen described with the mother she remembered and she'd had enough of these stilted phone conversations. 'I don't understand. Can we meet? Can we talk?'

'Of course. I would really like that.'

Now, the sun was trying its best to find them through the thick foliage overhead and Erin was beginning to regret her long sleeves. 'I know you don't think it's a good idea for you and Mum to meet, but I still don't really understand why.'

Imogen didn't respond straight away. They continued to crunch through the leaves, a lone bird called overhead and something bigger, a squirrel perhaps, scuttled past them in the undergrowth. Eventually she spoke. 'I've been thinking how to explain it to you. But I can't do that without explaining what it's like inside my head. How dark my days can get sometimes.'

Erin pushed the sleeves up her forearms; trying to keep up with Imogen was making her even hotter. 'I'd love it if you tried, I really want to understand.'

'Ever since that time I was really ill, I have suffered with bouts of clinical depression. Have you ever had depression?'

Erin shook her head. She'd had times when she felt down, of course she had, but that wasn't what Imogen meant. 'No. I've been lucky, I suppose.'

'Good. That's really good. The only way I can explain it to you – and maybe it's not like this for everyone – is that it's like a shadow, a person who slips silently into a room. No one else can see that they're there except you. They stand there behind you, getting closer. And you try, you really try to ignore them, to carry on talking with your friends, listening to their lives. But he waits for you, watching and you know that when you leave he is going to follow you and never let you go.'

Imogen resolutely faced forwards as she spoke and Erin couldn't watch her for fear of tripping over the network of tree roots along the mud path. But she couldn't mistake the tone of melancholy, the deep sadness this must have brought Imogen over the years. 'I'm so sorry it's been like that for you.'

Imogen seemed to pick up the pace even more, as if she

could outwalk the emotions hanging stagnant in the air. 'I can manage it. I have strategies. I'm okay.'

Erin didn't want to be cruel, but they also couldn't keep skirting the big questions she needed answered. If she was going to make sense of what happened, there were things that she needed to know. 'You don't have to answer this, but I keep coming back to the same thing. Why didn't you have any contact with us? Why did you have to give me up altogether?'

Imogen didn't miss a step of her stride, but she was shaking her head. 'I don't know how to tell you why. This depression has been my constant companion for over three decades, Erin. What kind of mother would I have been to you? You can't raise a child when you are lying in a dark room for days on end. I can't even hold a job down. This job at the pub? I've been there two years. That's the longest I've ever managed. When it hits... when he comes... I can't do anything.'

'I thought there was medication. I thought...'

What did she think? What did she really know?

'Yes. I've been on medication; I've tried different things. And it works. It does. For some people it's fantastic. A lifesaver. But the pills that work best for me are pretty strong and they make me feel so fuzzy and tired. When I can, I wean myself from them and try and go it alone for a while. Unfortunately for me, it always comes back. I've spoken to people about my experience with post-partum psychosis and they all tell me that most people fully recover. For me, it left a scar so close to the surface that I live in fear that the merest touch will start it all over again.'

When Erin had split from Simon, she'd had a really tough time of it, but she'd managed to keep it together because of Harriet. In fact, focusing on Harriet was the thing that had got her through. For her, being a mother came before everything else. If Harriet was okay, she would be okay, too.

But when Imogen spoke, it was only about herself. How *she*

felt. How *she'd* been affected. Did she ever think about how Erin's life had gone? Had she not cared how she'd been brought up and what her life had been like? How could she have ignored the fact that she had a living breathing daughter less than two hours' drive away? 'It must have been awful. I can understand that. But even though I know what happened wasn't under your control I can't help but feel... abandoned. You left me and that's really hard for me to understand. To... forgive.'

Imogen stopped dead in the middle of the path and waited for Erin to stop and face her. 'I haven't asked you to forgive me, Erin. I wasn't the one who came looking for you.'

Cold and hard, this change in tone was confusing. Erin wasn't sure how to respond. 'I know that.'

She shook her head again. 'Do you? Because I don't even *want* you to forgive me. Why would I when I can't even forgive myself?'

Her eyes were like dark pools down into the depths of her soul. There was such pain there that it would've been easy to pull back from the edge, to go back to the surface. But Erin was in pain, too. 'I understand why you had to leave; I do. And I know that you tried to come back that one time. But I don't understand how that was enough for you. Once I got older, once I wasn't a young baby who cried all the time, what about then? Why didn't you try again, and keep trying, to know me?'

Still Imogen stared at her. 'I did try, Erin. I did.'

THIRTY-ONE

Imogen had discovered the date of the school nativity by chance.

Whenever she went to the school playground, she took care not to stand close enough that her mother would spot her when she collected Erin. She also couldn't hang around the gates looking suspicious. She had to time it right so that she was walking past at the exact time that the stream of children flowed out of the classroom doors. Then the parents were so busy locating and directing their children that she could go unnoticed. Invisible. Which suited her fine.

Each time she was there, she would anxiously scan the sea of faces and then – when she located Erin, her two straight plaits flying behind her – she'd get a jolt of something that felt like excitement, followed quickly by an ache of longing.

Without moving from the spot, she'd watch her mother take Erin by the hand, listening as Erin chattered beside her. Imogen could never risk getting close enough to hear what she was saying, but she imagined they were stories about her day, her school work, her friends. Did she love reading like her grandmother? Or art like Imogen? Were her hands stained with paints and ink?

The worst part was watching them get further and further away down the street when every part of her wanted to follow them home, kneel down and speak to Erin, tell her that she was her mother and loved her so very much. But how could she risk that when she knew that the darkness would come for her again and take her away? She'd be doing it for herself, not for Erin. And Erin was what mattered.

That Tuesday, as she hovered nearby, two mothers were talking about the costumes they had to make.

'Jamie is a shepherd, so I'm making him a brown dress and sticking a bit of rope around it.'

'Sam is a sheep. It's costing me a fortune in cotton wool.'

Would this have been her? Chatting outside to other mums, laughing, joking, looking forward to taking her daughter home for tea? Why couldn't it have been her? Why couldn't she have this like everyone else?

Once the children started to come out of the building, the mums separated. 'I'll see you at the performance on Friday, then?'

'Yes. What time is it, again?'

'Two o'clock.'

She had gone back and forth in her mind several times about whether she should attend the show, but the temptation to see Erin on stage was too great. If she slipped in just as it was about to start and stayed at the back, what harm could it do?

Still, her stomach had been doing somersaults all morning. Imagining running into her mother or being asked to leave. In the event, it had been the easiest thing in the world to slip in with some latecomers. She'd even found a seat in the back corner.

A teacher introduced herself at the front of the room and

explained that they were doing a traditional nativity play and asked the parents to welcome the children to the stage with a round of applause. She didn't need to ask twice, the cheers and claps were on par with a West End show as a gaggle of five-year-olds made their way to the stage.

Imogen only had eyes for Erin. From the moment she ascended those three wooden steps, dressed as one of the innkeepers, she was captivated by every movement, every facial expression. Not caring about the performance, all she wanted was to see if her daughter was happy.

And she was. Holding on tightly to the sides of her chair, Imogen was blown away by how grown-up and confident her daughter looked. Remembering her one line, projecting her voice, looking out at the audience. She wasn't a baby any longer. Erin was a little girl with her own mind and her own personality. Those dark days of colic and sleepless nights must be years behind her. Hope prickled in Imogen's chest. Was it possible that she could cope with this older daughter? Be a mother to her? Be in her life at all?

She was so absorbed by her beautiful girl and the possibility that they could have a relationship, that it took a while for her to notice her mother, on the other end of the row, staring straight at her. In that moment, fear fell on her like a lead weight. Remembering the last time she'd wanted to take Erin, she wasn't ready to face her parents until she'd formulated a rock solid plan.

Once the performance was over, the children left the room to rapturous applause to go back to their classrooms to get changed. Imogen tried to get out of the main door as quickly as possible, but her mother caught her as she was about to leave. 'What are you doing here?'

'I only came to see her.'

Her mother had her by the elbow and was glancing around

to make sure that no one was listening. Clearly, she was still ashamed of her. 'Let's talk about this outside.'

The playground was full of parents waiting to collect their children, but they managed to find a quiet corner away from the throng. Her mother didn't waste any time in starting to berate her. 'You can't do this. You can't turn up like this, Imogen. It's not fair on Erin. She doesn't know about you.'

Imogen hadn't been sure how her mother would have explained her absence to Erin. But she certainly hadn't expected that she would have erased her altogether. 'What have you told her?'

'I haven't told her anything. How could I? It was easier this way.'

'She thinks that you're her mother?'

'What would you have had me do? I was trying to protect her. I am trying to protect you both.'

'How does this protect me?'

'You can start again, Imogen. You can get well. You can do what makes you happy. I can take care of Erin. She'll be fine.'

'But she's my daughter.'

'You barely know her.'

'That's not my fault.' She hadn't meant to raise her voice but she could see a couple of parents looking in their direction. Her mother didn't answer that, but Imogen could feel the judgement dripping from her. And she was right. She had left her daughter. What did she expect?

The doors to one of the classrooms flew open and children in various states of dress came stumbling out. Her mother turned to her, panic in her eyes. 'You need to go, Imogen. Don't come back. Stay away. It's the best thing for both of you.'

And she had. Tears streaming down her cheeks, she'd run from the playground into the street outside.

About a year later. She tried again. This time she'd prepared herself before knocking on the door of the house, ready to tell her mother that, whatever she thought, Imogen wanted to be in her daughter's life.

But they'd gone. They didn't live there any longer and no one could tell her where they were. Her mother had taken Erin away so that she could never come back for her again.

THIRTY-TWO

A bench under the shade of an oak tree was within a few steps and Erin sank down onto it. Imogen perched at the other end.

When Erin's shock subsided, it was replaced with the heavy pain of sympathy for Imogen. 'I can't believe they did that. I'm so sorry.'

Imogen wiped away her tears with the back of her hand. 'Don't apologise. You have nothing to be sorry for. You're right. This is all on me. I should have tried harder to find you again.'

What did it matter any longer? It was a mess. The whole thing. And she'd been so young. 'Mum should have helped you more. Maybe then you could have...'

She wasn't even sure how to end that sentence. Imogen turned towards her. 'I never stopped loving you, Erin. I don't know if you can believe that, but it's true. Ever since I left, there's a little hole in me, a part missing. Sometimes I lay in bed and imagine what your life is like. It never stops. I know that I'm not your mother in the real sense, that I'm just the person who gave birth to you. I've not been your mother, but you have always been my daughter. Always.' Her face crumpled and she turned away sharply to prevent Erin from seeing it.

It would have been the most natural thing in the world for Erin to reach out to her. If it had been Harriet sitting there crying, she wouldn't have thought twice. But something stopped her. After decades apart, she couldn't throw herself into Imogen's arms and pretend that it didn't still hurt. And what about Ava? She still didn't know what to believe; whose memory was the truth? This felt so disloyal to the woman who'd been her mother her whole life. 'You are my mother, too. I don't know how this is going to work, but I do want you in my life.'

The hope in Imogen's eyes was almost as painful as the darkness it replaced. 'I would like that so very much.'

'But I need this to involve Mum, too. Why don't you come over tonight? To our house.'

Imogen took a deep breath. 'I still don't think that's a good idea.'

'If we're going to make this work, it has to be all of us. I want you to see Mum. And I'd love you to meet Harriet when she comes home.'

That seemed to decide her. 'Okay. I'll come. Soon. I'll come soon.'

That meant it'd never happen. 'Please. Come tonight. Please.'

Imogen took a deep breath. 'Okay. I'll come tonight.'

When she arrived at work, Josh was at the reception desk. She walked straight past him but he followed close behind. 'Erin, can I speak to you?'

'I really need to speak to Andy about the food order.'

Now he was alongside her, his voice lowered. 'Please. I think you got the wrong idea yesterday.'

Was he going to pretend that nothing had been going on between him and Caitlin? 'Josh, it's none of my business. You don't need to explain yourself to me.'

'I can understand how it looked, but Caitlin was just... just helping me out with something.'

That sounded even worse. 'Like I said. None of my business.'

She pushed the glass door into the dining room. It was laid up for dinner but was otherwise empty. Josh sped up then turned around to cut her off. 'I've been staying in the hotel three nights a week.'

There were tables either side of her so she had to stop to prevent herself from bumping into him. 'But we're not supposed to do that.'

'I know. That's why I had to keep it quiet.'

'Why only three nights?'

'My ex-wife and I have shared custody of the children, but we decided to stay in the house for half the week each so that the children don't have to move. She goes to her boyfriend's house and I rented out a small place not far from here. But the landlord of the flat has decided to sell it. He chucked me out a couple of weeks ago. This was supposed to be temporary, but I'm finding it really difficult to find somewhere I can afford that's close enough to my kids and here.'

She'd heard of people doing this. 'That still doesn't explain why Caitlin was in your room.'

'Because I need whatever room I stay in to be cleaned on the day I move out each week. If the same room was permanently appearing as vacant on the schedule, I knew that you or Jasmine would realise there was something going on. I couldn't risk you finding out.'

It was against company regulations for staff to stay in the rooms without special permission and head office wouldn't think favourably about a hotel manager who couldn't organise his private life. It was admirable, though. 'It's great that you and your ex-wife are making that work. For the children, I mean. That they don't have to go between two houses.'

He ran his fingers through his hair, scratching his scalp so that it stood on end. 'Well, they're still pretty little. It'd be a lot of change for them. And it's not their fault that our marriage didn't work out.'

It was impossible not to think about Harriet. She'd been twelve when Simon and Erin had called it a day. The marriage had been over for a while before that; they'd been keeping out of each other's way for months, but not wanting to be the one to leave. Once Simon had found a flat closer to his office, she'd hated it when Harriet had stayed there every other weekend; the house had felt so empty without her.

But how must it have been for Simon? He got to spend two days with his daughter out of every fourteen. The final decision to end their marriage had been his, but that had nothing to do with his relationship with Harriet. Apart from the long hours he spent at work, he'd been a good father, she had to admit that. But he had missed out on a lot of time with his daughter since they'd separated. Was that why he was so adamant that he wanted her with him in America? What had he said? *Surely it gets to be my turn sometime.*

'I won't say anything to anyone, Josh. Not even Jasmine. You have my word.'

He smiled. 'Thanks. I appreciate it. But I need to sort it out really. I don't like the situation. Not having a proper home. I'm a settler at heart. Ironic, I know, for someone who works in hospitality.'

She knew what he meant. Like air stewards and cruise ship entertainers, hotel staff should be travellers at heart. But maybe it wasn't that. 'Not necessarily. Maybe it's people who love home who are the best people to run a hotel. They want to make it homely for others.'

A warm smile spread across his face like a sunny day. 'I like that. I like it a lot. You really should do it, you know.'

She frowned. 'Do what?'

'Open your own place. I've seen the way you work, this last couple of weeks. You'd be great at it.'

She laughed. 'There's a little problem called funding.'

'So start saving. Or look for an investor.'

His words were almost a challenge. It was true that she had more money now that she was living with her mother. For the first time in her life, she'd been able to start putting money away. But she'd anticipated that this was for Harriet. For university or a deposit on a flat or a car. But if she stayed in America, maybe there wouldn't be such a need for her to find this?

She shook away the traitorous thought. No. Harriet was going to come back. She had to. 'I need to get back to Jasmine. She can barely move.'

He blushed and took a step back. 'Of course. And thank you. For keeping my living situation to yourself.'

Back at reception, Jasmine was leaning so far out of her chair to try to reach some papers on the floor, that she looked as if she might topple over.

'You're going to break the other leg you silly woman.' Erin leaned down and picked up the scattered sheets.

'Well, you'd been gone so long I thought you'd left me for dead. Where have you been?'

'Sorry. I was talking to Josh.'

Her eyes gleamed. 'Were you, now? Did you find out anything about Caitlin and the pants?'

Erin kept her head down so that Jasmine couldn't see her face. Lying to her felt awful, but she didn't want to be a gossip either. And she didn't want to betray Josh's trust. 'No.'

Jasmine sounded disappointed. 'Well, did he say any more about giving you a promotion?'

She felt even worse about keeping quiet about the hotel. She'd have to think of a way of telling Jasmine without betraying Josh's confidence. She hated secrets. Even more so now. 'No.'

'Well, I think you should do it. You've been doing this long enough. You need something new. Something for you.'

'Where did you get that little rhyme from? The Live, Laugh, Love shop?'

Jasmine stuck out her tongue. 'Nope. That's all mine. I mean it, Erin.'

Erin sighed. 'I'm still thinking about it.' There was a part of her that wanted to go for it. Maybe this could be the beginning of a new chapter. Marcelle was arriving tomorrow. When she came to see her mother, wouldn't it be wonderful if Erin could greet her with the news that she'd reconciled with Imogen? And Jasmine was right about the new job; it would give her something to focus on if Harriet really did go through with the move to America. Maybe this was her opportunity to have the career she'd wanted after all.

Jasmine tilted her head. 'What are you smiling about?'

She hadn't realised she was. Maybe it was a little bit of hope that she could carve a life for herself out of all the chaos of the last few weeks. Starting tonight, when Imogen and Ava would be in the same room together for the first time in over three decades.

THIRTY-THREE

When she got home that evening, Erin could smell something familiar as soon as she walked in the door. Burnt sugar and sweet dough ticked at her nose. 'Mum?'

'I'm in the kitchen. I've got a surprise for you.'

She pushed open the kitchen door and the smell of French toast reached out for her like a warm hug. For a moment, she was back thirty years, home sick from school, watching cartoons and nibbling tiny squares of the soft sweet bread, covered in sugar and lemon juice. 'I haven't had that for years.'

Her mother's obvious delight in her reaction made Erin's throat tight. 'I thought it would cheer you up.'

It was such a thoughtful gesture that Erin didn't quite know what to say. 'Thanks, Mum.'

'Now go and wash your hands and you can tell me what you did at school today.'

Just like that, the spell was broken. Macy had said she should go along with her mother's version of life as it was, but how was that going to work when Imogen was due to arrive in an hour's time?

It wasn't worth rocking her mood yet, though. If she'd

learned anything in the last few weeks, it was that her mother could lose or find her moorings at the turn of a few minutes.

Upstairs in the bathroom, she washed her hands slowly and stared at her face in the mirror. How could her mother look at her and confuse her tired, lined face with that of her schoolgirl self? Maybe we only ever see those we love in the way we want to see them. It's only when we look back, at photographs, that we're forced to face the change that's taken place.

Harriet was always accusing her of treating her like a child, and Simon had said much the same thing. Maybe she needed to face facts. Her daughter was growing up and she didn't need her in the same way that she had. She was ready to stretch her wings a little. But why did she have to fly so far?

Erin was on her third round of French toast when the door-bell rang. It wasn't only that she'd missed lunch, it was the obvious delight in her mother's face when she slid each slice onto Erin's plate. Had she been like this back then? Erin could remember her mother's interrogation of her symptoms, her need to ascertain that Erin really was sick enough to stay home. But the smell – and taste – of the toast brought memories of a cool hand on her forehead, a blanket tucked around her as she drifted off to sleep.

The shrill notes of the bell made her mother frown. 'Who's that? It can't be your father home already.'

Erin's stomach tightened. She should've prepared her mother better for this. 'I'll get it. You stay here and make me another one.'

She closed the door to the kitchen behind her, then opened the front door to Imogen's back. When she turned, her face was white and pinched. 'Hi. I'm here.'

Erin stood back and motioned for her to come in. 'Come through to the sitting room. Mum's in the kitchen.'

Imogen glanced around her as she made her way down the hall, as if she was expecting ghouls to jump out at her from the wallpaper. When she pushed the sitting room door open, she gasped. 'This is the exact same furniture she had at the old house.'

'I know. I've tried for years to get her to let me get something new, but now – with the dementia – it's better not to change things apparently.'

'How bad is it?'

'It's difficult to say. She's past the merely being forgetful stage, but sometimes she knows exactly what's going on and you can almost forget that she has it.'

The irony of that statement wasn't lost on Erin, but Imogen was clearly too absorbed with her surroundings to pick up on it. 'Every piece of furniture is the same.' She pointed towards the sofa. 'I held you there as a baby.'

Erin followed her gaze, tried to imagine it herself. They were pulled away from the memory by her mother's voice from the kitchen. 'Who was it, Erin?'

Imogen froze on the spot at the sound of Ava's voice. 'Does she not know I'm coming?'

This was a delicate explanation. 'Well, I was going to tell her this evening, but then—'

Imogen's eyes were wild. 'She doesn't know? Maybe I should go?'

If she had to, Erin was prepared to lock her in here. 'No, please. You have to see her. We have to try.'

She didn't want to bring out the 'you owe this to me' card, but Imogen seemed to understand. She nodded. 'Okay, then. Let's get it over with.'

If she hadn't seen her perch onto the armchair, Erin might have locked the front door. Imogen had form for running away, after all. 'Give me five minutes.'

In the kitchen, her mother had already cleared away the plates and was washing the frying pan in a bowl of soapy water. 'Mum. You have a visitor.'

When she looked up, Erin tried to gauge where she was – here, now or thirty years ago – by the look in her eyes. 'Who is it?'

'Come with me. They're in the sitting room.'

As they walked into the room, Imogen got to her feet. For a few moments, neither of them spoke. Then Imogen took a step forward. 'Hi, Mum. It's me. Imogen.'

If Erin hadn't been standing behind her mother, she might've fallen. Her hands flew to her face and she wailed like a child. 'No. I told you not to come. I told you to stay away.'

If Imogen's face had been pale before, it was almost translucent now. 'It's been three decades, Mum. It's not the same any longer.'

'No. No. You have to go, you have to go.'

Imogen grabbed her bag from the chair beneath her and pushed her way past the two of them. 'I told you. I told you this was a terrible idea. I should never have come. You should have kept away from me.'

Though she wanted to follow Imogen, reason with her, ask her to try again, Erin's mother was in such a state that she couldn't leave her. 'It's okay, Mum. It's okay.'

Her mother was twisting her wedding ring round and round and round. 'Is Frank home? Did he see her? Where's Marcelle? I need to ask Marcelle to watch the baby.'

The front door slammed. Imogen was gone. 'Marcelle is coming, Mum. She'll be here soon. It's going to be okay.'

That was a lie. Nothing was okay. Imogen had gone. Harriet was going to live in another country. And her mother's dementia was taking her away faster with each passing day. Erin had no one.

THIRTY-FOUR

After the disastrous meeting with Imogen, Erin had no idea how her mother was going to react to Marcelle's arrival.

Her aunt had already refused her offer of a bed at the house. 'I've already booked myself into a hotel. I have this eightieth birthday to go to and about a million people to see, so it'll be easier. And I don't want to go upsetting Ava.'

The last was said almost nervously and made Erin wonder how things had been left between the two of them when Marcelle emigrated.

When she collected her from her hotel, though, Marcelle had been full of life and had folded her into her warm perfumed arms. She was younger and fairer than Ava. Ash blonde and tanned, she was a great advertisement for the Australian climate and, rounder in the face than Erin remembered, she was strong and fit and her hug was firm. 'It's so good to see you. I can't believe Harriet is fifteen already. Where have all of those years gone?'

'You'll get to see her soon. She's back from America in a couple of days. How long are you here?'

'A week. Then I have to travel up to Yorkshire for this birthday party. How's Ava? Does she know that I'm coming?'

Again, this nervousness. What had gone on between the two of them? 'I did tell her this morning but I don't know if she'll remember. She seemed pleased.'

That was probably an exaggeration. But she wasn't not pleased. She'd nodded and smiled when Erin had told her that her sister had flown halfway across the world to see her.

'Have you seen any more of Imogen?'

'Yes. And she came to the house yesterday but Mum made her leave.'

There was a sharp intake of breath. 'I was afraid of that. Oh, this is all such a mess. Do you think she'd come back? While I'm here? I want to help. I want to make this right.'

Erin had called Imogen late last night and tried to encourage her to come again. But Imogen had sounded pretty shaken up. 'I don't know. I've tried, but she seemed pretty adamant that it wasn't a good idea.'

Marcelle looked hopeful. 'Can I talk to her?'

Erin shrugged. 'If you want to. You can speak to her in the car while I drive.'

She dialled the number and gave the phone to Marcelle. Though Marcelle had it to her ear, Erin could hear the sound of the ringtone as she pulled out of the hotel car park.

She had to give it to Marcelle. She didn't give up easily. When the call went to voicemail, she pressed redial and tried again. And then a third time. Before she sighed. 'I'll have to leave a voicemail. Hello? It's Auntie Marcelle. I've come all the way from Australia, Imogen love, and I really want to see you. Please come to your mother's house. It'll be okay this time, I promise.'

She seemed pleased with herself when she disconnected the call. But Erin didn't fancy her chances. The look on

Imogen's face when she left last night did not make it likely that she was about to return for more of the same.

When they got to the house, Marcelle seemed to tense up again. Stepping over the threshold, she took a deep breath.

But when they walked into the lounge, the look on her mother's face was priceless. 'Marcelle?'

'It's me, Ava love. I've come to see you.' She was across the room in five steps and straight into her sister's open arms.

Erin watched her mother, the woman who had always been reserved and cool, crying like a young child. Watching these two older women holding on to one another like they were drowning, Erin sank down onto the sofa and wondered what had happened to make this reunion so powerful.

'I'm so sorry, Ava, I had to tell Erin about Imogen, you understand, don't you? I had to tell her.'

How could her mother understand when she barely knew who Erin was some days? And yet, she seemed to be responding to Marcelle in a very different way than she had to Imogen yesterday. Even so, Erin was stunned by her mother's next question. 'Are you going to look after her? Will you look after my baby girl?'

Which girl did she mean? Erin or Imogen? But Marcelle seemed to understand. 'She's safe now, Ava love. They're both safe.'

For the next three hours, Ava sat rapt as Marcelle recounted stories from her life in Australia. Erin knew that she'd been told these same stories at least twice before, but neither of them seemed to mind the retelling. Marcelle was halfway through an anecdote about her husband and a flying barbeque when the doorbell rang.

It was difficult for Erin to hide her shock when she saw who it was. 'I didn't think you'd come.'

Imogen's smile was weak, but it was a smile. 'I'm sorry for leaving and not answering the phone today. Running away seems to have become my default, but it needs to stop. And hearing Marcelle's voice message... well, I wanted to see her.'

Erin didn't push any further, she was just glad that Imogen was here. 'Come in.'

Like Marcelle before her, Imogen took a deep breath as soon as Erin pushed open the door to the sitting room. Two pairs of eyes looked around at them, then Marcelle was on her feet. 'Imogen. Oh, my love. It's so good to see you. I'm so glad you came.'

Imogen followed Erin into the room and Marcelle reached around Erin to clasp Imogen to her.

'Hi, Auntie Marcelle.'

There was something almost comical about a middle-aged woman calling someone 'Auntie' but, in the moment, Imogen looked young again. Maybe it was that which made her mother less anxious this time.

Once Marcelle had let her go, she took Imogen's hand and led her to Ava's seat. All the while, Erin felt like a bystander. This was playing out in front of her like a drama she had no part in.

'Ava. This is Imogen. She's come back to see you. It's okay, my darling. It's all okay now. I'm here and we're going to make this alright again.'

As her mother had watched Imogen, her brow furrowed. At Marcelle's words, her eyes widened and she whimpered like a scared animal.

Keeping hold of Imogen with her left hand, Marcelle reached out for her sister with her right. 'We need to tell the girls everything, my darling. Can I tell them? Can I tell Imogen and Erin the whole story?'

Her mother looked exhausted. And confused. Marcelle still

held onto her hand, but she looked to Erin for help. 'I'm tired. I might go to bed.'

Had she even understood what Marcelle had asked? It was so difficult to know what she was taking in and what was being lost in the mists of her mind. 'Okay, Mum. I'll come up with you.'

But her mother waved her away. 'No, no. You stay here with your friends. I'll be fine. Good night, everyone.'

As soon as she'd gone, Erin felt like she needed to apologise. 'I'm sorry. I think it's having us all here at once. It confuses her.'

Imogen shrugged. 'Well, she didn't throw me out this time. That's a bonus.'

Marcelle smiled at them both weakly. 'Your mother has been carrying everything for long enough. I need to tell you some things which might change the way you see her.'

THIRTY-FIVE

Marcelle had been looking forward to being an aunt. Thanks to the age difference between her and Ava, she was the only one of her friends to be one and she had plans to take the baby out in her pram and parade her around to everyone she knew.

Ava had laughed at her. 'I'm not giving birth to a dolly for you, you know.'

Marcelle had rolled her eyes at that. 'I'm twenty. I'm a little bit old for a doll.'

Despite the ten-year age difference, they were close. They had a brother, too, but he was hardly ever at home, so it had just been the two of them growing up. Ava had always been the clever one, her head in a book at all times. She'd always wanted to be a teacher and Marcelle had been her willing, if a little frustrating, pupil.

Even after Ava had married Frank – whose reticence had taken a turn into stern and joyless a few months after the ceremony – the two sisters had shared a lot of time together and Marcelle had planned to be the biggest help she could to her sister, especially in the first few days after Imogen's birth when she'd been so incredibly tired. But that was normal for a new mother, wasn't it?

Among the heaps of advice given to new mothers, someone had told Ava to sleep when the baby sleeps, so Marcelle hadn't noticed at first how often she took to her bed. What she did notice was how little Ava smiled, how difficult she was finding it to get dressed in the morning or to have the energy to even write a shopping list, much less cook a meal.

Then Frank had called her one night. It was so late that she and Ted were already in bed. The shrill ring of the phone on the table in the hall made her heart race as she took the stairs two at a time. '641730 who's calling please?'

'Marcelle. You need to come. She won't take the baby. I need to go to work tomorrow.'

Frank had sounded so abrupt and unfeeling. Not for the first time, Marcelle had wondered at her sister's choice of husband.

Ted – a much kinder man – had driven her to her sister's in their blue Triumph. And then driven her and baby Imogen back again. It was clear that she couldn't leave her there. She hadn't wanted to leave Ava there, either, but she was refusing to leave her bed. Frank had already gone back to the spare room and left them to it. 'I have to be up at five.' That might have been the exact moment that she started to really hate him.

Once they got the baby home, she'd insisted Ted go to bed, too. 'I can call in sick tomorrow, but you need to go in.'

She'd sat with Imogen in her arms until she'd managed to stop her crying and encouraged her to drink a little of the formula that Ted had made up in the kitchen before going to bed. Once she was quiet, she'd sat looking at her. 'Oh, baby girl. What are we going to do, eh? You need your mummy and she needs you.'

The next morning, she'd taken the bus back to Ava's house

with Imogen in her arms. The back door was open and she let herself in. 'Ava? Where are you, Ava?'

Upstairs, Ava was still in bed, in almost exactly the same position as she'd left her the previous evening. Marcelle perched on the edge beside her, shifting so that Imogen's sleeping face was close to hers. 'I've brought Imogen to see you. She's missing her mummy.'

Ava turned away.

For the next three hours, Marcelle tried everything she could to persuade her sister to get out of bed, wash her face, eat something. But nothing worked. 'We need to get you to the doctor, Ava. You need some help.'

It was heartbreaking. But when the doctor came, his verdict was cursory. He didn't actually say that she should pull herself together, but he may as well have.

Marcelle followed him to the front door, Imogen in her arms. 'Can't you give her something to help her?'

He had the front door open and was already crossing the threshold. 'If she doesn't improve, we can discuss antidepressants. But that should be a last resort.'

When Frank came home from work, he was no help at all. 'Can't you take both of them to stay with you until she's better?'

Initially, Ava refused to leave. It had been Ted, lovely gentle Ted, who'd persuaded her in the end. 'Come on Ava, love. I'm going to get it in the neck from your sister if you don't come.'

It had taken almost six months before Ava was well enough to look after Imogen again. Marcelle and Ted had given up their bedroom for her and they'd slept in the tiny spare room. He hadn't complained once. It'd made her love him even more. 'If her Frank was half the man you are, she might feel better by now.' Most nights, she ended up bringing the baby's crib into their room because Ava would just turn away when poor little Imogen cried. During the day, her elderly neighbour would come in and sit with Ava, give the baby her bottle and make sure that Ava ate something, too.

Eventually the doctor had been persuaded to prescribe medication and then – which took even longer – Marcelle had persuaded Ava to take it. Slowly, slowly she came back to herself and began to take an interest in her baby.

Leaving poor Ted alone in the spare room, she'd then spent two weeks in the double bed with Ava. It'd been like when they were young and shared a room together in their parents' tiny two-bedroom house. Except, instead of dolls and teddy bears, they had a real live baby for company.

When Imogen woke early in the morning, Marcelle would encourage Ava to go and pick her up, hold her. Sometimes she would lay her down on the bed between the two of them. She was the most beautiful baby; soft dark hair and big blue eyes that seemed to take in everything around her. She'd kick her legs as if she was running in thin air. One morning, when she grabbed at Ava's finger and held it tight, Ava looked up at Marcelle with her eyes brimming with tears. 'How can I have abandoned her like that? What kind of terrible mother am I?'

Marcelle told her again, as she had several times in the last few days. 'No, Ava. You were ill. It's not your fault.'

Imogen gurgled as if she was agreeing with her and, despite the tears, they both laughed.

A few minutes later, she spoke again without looking up. 'Will she ever forgive me?'

This time Marcelle reached across and held her hand. 'She doesn't need to forgive you, you silly thing. Look at her. She's a tiny baby. She won't even remember.'

Ava's tears fell on the blanket she'd wrapped around Imogen. She leaned in close and whispered in her ear. 'I'm so sorry, baby girl. I won't let you down again. I promise, from this point on, everything I do will be to keep you safe and happy.'

THIRTY-SIX

When Marcelle finished her story, the three of them sat in silence. From the look on Imogen's face, she was as shocked as Erin. She leaned back in her chair and rubbed at her eyes. 'I had no idea. She never told me any of this. That must have been so awful for her. I know first-hand how little support she would have had from Dad.'

Marcelle's face hardened a little. 'Don't get me started on your father. He was worse than useless. I know you shouldn't speak ill of the dead, but I honestly think she was better off without him.'

Erin's own memories of her father were patchy scraps: the rustle of his newspaper on a Saturday morning, the smell of Golden Virginia tobacco, the crisp bark of his voice. Only twelve when he died, she struggled to conjure up a whole person in her mind. Even those events she remembered, were indistinguishable between her own memories and brief references and anecdotes from her mother. Did she know that he'd liked war films and strong tea or was it only because she'd been told?

Imogen's hands fluttered from her lap to her face. 'I wish

she'd told me. It might have helped. It might have prepared me for what happened.'

Reaching for Imogen's hand, Marcelle's whole body softened towards her. 'Your mum felt guilty about it her whole life. She was sure that she'd damaged you in some way because she'd neglected you in those first few months. And then...'

'Then I got ill and she thought it was her fault.' Imogen rubbed at her temples. 'Oh, Mum.'

Fog was clearing, cogs were turning, and they were beginning to make sense of everything that had happened. Thinking back to her own pregnancy, Erin could remember how interfering her mother had been. How overprotective. Particularly when she was a new mother. It had been almost suffocating. She'd felt judged, untrusted, found wanting. But what she'd seen as her mother not believing that Erin could do it, now felt like love. And fear. Fear that what had happened to her and – worse – what had happened to Imogen, would also happen to Erin.

Marcelle and Imogen now held both hands, looking so intently at one another that Erin was merely an observer. 'I'm sorry I kept this from you for so long. After we emigrated, it was a lot easier to put the decision out of my mind. I wanted to try and contact you, Imogen, but Ava made it sound as if you wanted to be left alone. There was a part of me that wondered if there was a little jealousy there. Ava always felt jealous that I'd had the first six months with you. So, I persuaded myself that I had to do what Ava wanted. I had my own daughters with me over there, but I often thought about that baby. My first baby. You.'

She shifted forward in her seat so that they were even closer. How strange it was that Marcelle had been her mother for six months and yet these were months that Imogen would never be able to recall.

When Imogen looked up, her face was full of tears. 'I didn't know. That she'd been through it too. She never said.'

'She was ashamed, love. And she blamed herself for what happened to you. She loved you so much, Imogen. She wanted for your life to be so much easier than hers. She might not have made the right choices, but she did it for the right reasons. You have to believe that.'

A strangled sob escaped from Imogen and she covered her face with her hands. Marcelle pulled her gently into her arms and rocked her like a baby. 'It's okay. It's okay, sweetheart.'

Erin would've had to have a stone in place of her heart not to feel sympathy for Imogen, for Marcelle, for her mother. Especially after the stories she'd heard from both of them today. But there was still a part of her that dragged its heels. Had she not been wanted like this? Imogen had left. Her mother had looked after her because... why? Because she wanted a better life for Imogen, the daughter she'd loved and wanted?

Maybe she was being cruel. Her mother had looked after her, had protected her to the point of suffocation. But what love had there been? When had she pulled her onto her lap to be cuddled? Tickled her to make her laugh? Told her how amazing, clever, beautiful she was? All the things that Erin had done for Harriet had been because she'd felt the lack of them in her own life. Was this because her mother – Ava – had never really wanted her at all?

Once they pulled apart, Marcelle sighed. 'I'm so exhausted, girls. I'm going to need to go back to my hotel. I'll be back in the morning to see Ava. We can talk about this more then. Whatever you want to know.'

What else was there to know? It seemed as if the whole sorry mess was out there now. The only thing they could do was pick through it and work out how they could put it all back together.

Once they'd hugged again, Erin drove Marcelle the fifteen minutes to her hotel.

'I feel bad that you're not staying at the house. You could have had my room.'

Marcelle shook her head. 'I'm getting too old for sleepovers. I like a hotel room with my own bathroom. And you three need time to be together without me there.'

There was something in her tone that made Erin wonder how heavily the guilt of this secret had weighed on her over the years. Carrying the burden of someone else's secret. How had it affected her own mother, too? It made Erin want to pull out the memories of her childhood and pore over them through a different lens.

'She was difficult, you know. Growing up, Mum was difficult to live with sometimes.'

She felt Marcelle shift in the passenger seat to look at her. 'In what way?'

Even saying this aloud felt disloyal, but the time for pretence was over. 'She was pretty strict.'

Marcelle's voice was kind and gentle. 'Well, maybe that makes a little more sense now that you know the history?'

'And she wasn't very loving. Or warm. Or affectionate. Listening to you talk to Imogen tonight. It's made me realise it even more.'

She couldn't bring herself to say what she was really feeling. That her mother hadn't really loved her at all. She was the grandchild she hadn't expected. Then the foster child she hadn't wanted. Had she ever even thought of her as her daughter? A sick feeling of dread was seeping into her.

But Marcelle didn't seem to understand what she was asking. 'It's the way she was. Your father wasn't a good husband, Erin. She didn't have a lot of love in her life. I left, Imogen left. You can see how she wanted to make sure you were safe. Maybe that's what made her like that.'

Erin could think of nothing that would stop her wanting to hold Harriet close, love her, kiss her, be with her. The mere thought of seeing her again in two days' time made her heart yearn as if it was reaching across the ocean to find her. But Marcelle was carrying enough tonight. Why make her feel worse? 'Maybe.'

After seeing Marcelle safely to reception, she returned home to find Imogen waiting up for her. She'd changed somehow. The stiffness in her had gone, her shoulders softened, her face less constricted. 'I made tea. Would you like some?'

'No. I can't drink caffeine this late. I'm fine.' As much as Imogen looked relieved, Erin felt more confused, more adrift. She knew how rude she must sound, but – like a hormonal teenager – she couldn't stop herself.

Imogen merely nodded. 'I'd really like to hang around tomorrow if that's okay with you.' She twisted the cuff of her jumper. 'I was hoping to spend a bit of time with Mum. Maybe see if we can, I don't know, reconnect.' She laughed at the word and made inverted commas with her fingers. It was strange in Erin's ear. Was that the first time she'd ever heard her laugh? And why did it make her feel worse?

She swallowed. 'Of course. This is your mother's house after all.'

She attempted a laugh, too. But it didn't come out quite right. There was a maelstrom of emotion fighting for precedence and she didn't want to poke at it too much.

'Thanks. Look I—'

'Actually, I need to go to bed, too. Today's taken it out of me. Can I leave you to find your way to Harriet's room?' She didn't want to sound rude but there was no capacity in her right now for any more deep and emotional conversations. She needed time for this to settle.

Imogen almost shrank back into herself. 'Of course. Sleep tight.'

Those two words – something a million mothers have said to their children – made a lump in Erin's throat which meant that she could only nod and smile before leaving the room.

Imogen had clearly gained a lot from Marcelle's stories. Enough that she was hoping to build bridges in the morning. But where did that leave Erin and her mother? Either of them.

THIRTY-SEVEN

Erin hadn't slept well. Aside from the turmoil of the day before, a message from Simon pinged onto her phone around midnight to inform her that due to 'work issues' he and Carmel were staying another couple of days and Harriet was going to fly home alone. Her anger with him fought with her desperation to see Harriet as soon as possible and neither were helpful for sleep. Around 5 a.m. exhaustion must've claimed her because she woke at 9 a.m. with a start.

Her first thought was about work, but she wasn't due in until the afternoon, so that was fine. Then she remembered that Imogen was here and her mother might not be expecting her. She grabbed her dressing gown and made her way downstairs, unsure what she was about to find.

Downstairs, everything was quiet. No one in the kitchen, no one in the lounge. Then she noticed there was a note on the kitchen table. *We've gone for a walk.*

It had been so long since Erin had been alone in the house that she wasn't quite sure what to do with herself. She made a coffee and picked up her phone to scroll through Facebook. There was a memory from nine years ago, a seven-year-old

Harriet pretending to be a YouTube presenter. 'Hi, I'm Harriet. I'm going to show you how to paint a sunrise. Look, here's my paint, I'm going to start with the orange.'

She was so confident, so bright and clever. Erin watched it through three times before flicking through the memories from this day four years ago, five, six, seven, backwards in time at the flick of her thumb. Was it easier now that they stored so much of their lives online? That those memories would be there for them to access in ten, twenty, fifty years. She could barely remember Harriet being this small, her soft breathy voice as she recited a nursery rhyme in one video, her tongue poking out in another. There would be no biscuit tin of faded photographs for their generation: everything would be laid out in full colour to prompt their nostalgia.

She was jolted from her reverie by a knock on the door. Imogen and her mother both smiled at her from the doorstep. She was struck again by their likeness. Imogen followed her mother through the door. 'Sorry. I didn't know where you kept a key.'

'Where did you go?'

'There were no eggs in the cupboard so we decided to go for a walk to the shop, get some fresh air.'

Erin glanced between them; it was as if they had been doing this every day for the last thirty years. 'Are you okay, Mum?'

'Yes, dear. We're going to make some scrambled eggs. Would you like some?'

'No, I'm fine. Why don't you sit down? I can do it for you.'

Her mother laughed and waved her away. 'I'm fine. You two go and play.'

They watched her disappear into the kitchen. Who did she think they were? Was she currently in Imogen's era or Erin's? Either way, at least she seemed happy.

Imogen slipped off her jacket and hung it in the hall. Why

was Erin finding it so irritating that she was making herself at home so quickly? 'How was she? At the shops?'

Imogen smiled and her face seemed lighter, clearer than it had since Erin first met her. 'Fine. We were talking about our neighbours from the old house. She remembers so many details that I'd forgotten.'

That seemed to be the way the dementia was going. As she remembered less recent history, the distant past became clearer. 'Did she talk about anything else? The stuff Marcelle told us last night?'

'No. I stayed away from anything that might upset her. It's strange but it makes me feel closer to her than it did before. Knowing that she'd been through it, or something like it. It makes me understand her fear a little better.'

This was a good thing, so why was Erin feeling so awkward? 'Great. I'd better get into the kitchen and make sure she's okay with the cooker.'

'I can do it. Why don't you have some time to yourself?'

Erin was about to protest, but Imogen was already opening the kitchen door. 'Okay, Mum. What do you want me to do?'

Upstairs in the shower, Erin let her head fall back and the water run across her forehead. She wasn't proud of the way she was feeling, but hearing Imogen call her mother 'Mum' had been distinctly strange. Having been an only child all her life – a state she'd bemoaned frequently – it brought up unexpected feelings hearing someone else call her mother. Even more strange because, as she had to keep reminding herself, Ava wasn't *actually* her mother. Had she ever felt that she was Erin's mother or had she always, albeit privately, regarded her as the grandchild she was?

She didn't want to sit downstairs with them and play happy families, not yet. After her shower, she took her time getting dressed and drying her hair, so that the egg scrambling was over and her mother was in the sitting room watching television by the time she came back downstairs.

Imogen was cleaning up the kitchen, humming to herself. How could she have changed so quickly? She looked up at the sound of the kitchen door opening and coloured a little when she saw how stiffly Erin stood on the threshold.

'I was about to put the kettle on. Can I make you a drink?'

She sounded so tentative that Erin softened; this was strange for all of them. 'It's okay, I can do it.'

She filled the kettle and flicked it on, reached into the upper cupboard for some mugs.

'When is Harriet getting home?'

Erin turned in surprise. 'Tomorrow lunchtime. I'm collecting her from Heathrow.'

Imogen didn't make eye contact as she wiped down the kitchen counter. 'I'd love to meet her, if that's okay with you?'

Again, that awkwardness. 'Of course. I'm sure she'd love to meet you, too.'

What would Harriet make of Imogen? For the first time, Erin realised that this altered reality affected her daughter, too. Although she could imagine Harriet just taking it all in her stride. After all, who is more self-centred than a fifteen-year-old?

Up until now, she'd only told Imogen that Harriet was on holiday with her father. The whole moving across the ocean thing had been too much to get into. But if she was going to meet her, she needed to tell her the truth.

One of the things that her mother had been good at – whether she chose to take it or not – was dispensing advice. It was one of the many things that the dementia had taken from them. Throughout this process of decision-making, Erin hadn't really had anyone to talk to about it. Jasmine was great, but they hadn't been friends that long and she didn't have kids. It was difficult to explain how she felt about losing Harriet to Simon.

'She's considering whether to move there. To America. Permanently. Her father has a new job there and he wants her to live with him. With him and his new wife. And their new baby.'

She was well aware of how many times she'd used the word 'new' in that sentence. And how bitter she must sound.

Imogen raised her eyebrows. 'I see. And how do you feel about that?'

How did she think she felt? What a stupid question. Although, she was a mother who had voluntarily stayed away from her child. How could she possibly understand?

Anger flashed through her and made her brutal in her honesty. 'I don't think I can bear it. I feel as if I want to hold onto her and never let her go. Try anything to keep her here, keep her close. That's what any mother would feel, isn't it?'

If Imogen was hurt by her words, she didn't show it. 'Yes, I suppose it is. That need to protect your child runs deep. It's primeval.'

Her words hung in the air. The need to protect your child. Erin had been wrong to say what she had. 'I'm sorry. I shouldn't have said that.'

'It's okay. You should say what you feel. But your situation is very different from mine. Your Harriet knows that she is loved. She knows that you are here. That she will always have a home.'

'But she won't be here with me. She'll be with Simon and his wife. They'll be the ones who see her every day.'

'What's she like, her stepmother?'

Carmel was great, Erin had to admit that. 'She's lovely. And kind. And young and beautiful. I mean, I want to hate her but...' she smiled. 'And Harriet loves her.'

She'd wrestled with her jealousy a long time ago and, largely, she'd won. But it was a different scenario now. Carmel would be the woman who was there, that Harriet would talk to about boyfriends and school and life. She'd speak to Erin about it too, but it would be the later version, the considered, ameliorated version. Not the riot of emotion that would come tumbling out of her as she threw herself on the bed and vented about whatever was today's perceived injustice from her friend or teacher or a boy she 'kind of' liked. So many moments that Erin had taken for granted. Would she ever have them again?

Imogen was watching her closely. 'I understand.'

How could she? She might have given birth to Erin, but she had not been her mother. She couldn't let it go. 'I'm not sure you do.'

'Watch another woman step into your place and raise your child? I completely get it.' Imogen raised a hand to stop Erin's interruption. 'I know you're going to say it's completely different and you're right. But at least Harriet knows that she has a mother who loves her desperately. Who would be with her in a heartbeat if she needed her. Who's been there for her and been everything a mother should be. You've never let your daughter down, Erin, and she knows that. She knows that you love her. That you have always loved her.'

A single tear made its way down Imogen's cheek. Erin no longer knew if she was talking about Erin's situation or her own. But she knew what she was trying to say. What she *was* saying. Again, there was that fight within her, like a teenager who wants to hug their mother but cannot ask. 'Well, I'll know tomorrow what she's decided to do.'

Much as she was desperate to see Harriet tomorrow, it also felt like waiting for the executioner. Tomorrow she'd know for sure whether she got to keep her daughter a little while longer.

THIRTY-EIGHT

If Erin could have leaped the barrier to get to Harriet, she would've done. It felt like hours since the text had arrived.

I'm here! Just getting my bag.

How long did it take to collect a suitcase and walk through to arrivals? She'd been here for an hour before the flight was due at 3 p.m. and was currently flanked by two weary taxi drivers and a young man holding flowers and a hopeful expression.

Imogen had returned home yesterday and Erin had made sure that Harriet's room was ready for her return this morning before going into work. Josh had met her at reception with a smile that had made her blush for no reason at all. 'I wanted to remind you about that job application. It closes tomorrow.'

He clearly hadn't realised that Jasmine had been in the office and overheard him. As soon as he'd gone, she came out and confronted Erin. 'What job application?'

'Good morning to you, too.'

'Good morning. What job application? Have you decided to go for the hotel manager job?'

There was no getting around it this time. 'It's not for hotel manager here. It's an area manager position. Like Josh does but for northwest Kent. He thinks I should apply for it.'

Jasmine folded her arms. 'And when were you going to tell me?'

For a second, Erin faltered. She'd really grown to like Jasmine and didn't want to upset her. 'I haven't even decided whether to go for it or not. There seemed no point in saying anything.'

'But you're considering it? Thinking about leaving me here alone?'

Her mouth was so dry that Erin could barely speak. 'I'm sorry, I—'

Jasmine grinned. 'I'm messing with you, you mad woman. Of course, you should go for it, it's a great idea!'

Jasmine's encouragement made her feel guilty about what else she knew. 'I'm worried about the hotel, too. We've been so quiet lately and I'm worried head office might—'

She stopped when Jasmine held up a hand. 'I'm not silly, Erin. I know it's tough for us at the moment. But you forget that I'm amazing. I'll be fine. And you need to apply for that job. Because you're amazing, too.'

Erin breathed out in relief. 'Thank you. But I don't know if I will. There's so much going on right now and I don't know what I'd do with Mum. And I don't know what's happening with Harriet.'

'Isn't she coming home today?'

'Yes. She gets in at three. Simon needs to stay another couple of days, so she's travelling back on her own. Josh has let me book the afternoon off.' It was good of him to let her do so at such short notice. Although it meant she'd had to come into work this morning, it'd actually helped the hours to go faster. Waiting at home would have been intolerable.

'Have you thought about what you're going to say to her?'

Erin had called to check with Harriet that she felt okay about flying home alone, but they hadn't discussed anything else. 'What can I say? It has to be her decision, doesn't it? She can make it for herself in a few weeks when she turns sixteen. I've got nothing to gain by holding her back if she's made up her mind.'

She could feel herself close to tears again, so was grateful that Jasmine merely nodded and didn't press her. 'Look. If the closing date is tomorrow, why don't you apply? It doesn't mean you have to take it, does it? What have you got to lose?' She softened her voice. 'And then, if Harriet does decide to go, you'll have something to focus on.'

Thinking about that was painful, however likely it was beginning to seem. 'Maybe you're right.'

'Of course, I am. I always am. Go and fill out the application now while we're quiet. And then I can tell you all about my fabulous date with Dr Anthony.'

Erin raised an eyebrow. 'That sounds promising.'

Jasmine grinned. 'It is very promising. We've been texting non-stop. He's funny and clever and kind.'

This was high praise indeed. 'I'm so pleased for you, Jasmine.'

Jasmine blushed; this must be serious. 'I'm pleased for me too. And I'll be pleased for you when you get this job. If you ever get in that office and apply, that is.'

They'd been busier than expected all morning, but she'd got the application completed and emailed before driving to the airport an hour before she needed to be there. Apart from grabbing a coffee, she'd been rooted to the spot in arrivals ever since.

At last, the sliding doors in front of her squeaked open and – interspersed with business people and couples – families tumbled through carrying sleeping toddlers, older children stumbling behind with fractious faces, rubbing at their eyes. It was hard not to grab their arms and tell them to make the most of every difficult, irritating moment.

And then she was there. Tired but beautiful, dragging behind her a smaller case than Erin was expecting, but she didn't care about anything right now other than having her daughter in her arms.

'Harriet!' She waved furiously in a way that would normally make Harriet roll her eyes, but this time a smile spread across her face like honey on toast and she quickened her step.

And then she was in her arms. Fiercely, Erin held her tight, her face buried in Harriet's hair. Breathing her in, trying to almost absorb her back into her own body. Harriet held her tightly too. 'I missed you.'

Were there any three words more beautiful in the English language? Erin tried not to sob. 'Oh, baby girl, I missed you so much, too.'

Reluctantly, she'd let go of Harriet long enough to drive her home. Initially she was full of chatter, but – like a clockwork toy – as the effects of the time difference and the overnight flight took hold, she started to slow down and her eyelids got heavy. Until she nodded off.

At home, Erin had made sure she had all of Harriet's favourites available – Honey Loops, crumpets with Marmite, ham and cheese croissants – and had laid them out on the kitchen table like a hotel buffet, adding a banana and apple for garnish. 'I know it's gone lunchtime, but I assumed you'd still be on US time and want breakfast. You need to eat something and stay awake, otherwise you won't be tired enough to sleep tonight.'

Harriet groaned, but she dutifully slipped onto one of the chairs and started to eat. 'Thanks, Mum. Where's Gran?'

'Well, her sister is here from Australia and she's taken her out for the day. I've mentioned Auntie Marcelle before, haven't

I? You'll get to her meet her later if you promise not to fall asleep.'

'Wow. I promise to try.'

That smile was infectious. It was so good to have her home that Erin couldn't stop looking at her. How had it only been a few days?

'So, how was everything?'

'It was really great, Mum.' Her tone and face belied her words. It was as if she was trying to break bad news.

Erin wasn't quite ready for the answer to the big question. 'And you said the house was great.'

'Really great.'

She'd heard all about this on their FaceTime chats, so she wasn't sure why Harriet was being so reticent now.

'And the area?'

'That's great, too.'

She tried to keep her voice light. 'Well, that's a lot of great things. Anything you didn't like?'

She laughed but it sounded hollow and Harriet didn't smile. 'I didn't like that you're not there.'

She couldn't have sliced into Erin any more sharply if she'd used the knife in her hand. For a moment she was winded. What could she say to that?

Harriet seemed to realise that this was her moment. 'I really want to go and live there, Mum. But I don't want to make you sad. And I know that I will really miss you.'

As hard as she'd tried to lie to herself, she'd known that this was coming. But it didn't make it any easier. All she could do was keep breathing and hope that the right words would come. 'If it's really as great as you say, then you have to go, love. I know that your dad wants you to go, too. It'll be an adventure.'

Lack of sleep and emotional subjects were never a strong point for Harriet and the corners of her mouth turned down before her lip began to wobble. 'I don't want to hurt you. I don't want you to think that I'm choosing Dad over you because I'm not. I'm really, really not. I love you so much and I missed you like crazy every day.'

When you're told that a mother makes sacrifices, you think of the sleepless nights and the wrecking of your body and the nights you have to stay home. But they are easy when compared with the biggest sacrifice. The one where you have to let them go. Worse; you have to make them feel as if they can walk away and not look back. Freedom without strings.

Erin forced a smile onto her face in the hope that she could mask the grief that was fighting to get through. 'I'll be fine, baby. I've got your gran and I'm going to apply for a new job. A promotion.' Jasmine was right. If this was really happening, she needed something big to throw herself into.

'Really?' The relief on Harriet's face was palpable. 'That's so great, Mum! I'm so proud of you. You'll really be okay without me?'

That was too much to ask. But she had to say it. 'Of course, darling. I'll miss you every single minute. But I will definitely be okay.'

The kitchen chair scraped on the floor as Harriet pushed it backwards to get to Erin. Though she was far too big to fit on Erin's lap, she tried her best and – just for a moment – she was Erin's little girl again.

At around five, Marcelle and Ava arrived home and it was as if her mother had had a new lease of life. She greeted Harriet with a hug and asked where she'd been today. Though she got a little confused when Harriet tried to explain that she'd been in America, she was happy enough to go along with the conversation. Erin managed to keep Harriet awake until 8 p.m. before she was so exhausted that she begged to go to bed.

Marcelle whispered to Erin in the corner of the kitchen. 'I didn't realise how bad it had got.'

'The dementia? I know. It's hard to know what she takes on board and what she doesn't.'

'She talked a lot about Imogen today.'

Again, a streak of jealousy ran through Erin. She was pleased for them both, but couldn't help feeling that, the closer they got, the more she was squeezed out. 'Oh, yes?'

'I'm so pleased that they've had the opportunity to come back together like this. Before it's too late.'

She knew what Marcelle meant. Before the dementia had taken so much of her mother that they could no longer find a way back to each other. 'Yes.'

Marcelle paused. 'You did that for them. You were stronger than I was.'

Erin hadn't thought about it like that. What would've happened if she'd never found out about Imogen? Or if she'd been put off by that first abrupt phone conversation and let sleeping dogs lie? Right here, right now, she still wasn't sure if she was better off than she had been back then. 'Well, it's up to them now, isn't it?'

Marcelle tilted her head. 'And what about you? How do you feel about Imogen?'

How could she sum it up? 'I... don't know. It's been a lot to take in.'

'They both love you, you know. I know it's hard to see it that way, but it's like you've had two mothers instead of one.'

She didn't want to upset her aunt or make a scene. But Erin couldn't see this situation through the same set of rose-coloured spectacles. In many ways, she felt the opposite. Like she'd not really had a mother at all. 'Maybe.'

'I'm not saying they got it right. But we're all flawed aren't we, us mothers? None of the decisions we make are impartial because we're programmed to protect our children: it's in our

DNA. It's why mothers throw themselves over their children when a bomb goes off, or in front of them when there's a rabid dog. Or push them away when they think that they will be better off without them.' Marcelle reached out and rubbed her arm. 'Give them a chance, Erin. Both of them. Let them show you that they love you.'

THIRTY-NINE

It was the most surreal of experiences introducing Harriet to Imogen. Erin had dropped her mother off to The Oasis an hour before Imogen arrived, so it was just the three of them.

'So, you're my grandmother?'

Imogen look startled, then glanced at Erin who shrugged. 'I suppose I am.'

Harriet looked between the two of them. 'I can see a likeness.'

That surprised Erin, she'd been more focused on the ways in which Imogen looked like Ava.

Imogen seemed to enjoy the comparison. 'I can see your mum in you. And,' she paused as if to test the water before she spoke, 'I can see some of your mum's father in you, too.'

'Wow.' Harriet was nodding. 'I'm made up of scraps of people that I don't even know about yet. That's pretty interesting.'

As understatements went, that was a big one.

Once Harriet had disappeared to her bedroom to call her friends, Imogen repeated what she'd said about Harriet looking like Erin's father. 'It's not a bad thing. He was a nice guy. And very handsome.'

'Where is he now?'

'I don't know. But I can help you to find him if you'd like to?'

'I'm not sure. I'm assuming that he wasn't really interested in me?'

'He was very young. And his family were pretty persuasive. I think he probably deserves a chance.'

At the moment, Erin was finding it difficult enough to navigate two mothers. Maybe in the future she could think about finding her father, too.

Imogen was clearly thinking about something else. 'Were you like Harriet? When you were sixteen, I mean.'

'She is prettier than me. And more talented. Possibly more sarcastic.' She smiled. 'But, yes. I think we are alike.'

Imogen's smile turned down at the edges. 'I wish I'd known you then.'

That reminded Erin of something. 'I have something to show you. Wait there a moment.'

She ran upstairs to her wardrobe and found what she was looking for. As she walked past Harriet's bedroom, she heard her laughter and then the tinny responses of her friends on their group chat. Even ordinary moments like that felt inordinately precious now she knew that Harriet was going.

Imogen hadn't moved from her seat and she looked up as Erin came towards her. 'What are those?'

Erin held out the box of envelopes, different shapes and sizes but stacked in order from the first to the thirty-eighth. One for each year of her life. 'They're addressed to you.'

Imogen took the box from her as if it were an incendiary device that might go off in her hand. 'Where did they come from?'

'I found them in Mum's loft. I've been keeping them in my room. Waiting to give them to you.'

Imogen raised an eyebrow. It occurred to Erin for the first time just how much she looked like Ava when she did that. 'And you weren't tempted to open them? Read what was inside?'

It had become increasingly difficult to resist them, but she'd managed it. 'They're not addressed to me.'

With trembling fingers, Imogen took the letter on the top, then a second, then a third. Her eyes were full when she looked up at Erin again. 'They're dated. Your birthday.'

Erin swallowed. Nodded. 'I assume she wanted to tell you about me. Maybe she planned to send them to you someday.'

Imogen stared at the three envelopes in her hand, brushing her finger over her name on the topmost one. A butter yellow rectangle, thick enough to *shush* as she moved her finger across each letter. 'She didn't know where I was.'

It was as if this had just occurred to her. The thought that her mother had sat down to write to her each year, with no idea where she lived, what she was doing. Had she hoped to send them, that maybe that was the year that she would see her daughter again? 'Are you going to open them?'

Imogen looked up at her. 'I'm not sure where to start? Do I go backwards or forwards?'

'It's up to you. Maybe starting at the beginning makes sense.'

She nodded and smiled weakly. 'Okay. I'm going in.'

That first envelope had sat in the box for over three decades, so the glue which held it closed had dried and it was easy to pop it open without tearing. That was the easy part. Imogen slid the folded pages from its embrace and held them between her fingertips as if waiting for the voice within to begin. Maybe she felt conspicuous. 'Should I leave you alone to read them?'

She shook her head. 'Please don't. Why don't you open some of them? This is your history after all.'

Erin wanted to. Since finding the letters, they'd called to her from their resting place at the bottom of her wardrobe. But now she was anxious about what they might reveal. Yes, it was her history, but it was also another country that she didn't know she wanted to revisit. 'I'll read them after you.'

With trembling fingers, Imogen read through the letter in her hand. Erin watched as her eyes hungrily ate up the words, her face twitching from smile to frown and back again. When she finished, she closed her eyes, then handed it to Erin. 'It's all about you. About the things you did. You should read this.'

Erin had barely taken it from her when Imogen picked up another. Now she'd begun, she seemed almost desperate to absorb everything from it.

Her mother's handwriting had been so precise and perfectly formed. Now, if she wrote anything at all, there was a shaken form to it which sometimes made it difficult to discern the *o* from the *a* and the *e*. Here though, was the hand of the schoolteacher she'd known as she grew up.

But if she was expecting the practical, prosaic informative letter she'd seen her mother write in the past, this was not what she found.

My Dearest Imogen,

How have you been gone for almost a year? Erin has changed so much in the last few months and my heart breaks that you are missing her becoming a little girl. I wish you would come home.

Erin looked at the date in the corner of the envelope. She would have been two when this letter was written. This must have been before Imogen's last disastrous return to the house.

Erin's favourite toy is the little kitchen that your Uncle Ted made for you, do you remember? I found it in the garage underneath some tarpaulin. It needed a rub down and some paint, but I was pleased with the result and Erin loves nothing more than making us 'dinner' and setting the table for us to sit and 'eat'.

She'd forgotten that kitchen. Now she remembered a red plastic saucepan and plastic food. There was a strange green vegetable that she'd never recognised. And plastic tins of tomato soup and packets of cereal. She'd never known that the kitchen had once belonged to anyone else. How must that have felt for her mother to watch her following in Imogen's footsteps?

She's very quick to learn anything. Much like you were at that age. And she charms everyone she speaks to. The postman, the lady at the shop on the corner, people on the street. People seem to gravitate towards her and then she rewards them with a smile. Sometimes it takes my breath away. She has your beautiful smile. You would love her so much, Imogen. It's impossible not to.

That final sentence was like a punch to the heart. It was impossible not to love her? Her mother had loved her? She read to the end of the letter. Details about her favourite food and the words she could say and the nursery that she'd been enrolled in. Then the final paragraph was a plea to Imogen.

I don't know if I'll ever be able to show you this letter, but I wish you would come home my darling girl. I am doing my best, but Erin needs her mummy. And I need my daughter home. Please come home.

Imogen was reading much faster than her. Already, she'd dropped another letter onto Erin's lap and she was busily reading a third. Erin picked it up and started to read as much as she could through blurred vision. As she unfolded another letter, her mind unfolded the memory that went with it. How had she thought that her mother didn't love her enough?

Was love any less because it wasn't displayed for all to see? Did it have to manifest in physical touch – kisses, hugs, strokes of the hair – or was it just as valid in acts of service? Making sure that her clothes were always pressed and ready to wear. Attending every parents' evening, sports day and school play. Always leaving her favourite flavour of crisps in the multipack of flavours even though she, too, liked salt and vinegar best.

Because her mother had done all of those things for her. And many many more.

'You're crying.' It wasn't so much a question as a statement of fact, but Imogen looked at her with curiosity.

'I'm remembering. All of these things. I'd forgotten. You're crying too.'

Imogen's face wasn't crumpled like hers. But the tears were there all the same. Her expression was more that of one who had grown used to sadness. She wore it lightly. 'I wish I had those memories. I wish I'd seen you at each of these ages. I've missed so much.'

There was no getting away from it. She'd missed out on all the years that'd made Erin who she was. Day after day, week after week, like bricks in a wall, she'd built herself into the woman she was. Some of those bricks had been made by her mother, others she had made for herself.

Like waves, memories coursed through her of the events in these letters. Primary school shows where her mother had been at work all day but had sat up late to make her costume, evenings when she'd helped her to practise for a French test when the vocabulary wouldn't stick, mornings she'd run to the shops to get ingredients for a cooking lesson which Erin had forgotten until the last minute.

Where she'd felt overlooked and unimportant, her mother had been fighting a battle she didn't know about. She'd been a woman who'd lost her daughter, been thrust into a role she didn't want, had to juggle and sacrifice and struggle to do what she could. 'It wasn't her fault.'

Imogen winced, her face taut. 'No. It was my fault. All of this is my fault.'

She didn't want her feeling like that again. 'You were ill.'

'Yes. I was. And then I was scared. Not just of being ill again, but of hurting you. Of ruining your life. But I shouldn't have let the fear win. It's taken everything from me. And from Mum. And from you.'

It was time to let all of that go. Erin reached out for Imogen's hand. 'I want you to stay here. With us. With Harriet gone, there'll be a spare room and we don't know how long we have with Mum as she is. At the moment, she still knows who we are, but that won't last forever. Come and stay with us.'

Imogen wiped at her cheeks. 'Really? Do you think she'd want that? Mum? What if she gets upset and asks me to leave again?'

It was a distinct possibility. 'She might do that. As her memories wax and wane, she might push either of us away. But there's still time for us to try. Look at these letters. She never stopped loving you. She loved both of us.'

Now Erin's eyes filled with tears. She *had* loved them both. She'd been scared too. But she'd loved them in the only way she knew how.

Imogen gave her a watery smile. 'If you want me to come, I would love that.'

Suddenly, it wasn't confusing any longer. It was a mother

and it was love. Erin reached for Imogen at the exact same moment as Imogen reached for her and then they were in each other's arms and neither of them ever wanted to let go.

FORTY

Erin had planned to book a day off for Harriet's last day in England, but Harriet's friends wanted to see her that morning, so she'd come to work after making Harriet promise that she would return home by five so that they could spend some time together tonight.

Jasmine was halfway through telling her about her latest conversation on Bumble when Erin's phone dinged with a new email. When she glanced down and saw who it was from, she couldn't help but squeal.

Jasmine stopped mid-sentence. 'What? What's the matter?'

'I've had an email. About the job.'

'Really? Open it! What did they say?'

Erin scrolled through to the second paragraph. 'They want me to come in for an interview next week.'

'Well, that's great, isn't it? Well done.'

She felt sick at the very thought. And it wasn't helped when Josh arrived and Jasmine announced it to him.

'I know. I heard. That's great news.'

Jasmine was called away to check out a young couple with a really long bar bill that they wanted to verify line by line. The husband was counting the number of glasses of Chardonnay that his wife had drunk every night, while she rolled her eyes at Jasmine.

Erin turned to Josh. 'I'm nervous about this interview. What kind of things will they ask me?'

'I can coach you, if you like? I've been part of the interview panel for these kinds of positions. Funnily enough, I was supposed to be on the panel for this one.'

She frowned. 'And you won't be?'

He flushed. 'Ah, no. I didn't think it would be appropriate in the circumstances.'

Now it was her turn to feel the heat creep up her face. 'Because we work together?'

He laughed. Then coughed. 'No. Because then I wouldn't be able to ask you if you'd like to go out afterwards. For a drink. Or coffee. Or whatever.'

Was he asking her on a date? Before she could answer, Jasmine had sidestepped towards them and spoke through her grimace-like smile. 'See, this is why I don't want to ever get married. He's asking her whether she ate the nuts from the minibar now.'

She sidled back to the couple in time to see the wife snatch the bill from her husband's hand and slap it onto the counter. 'Just pay it.'

Josh grinned at her and she returned the smile. 'A drink afterwards would be lovely, as long as you don't count how many peanuts I have.'

Initially, she'd planned that evening to be just her and Harriet, but Marcelle was back from Yorkshire before her flight home and she'd wanted to see Ava and Imogen again before she left. 'This might be the last time I come back.'

In actual fact, it was probably better that they were all there.

In company, Erin was less likely to break down and beg Harriet to stay.

Harriet herself was on really good form. She sat on a footstool at Ava's feet and told them all about the art department in the school she would be going to.

'I loved art at school.' Imogen spoke so softly that she was almost speaking to herself.

Harriet grinned at her. 'Really? No one else in the family is interested in art. Maybe I get it from you.'

Imogen laughed. 'I'm sure you're far more talented than I was. Do you remember me drawing pictures, Mum?'

Now Ava laughed. 'You used to draw on everything. Your books. Your napkin. Your father's newspaper. He used to get so cross.'

The whole evening was rather lovely. The five women, four generations, sharing memories until Ava's grandmother clock chimed 11 p.m. and Harriet yawned.

Erin reached over and tapped her on the knee. 'I hate to be a party pooper, but I think it's time for you to get to bed, sweetheart.'

She glanced at the time on her phone. 'You're right. But, before I go, I have something for you, Mum. Well, it's for you and Gran really.' She frowned as she looked around the room. 'Maybe for all of you. It'll make sense when I show you.'

Once she'd gone, Marcelle reached over and patted Erin's hand. 'She's a lovely girl, Erin. You've done a good job on her.'

Ava surprised them by adding her voice. 'She is a lovely girl.'

This unexpected praise choked Erin. 'Thanks, Mum.'

The door opened and Harriet walked straight to the dining table holding a huge sheet of paper. 'This is the project I was supposed to do for the sixth form college. I won't need it now, but I wanted to finish it.' She laid it out on the table. Slightly bigger than A3, it took up half the space. Standing back, she held out her hands towards it, looking equal parts proud and unsure. 'It's my collage. I've called it Memories.'

Marcelle helped Ava to her feet and the four women approached the table. The collage was beautiful. There were photographs of Ava and Marcelle as little girls, the photograph of Ava holding Imogen in Marcelle's garden, school photographs of Harriet, family groups of Erin, Harriet and Ava. Interspersed with the photographs were scraps of fabric which Erin recognised as belonging to Harriet's school uniform, an old blanket she'd had as a baby, a crocheted square that'd been donated by Ava from a collection under her bed. Then there was text. Printed screenshots of WhatsApp messages between Erin and Harriet, a torn section of a letter in Ava's handwriting, a white square with calligraphy: *Memory believes before knowing remembers. William Faulkner.*

'This is amazing, Harriet.' She couldn't believe the scope of this, the way each piece connected and overlapped in a way that seemed natural and perfect.

'Thanks, Mum.'

'It really is.' Imogen held out a finger and stroked the picture of Ava and her, unwittingly echoing her mother's actions weeks before. 'You have a real talent.'

'I like it, but I don't understand it.' They laughed at Marcelle's frown and her hands on her hips.

'It's a collage, Auntie Marcelle. It comes from the French *coller*, which means to paste or glue.' Harriet pointed to the overlap of paper and fabric. 'It's Modernist. Picasso did it.'

'Oh.' Marcelle paused. 'Nope. None the wiser.'

Harriet didn't seem remotely put out. 'You paste or glue fragments of different media, like photographs or pictures or text, anything really. You bring them together to make something new. Some of the pictures are copies of the ones in Granny's tin and some are from Mum's computer.'

Marcelle still had questions. 'So why are they torn? And why do some of them have pieces missing?'

Erin looked closer; she hadn't noticed that. In some of the text, words had been cut out, or it had been clipped mid-sentence.

'I wanted to show that that is what memory is like. Sometimes it's not perfect, things are missed or get lost.' She glanced at Ava. 'Sometimes it dissolves.'

'And why are some of them on their side? Or upside down?'

'Because,' Harriet reached for the corner of the page and turned it through ninety degrees, 'everyone will see it differently according to where they are standing. Like memories. Everyone has their own version. And sometimes you have to look at something a different way to get to the truth.'

Through blurred eyes, Erin saw Imogen's hand flutter to her mouth. She reached an arm around Harriet's shoulder and kissed her. 'My clever, clever girl.'

She felt a light touch on her shoulder and looked left into Imogen's tearful face.

Her mother sighed. 'Look at my beautiful girls. Where are they?'

'We're here, Mum.' Erin's throat was so thick that she could barely get the words out. 'I'm here. And Imogen is here, too.'

'My Imogen?' Her voice was so eager, so hopeful.

Imogen stepped closer, tears running down her cheeks. 'I'm here, Mum. I'm back and I'm not going anywhere again.'

Ava looked from one to the other of them, back at the collage, and then at their faces. Hope prickled in Erin's chest at the recognition in her mother's eyes. Was she here in the moment? Did she understand who they were?

She turned to Imogen first. 'He said it was my fault. Frank. Your dad. He said I'd made you like that. After I was ill, I tried to make it up to you. I loved you so very much. But Frank said I'd made you weak. He said it was my fault.'

Imogen shook her head. 'It wasn't your fault, Mum. I was ill, too.'

Ava rubbed at her temples as if she was retrieving slivers of memory with her fingertips. 'But that was my fault, too. You must have got it from me. That's what Frank said.'

Was there any substance in the world as heavy as maternal guilt? And her mother had carried this weight for the whole of Erin's life. She could see the pain in Imogen's eyes as she reached for her mother's hand. 'He was wrong, Mum. My illness wasn't your fault.'

Her mother grasped the hand that Imogen was reaching towards her. 'But I was still wrong. I stopped you being with your baby. I was scared. Frank said that if you came back, I had to make you take the baby. I begged him. I got down on my knees and begged him to let me find you. Pleaded with him to let you come and stay with us again. But he wouldn't have it. If she comes back here, she's leaving with that child. That's what he said.'

Erin flinched at the reference to herself. She hadn't been close to the man she'd called Dad, but she'd had no idea how cold he was. Marcelle was shaking her head in anger. 'That man has so much to answer for.'

'But it's my fault. I shouldn't have done it, should I?' Ava's eyes searched Imogen's face; was she looking for denunciation or absolution? 'I was so certain that you wouldn't cope on your own. I thought I had to be strong for you. Take care of your baby. So that you had a chance to start again. I'm sorry, I'm so sorry. I should have trusted you.'

Imogen had to fight to get the words out. 'How could you have trusted me when I didn't trust myself?'

Keeping a fast hold on Imogen's hand, Ava turned to Erin. 'I was so scared for you, too. You were so tiny, so helpless. But I knew I couldn't make the same mistakes. Couldn't let my feelings get in the way. I had to be strong for you. I had to help you to be strong. I thought that, if I told you about your mum, you would go looking for her and I was terrified what might happen. And I was terrified that I would lose you both. I'm sorry, Erin. I was wrong and weak and I don't expect you to forgive me.'

Erin had been lied to her whole life. It was too big to ever forgive, yet it was the only thing she could do. Who knew how long before these fragments of her mother's memory no longer existed? The past must be allowed to go with them. They had to look to the future now: it was all they had. 'I forgive you, Mum.'

Imogen nodded. 'We both do.'

When her mother began to quietly weep, Erin realised that she'd never seen her cry before. Not when she sliced the top from her finger cutting carrots, not when she'd first been diagnosed with dementia, not even at her father's funeral. Now the sobs shook her frail body as if someone had their hands on her shoulders. As one, she and Imogen moved to hold her close and the three of them entwined their arms around one another like a statue of the fates.

Marcelle had her arm around Harriet. 'Oh, Ava. You've got both your girls. They're here.'

Daughter? Mother? Grandmother? Did it matter any longer? Erin felt her mother's arms tighten around them. 'My girls. My beautiful girls. They're safe. They're home.'

FORTY-ONE

Heathrow airport was huge. Erin checked Simon's email several times to check that they had the right terminal and gate. They'd also set off from home an hour before they needed to, so it was hardly surprising that they were early.

Simon had suggested he collect Harriet from home the night before so that she could come in the taxi with him and Carmel today, but Erin had wanted to come. Even one night more with Harriet felt precious right now and she wanted to take her as far as she could.

The car trip had been strained, Harriet was clearly nervous and Erin felt the need to be unnaturally positive and enthusiastic about how lovely it would be to fly business class with her dad. It was when she'd recounted the stories she'd heard of tiny little individual salt and pepper shakers that she realised Harriet wasn't even listening, so they'd driven the last fifteen minutes in silence.

The short stay car park was only a five-minute walk to the terminal. Harriet had insisted on dragging her own suitcase and carrying her bag despite Erin's offer to take one of them. 'I need to learn to do it all myself.'

Her tone was sharp, as if Erin was the one abandoning Harriet, as if Harriet was cross with her for something she'd no idea that she'd done. Still, she didn't want any kind of argument with her today. 'Okay, love.'

Once they'd found the number of the desk where she'd check in – which was also where they'd arranged to meet Simon – they found a Costa with a spare table. Harriet sat with the bags while Erin queued for drinks.

Waiting behind a man who was ordering as if he'd never been in a coffee shop before, she looked over at Harriet who was scrolling through something on her phone. Her face serious and heartachingly beautiful. Even in the last six months she'd grown so much, yet she still looked to Erin like the little girl who'd loved coming to Costa to get a tiny babycino in a tiny cup and saucer. In those days, she'd wanted to be like Erin in every way – *let's both wear our black boots, Mummy, let's both have a ponytail, Mummy, let's both wear blue today, Mummy* – and now her child was going to be thousands of miles away and she would spend the next weeks, or months, only seeing that face on a computer screen.

She took a deep breath so that she could order the drinks. She was not going to cry; she was not going to make this difficult for Harriet.

Back at the table, with their drinks in their hands, she tried again with the upbeat conversation. 'I wonder what the temperature is like over—'

'I don't want to go.'

Harriet cut off her words and took the wind out of her. She hadn't been expecting this. Harriet was staring down into her teacup, her cheeks flushed in the way that had always precipitated tears.

It took every ounce of self-control not to blurt out *don't go, then* and take Harriet home. But she knew that this was only a momentary fear and it wouldn't be right to use it to her advantage. 'It's going to be okay, sweetheart. Dad is going to be here soon and then he'll sort everything out and you'll feel better about it all.'

Harriet's voice was thick and her eyes were full of tears. 'But I don't want to leave you, Mum. I don't want to be away from you. I'll miss you too much.'

'Hey.' She put down her cup and pulled Harriet in close, pressing her face into the top of her head and rocking her gently. The smell of Harriet's coconut shampoo was so familiar it made her heart squeeze. Harriet was properly crying now, not caring who could see her and Erin let her own tears fall into her daughter's hair. Those were the words that Erin had longed to hear these last two weeks. But she knew that they came from fear. And hadn't that been her job since Harriet was a small child waking from a nightmare, a four-year-old starting school, a teenager going to her first sleepover. Smoothing away her fears with a gentle hand and a soothing voice?

After a few moments, she pushed herself away from her daughter and looked into her red eyes. 'I'll miss you, too. So very much. But we can talk every day. Twice a day if you want. And I'll come and visit and you can come home.'

Harriet's trembling lip was almost unbearable. 'But what about you? How are you going to be without me there?'

'I'll be fine, sweetheart. I've got Granny to look after and Imogen to get to know better. And there's the new job.'

'And Josh?'

There wasn't much that got past her. 'And maybe Josh, yes.'

'I'm glad.' Then her face crumpled again in a way that belied her words. 'But what if I don't like it over there? What if I don't make any friends? What if I'm lonely?'

These were all the same fears that had kept Erin awake last night, that Harriet would be lost and isolated and scared. Except that the opposite was almost as terrifying for her: that she loved it so much that she never came home. 'No friends?

That would never happen to you. You will always have friends because of how lovely you are. People can sense that. Plus, you'll have an English accent in an American school. We've both watched enough high school movies to know how that turns out.'

A fragile smile appeared on Harriet's lips. 'Are you sure you're going to be okay?'

Bless her generous-hearted, thoughtful girl. 'I'll be fine. I can't wait to hear all your stories of what you get up to.'

'And Dad said you can come and stay whenever you want. There's a whole guest suite you can use.'

She wasn't so sure about that, but she nodded. 'That will be lovely.'

As if they'd summoned him, Simon appeared beside their table, on the other side of the waist-high barrier. 'Hello. I thought I'd find you two in here. Check-in has opened. Shall we go?'

Erin waited while they checked in their luggage and then walked with the three of them to departures. Carmel, looking like an advert for an airport magazine, was particularly friendly and she took the opportunity to speak to Erin quietly. 'Thank you for letting Harriet come. I know it can't be easy, but I promise we will make her happy. Keep her happy, I mean.'

'Thank you. I know how kind you are to her. Thank you for all you do.'

'It's my pleasure. Like I said, I know I'm not her mum, but I do love her like a daughter.'

Even a few weeks ago, Erin would've been jealous at the very thought, but the events of the last couple of weeks had changed her. Maybe two mothers *was* even better than one. 'I know. Thank you.'

The departure gate was difficult. She held Harriet close and didn't want to let go. She wanted to absorb her sharp elbows and soft skin, the smell of her moisturiser and shampoo. When she let go, it would be the last time she held her for a long, long time.

But let go she must. She kissed her soft cheek. 'Have a wonderful flight, baby.'

'Thanks, Mum. I'll be sure to use the little salt cellar.'

Her words made Erin laugh, but her damp smile pierced her heart. 'I love you.'

'I love you, too.'

She stood and watched them walk away. Just before they joined the queue, Simon broke away from the group and came back to her. Unexpectedly, he reached out his arms to hug her. 'I know how hard this is for you. Thank you.'

A sob lodged in her throat and made it hard to speak. She could only manage a whisper. 'Look after my baby.'

He looked her dead in the eye. 'I will. I promise.'

Then he jogged back to Carmel and Harriet and put an arm around Harriet's shoulders. She must've been feeling apprehensive because she slipped an arm around his waist, something Erin hadn't seen her do in public for a long time.

Then her face turned to look at Erin and she mouthed, 'I love you, Mum.'

'I love you, too.'

So very much, she loved her. And that's why she had to let her go.

FORTY-TWO

When she emerged from her job interview, Josh was waiting for Erin in the lobby. 'How did it go?'

It had been a pretty intense hour, being quizzed by the HR manager and two of the senior managers from head office, but Erin had a feeling that they'd been impressed with her answers. 'Good, I think. They asked me about my past experience and how many hotels I've worked at. They even asked me about the fast-track programme because I put it on my CV. They wanted to know why I hadn't taken the move into management sooner.'

The revolving door to the outside stopped their conversation until they were out in the fresh air. 'And did you explain?'

She'd been completely honest about her desire to put her daughter first back then. And how her circumstances had changed. 'Yes, I told them everything. So we'll see how painful honesty pans out.'

They were outside a coffee shop by now and Josh pointed to a table in the sunshine. It was lovely to feel the warmth on her face and she closed her eyes for a moment. When she opened them, Josh was smiling at her. 'Well, I think they want to get someone in quite quickly so I reckon you should hear pretty soon.'

No sooner had he spoke, than his phone dinged with a message. He glanced at her then, grinning, read the text aloud. 'Thanks for the recommendation, mate. Erin is exactly what we're looking for. HR are emailing her now.'

She couldn't quite believe it. 'What?! Wow! That was really fast.'

'Congratulations! Maybe we should be ordering champagne rather than coffee?'

Feeling giddy and overwhelmed, there was no way she'd trust herself with alcohol right now. 'A latte will be fine. Thanks for putting me forward for the position, Josh. I really do appreciate it.'

He held out his hands as if it was nothing. 'It was a no-brainer. I knew you'd be great for it.'

Despite being happy she'd got the job, something was still troubling Erin. 'What's going to happen to the hotel, though?'

She couldn't help but worry about Jasmine and her colleagues. They were good people and were good at their jobs. It wasn't their fault that the business had taken such a hit. Josh sat back in his chair, his blue eyes inviting her to trust him. 'Look, nothing has been decided for certain yet, but don't worry, everyone else will be offered a job within the group. Whatever happens, I'm planning on offering Jasmine a promotion in one of the other hotels. If you don't poach her first, of course.'

She returned his smile. 'And how about you? Will you be off to save another part of the business?'

Josh shrugged. 'I don't know, I'm getting a little tired of troubleshooting. But at least we'll be colleagues now. I won't be your boss any more.'

She realised that she was going to have to start learning how to be a boss. How to manage other people. Her stomach thrilled at the thought of a new challenge. She was going to learn so much in the next year. Maybe she would learn enough to get her own hotel one day. Maybe it wasn't too late? 'I guess we will.'

His expression became a little more serious. 'And if I'm not your boss... maybe I can take you out for a proper drink sometime, rather than just a supportive post-interview coffee?'

Now her stomach flipped for a whole other reason. It'd been a long time since anyone had looked at her like that and she felt as light-headed as a teenager. Her smile was so wide, it made her ears tickle. 'Yes. I'd like that.'

By the time Erin got home, though, the adrenalin of success had subsided and the reality of the extra responsibility – and hours – was starting to erode her confidence. The email from human resources had arrived with a formal offer of the job, but she hadn't yet replied.

In the sitting room, Imogen was with her mother going through the tin of photographs that Harriet had found all those weeks ago. Despite having several days to serve on her notice at the pub, she'd begun to move her things into Erin's bedroom. Though Harriet had said it was okay, Erin hadn't wanted Imogen to move into her bedroom. She wanted it to be left as it was, waiting for Harriet to come back whenever she chose. Instead, she herself was planning to sleep in Harriet's room while she was gone. It meant she felt a little closer to her, too.

Imogen smiled as she came into the sitting room. It was surprising how quickly it'd felt as if she'd always been here. 'How did the interview go?'

Erin sank down onto the chair. 'It was good! They've offered me the job.'

Imogen put down the photographs she was holding. 'Wow, that's amazing. Congratulations.'

'Thanks.'

Imogen frowned. 'You don't look very happy about it. I thought you wanted the promotion.'

She did. Very much. But now that the excitement of being found good enough was over, she couldn't help but consider the logistics. Yesterday, she'd taken her mother for an appointment with her consultant. From a few simple tests, he'd confirmed what she'd suspected: the dementia had progressed. Again, he wouldn't be pressed into giving her a specific timeline for what they could expect, but he had told her to be prepared for her mother to need more care.

'I do want the promotion. But I might be needed here. What if anything happens at home and I am two hours away in the car?'

She was trying to be tactful with her mother sitting right there and Imogen knew that. 'But I'll be here.' She turned to their mother. 'We'll be okay, won't we, Mum?'

'Yes, dear.' Their mother had got used to Imogen being there surprisingly quickly. Erin wasn't sure if she always had it clear in her head, who was who, but did that matter? Yes, it was going to get more difficult and they had some tough times ahead, but right now she was going to enjoy having the three of them together. Still. It was a big ask for Imogen to take over her care.

'I can't expect you to do that.'

Imogen turned back towards her. 'You're not asking me. I want to do it. I need to stop running, Erin. You asked me if I wanted be part of this family again. Isn't that what families do? Support each other?'

It was a lovely sentiment, but it wasn't as easy as that. 'I don't want to be unkind, but, well, what if you're not well again?'

Imogen didn't appear to take offence. 'That might happen. But we can deal with it then. Being with the two of you feels... it feels really good. I want us to be a family. I want us to make new memories together, Erin. And we don't have all the time in the world.'

They both looked at her mother, who was choosing photographs from the biscuit tin, smiling at faces from her past. Imogen had brought the picture frame from her flat, the one of her with a baby Erin, and now it sat proudly on the mantelpiece in its rightful place. Erin still had the copy that she'd given her in her handbag, and she pulled it out and gave it to her mother.

Her mother beamed. 'Look at that. My two beautiful girls. I'll put it with the others, where it belongs.'

For so long, Erin had felt like she had no one to turn to, no one to look to for help. And here was Imogen, a mother that she didn't even know she had, supporting her and being there for her. And it was more than that. Learning the truth about her childhood had brought a new understanding and brought her closer to Ava than she'd ever been before. She'd thought she wasn't wanted by either of them, when they'd both loved her all along.

As she placed the photo on the top of the pile in the old biscuit tin which held their family history, Erin smiled at her mother. Both of them. They were all where they belonged.

A LETTER FROM EMMA

Dear reader,

I want to say a huge thank you for choosing to read *Please Take My Baby*. If you did enjoy it, and want to keep up to date with all my latest releases, just sign up at the following link. Your email address will never be shared and you can unsubscribe at any time.

www.bookouture.com/emma-robinson

Please Take My Baby has the theme of memory at its core, which is something that has always fascinated me. Why do we remember some things and not others? Where do those memories live? Why do people remember the same event in different ways? Ava and Imogen see the same events from different perspectives and Erin has to accept, as we all do, that sometimes you need to leave the past where it is and look to the future.

However, when I get to the end of a first draft, I often read back and realise that, beneath the story, I have been processing something from my own life. This time, Erin's feelings about Harriet are really my feelings about my eldest child becoming independent and needing (and wanting) me less. While I know that this is natural and right, it is difficult to let go and – like Erin – it makes my heart sore. When I wrote the line, 'She was ready for her to grow up, but not for her to grow away' it made me cry because this is exactly how I'm feeling right now. Letting go is perhaps the most difficult thing a parent has to do.

Another big change for me this year is that I am leaving teaching, after twenty years, to write full-time. While this is very exciting – and a lifelong dream! – I will miss my classes and colleagues very much. It's impossible to explain to anyone who hasn't been a teacher just how demanding it is. But it is also the most rewarding and joyful career and I am grateful that I have taught so many wonderful students in that time. This book is dedicated to my last A level class, who arrived at our last lesson together wearing badges that read 'Our teacher is THE Emma Robinson.' Reader, I cried.

I love hearing from my readers – you can get in touch on my Facebook page, through Twitter, Goodreads or my website.

Emma

www.emmarobinsonwrites.com

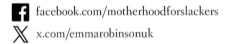

facebook.com/motherhoodforslackers

x.com/emmarobinsonuk

ACKNOWLEDGEMENTS

This book wouldn't be half what it is without the help of my fabulous editor Susannah Hamilton. Plotting this book together was an absolute dream. Let's do lots more plotting days, please!

Thanks also to Kim Nash, Sarah Hardy, Noelle Holton and Jess Readett for all your PR work and to everyone else at Bookouture who works so hard for our books. I am so grateful to be in the position to make writing my full-time career and this is because of all of you.

For razor-sharp editing, thank you to Laura Gerrard and Deborah Blake for your attention to detail which ensures I don't make an epic mistake in timelines or other details. And my friend Carrie Harvey for being my final proofs safety net! Thank you Alice Moore for this gorgeous cover which I love.

The book is dedicated to my last ever A level class who are: Muttaya Agbolade, Jasmine Banga, Ella Berry, Emily Cooper, Jasmine Elworthy, Megan Foster, Ronnie Griffin, Keane Handley, Freya Martin, Henry Morgan, Isabel O'Connor, Merlin Santosh, Vivan Ton and Molly Townsend. Fourteen wonderful human beings who have made my classroom a happy place to be. Thank you and fly high!

Lastly, as always, to my family, for your patience and support when I am on a deadline and not easy to live with. I love you. Please never leave me.